BONES ALONG THE HILL

By Nancy Sartor

FRIEND OR FOE?

Neva flattened herself against the wall.

Uncle Rex was outside. There was nothing to worry about. Then she remembered that Davis had soundproofed his walls during the renovation, saying the houses here were so close his neighbor could hear a half-hearted fart. She'd thought it funny at the time. A rush of adrenaline sent her heart galloping.

You are such a coward. There's nobody in here.

Unless it was Davis. Davis, who was not in England, who came home to find someone in his house and noises from his sanctuary. In which case the gun was in his hand.

She should call out.

If it wasn't Davis, she'd lose any chance at surprise.

She turned the scissors so the sharp end was poised to stab.

BONES ALONG THE HILL

By Nancy Sartor

www.BOROUGHSPUBLISHINGGROUP.com

BONES ALONG THE HILL

ISBN 978-1-941260-8-14

To Dave, whose love forms the beat of my heart

ACKNOWLEDGMENTS

Like almost every author, I have many people to thank for their help. First, David Thomerson, who took two books on undertaking from his private collection and allowed me to keep them for far too long, then answered all my stupid questions. Beth Terrell, Chester Campbell, Nikki Nelson-Hicks, Nina Fortmeyer, Kay Elam, Hardy Saliba, Richard Emerson, Nick Padron, and Wendy Campbell slogged with me through endless rewrites of BONES, giving their expertise and opinions and exhibiting amazing patience.

Donald Maass, whose style of teaching and incredible knowledge first made me believe I could do this. I did the hard work, as he said when I thanked him, but he gave me the Rosetta stone to writing, pounded the need for tension until I got it. He is and will remain my ultimate guru.

CONTENTS

CHAPTER ONE

Except for his jaw, the baby's new head looked exactly like his old one.

Neva Oakley took in little Jared Nelson's forever-closed eyes, the pale, delicate brows arched like butterfly wings on either side of his upturned button nose. A beautiful child, rounded in the way only a six-month-old human could be, perfect. His life had stretched ahead in promise and opportunity.

Babies should be exempt from the meanness of life, coddled and tickled and hurt only when they had to be. A baby should never be collateral damage in a savage attack on his mother, as Jared had been yesterday.

Neva couldn't change the unchangeable, couldn't will the child back to life. She could only close the gaping wound in his head, replace his missing ear and present him to his mother looking like her child. Neva knew only too well that this illusion would not erase the stark image of Jared's death, but she hoped it would give Larissa Nelson a few moments of peace, a tiny respite from her grief.

If she could fix whatever was wrong with his jaw before the putty dried.

With a sigh that came from her toes, she went over it one more time. His ears were equally placed in relationship to his head. The natural left was about the same distance from his jaw as the newly formed right one. The jaw had been pretty much intact. So, what the hell?

She dropped into a modified downward-facing dog yoga pose with her arms hanging free. As she visualized tension flowing from her shoulders down her arms and out her fingertips, her fingers tingled. The ache between her shoulder blades eased.

Her father cleared his throat.

She swung up, turned to face him.

"Got a problem?" he asked.

"His jaw." She waved a hand at Jared. "It's lopsided, and I cannot tell why." As she had so many times, she waited for his thirty years' experience in the mortician trade to rescue her. That he knew little about restoration or sculpting was irrelevant. He had a keen eye and years of peering at dead faces.

He stepped around her, leaned over the baby.

For the purposes of sculpture and restoration, people were made in two separate and slightly disparate halves smashed together. She'd measured Jared's cheeks. They had the right variances.

"Maybe it's not the jaw." Her father cupped his big hands on either side of Jared's head, framing the ears. The problem suddenly shimmered against his right palm. The right lobe was a hair thicker than the left, the natural one. That created the illusion of wrongness in the jaw.

"Why didn't *I* see that?" Neva asked as she shouldered her way in beside him.

She'd consciously chosen fast-drying putty for the ear to minimize the chances of denting it as she worked. Now, time ticked in her head like a windup clock. The clay was grainy, barely pliable. Slicing would require the lightest of touches.

For the millionth time, Neva blessed her strange hands. The subject of incredible ridicule when she was a child, her hands were long, thin, so narrow her wrists were practically nonexistent. She was also blessed with a double-jointed thumb on her right hand. She cocked the thumb back, felt it catch, moved it forward a half-inch into her palm. In this position, it was little more than a length of bone and skin, able to exert almost no pressure. Which was exactly what she needed right now: a way to balance the tool without adding pressure.

Breathless with the need to hurry, she grabbed the double-ended sculpting tool from her metal tray.

"Be careful," her dad said from her elbow.

She nodded, already planning the width of the slice, how deep the cut, knowing she had a minute, tops.

She set the angle of the blade against the lobe, bit lightly and cut all the way to the bottom, widening without deepening, then flung the slice into her metal tray, flipped the tool upside down, moved it to her left hand and smoothed the lobe. With her thumb and forefinger, she rolled and further smoothed it to make sure no sign of the tool remained.

When she thought it was good, she pulled the telescoping light down and peered over every inch. The ear was perfect. Now, if the jaw was okay.

She flung the light up again and stepped back. The jaw looked right, didn't it? She rubbed her tired eyes, looked again. Was that an eyelash on his cheek? She reached toward it, her finger trembling with exhaustion, afraid to touch the putty again, unable to stop herself.

"He's perfect!" her father said and exploded her compulsion into a billion fragments.

"Bless him," she said as she released a breath she hadn't realized she was holding and dropped her hand to her side. There was no eyelash. It had been a figment of her insatiable need for perfection.

They gazed in silence at the baby's innocent face. "You thought you knew the mother?" her father asked.

"Yes."

Knew was a strong word for what they'd shared at Hume Fog Comprehensive High School. Larissa Dudin, later Nelson, was a strange, withdrawn child. Neva had touched the girl's arm once and been shocked when Larissa jerked away as if she'd been burned. Larissa joined no groups, ate alone in the cafeteria, had no besties, offered no opinions, joined in no conversations, never raised her hand in class. Now, with the advantage of an adult brain, Neva realized Larissa's isolation had spoken perhaps more loudly than the overt acting-out obvious in some other children. A silent cry for help.

In that same silence, Larissa had communicated her love for her child this morning when she and her husband came to make the arrangements. Stiff, dry-eyed, Larissa had seemed lost in her own personal hell until Neva's father mentioned a closed-casket funeral with perhaps a nice picture of Jared on the lid.

The woman jerked up. Her eyes flared. She spoke rapidly to her husband in a voice too low for Neva to hear. He nodded without looking at her, then said to Neva's father, "How much more to make him look right, to let us open the casket?"

Neva was recognized as one of the best facial reconstructionists in the business, as witnessed by the newspaper article her father recently taped to her wall. But funeral restoration, like the repair of a living being, required that certain things be in place. Like a skull, which in Jared's case had imploded when his mother's attacker knocked him to the sidewalk. To fix it, Neva had to create half a head, not repair one.

Her father had must have caught Neva's discomfort because he began to explain the reasons a restoration might not be possible. Laser-focused on Larissa, Neva had felt more than seen Larissa jerk with his every word as if they were rocks. Larissa's pain was so raw, so fresh, it seemed to fill the room and then to finally fill Neva with a miserable ache she remembered well.

"I can do it, Dad," she'd said, the words feeling torn from her tight throat.

Larissa held Neva's gaze for a long and painful moment before she lifted a hand, a salute, Neva thought, a thank-you for giving them the one and only gift that could matter at this point.

Now, with the baby almost whole again, Neva gave her father a quick squeeze. "Don't know what I'd do without you." She meant that in every respect of the word. He'd held her tight when life was so devoid of light she didn't want to be in it. Even now, when her life was pretty calm, he was the anchor from which she lived it.

"That Pratt guy hangs around here long enough," he said while she moved her thumb back to its first joint, "you'll be saying good-bye to your old dad to go make babies."

"Better slow that one down a step or two," Neva said as she dumped her tools into the deep sink in the far corner, its porcelain surface stained and scarred from decades of use. "He and I are sorta just getting going here. No commitments."

Her father's eyes widened. "Gave you a key to his house."

"Yes."

"Sounds serious to me."

From habit, Neva checked the bust on the tall stool beside her before she washed up. She'd started it ten long years ago when her first love, Gray Ledbetter, took his life. She picked pieces of clay from her fingers and wondered again why she could easily sculpt anyone else's likeness, recreate a child's head, a woman's face, anything but *Gray's* face. Each time she worked on it, the head, shoulders, pecs and upper arms almost sculpted themselves. But his face …not the whole face. It was mostly his eyes. She could get his turned-up nose, the high cheekbones, but when she tried to add the eyes, in some reverse synergy, the total became much less than the sum of all its parts, a face as lifeless as Gray's real one had been after his inexplicable suicide.

"Throw it away," her father said from the other side of the room.

"When I get his face right," she said. She didn't offer any more explanation although she'd had many over the years. Professional pride, a need to complete what she started, dogged determination not to let the thing defeat her. But the secret truth was she'd never completely recovered from Gray's suicide, never quite let him go. She was positive if she ever got his face right, she could turn him loose. Even though she'd just denied it, she and Davis were growing ever closer. They'd not discussed marriage, exactly.

Not yet.

Gray would always be a part of her, always have a place in her heart, but she didn't want his ghost in her trousseau.

She tore her gaze from the bust, forced herself to focus on Jared. That fine baby hair would be hell to replace because it was thin and sparse. Far different from thick, adult hair. After the embalming, she'd added protective undergarments to ward against any leak of fluids, then dressed the baby in a tiny pair of dark blue trousers and a white dickey with a navy blue tie. Topped off with a tiny navy jacket, he looked like he was on his way to church. Which, in a way, he was.

Six o'clock. Davis would be in soon. They had this one night together before he left for Europe for a week. Her gaze moved to Jared's head. She could cheat a little, make the hair thinner on his left side, the side that would face the casket lid. The shadow of the lid would hide it. She could save several hours.

With her hands and tools clean and dried, she turned back to the room.

Her father was still at Jared's side. The basement prep room's ultra-bright ceiling lights sparked off the new strands of silver in his dark hair, accentuated the deeper slope of his shoulders. As if he felt her gaze, he said, "Will you be working late?"

"First viewing's at nine tomorrow. He needs hair. I'm using angora. Might as well be a spider web, it's so thin and fragile. It'll take forever. Besides, Ice hasn't picked up his bodies yet."

Her father glanced at her, his face stretched in mock surprise. "Didn't we give that old bird a watch last Christmas?"

"Shoulda included a tutorial."

They *had* given Ice a watch. One with a ginormous face. Meant to be funny, true, but also given with a definite message.

Ice had worked for Oakley's Funeral Home for twenty years, bringing bodies to Oakley's for embalming and restoration from outlying funeral homes that had no morticians. Her father got a fee for *their* work on these bodies, twenty percent of which went to Ice. He'd quickly dubbed the refrigerated truck in which he brought the bodies the "Ice Wagon," which had spawned his nickname, "The Ice Man," who, he often quipped, cometh when he cometh.

Trouble with that philosophy was somebody had to log those bodies out of Oakley's system, have Ice certify all their belongings were there.

She'd waited until midnight more than once for him to pick up.

Her father, who was still staring at Jared when she moved up beside him, said, "I've buried probably a hundred of these little guys in my career. It never gets easier." With a deep breath, he finished, "Don't stay too late. Call me before you leave so I won't worry."

"Davis is around somewhere."

Her father turned with a teasing smile. "Ah, the grave-digging architect. Tell me he's better at designing buildings than he is at digging graves."

Delighted to shake off the somber mood of this day, Neva said, "You are such a comedian."

"Don't get sassy, girl. You may be too old to spank, but I'm still your father."

"Indeed you are." She tiptoed to kiss him good-bye. "The best father a girl could have."

"Flattery is the favorite tool of a naughty child," he said as he returned her kiss.

She watched him cut his usual path between the long embalming tables, his head barely passing beneath the lights. As always, he sidestepped the floor drains, but his once-jaunty step was slower.

He tried to keep a cheerful front, but he wasn't fooling her. Her mother's illness and his mounting business problems were wearing him down.

CHAPTER TWO

The silky, thin and preciously expensive angora was piled on the small rolling table. The right side of Jared's head was covered with soft, slow-drying flesh-colored clay. Neva separated the two-inch strands with a pair of long, thin tweezers, grabbing only two or three at a time, then doubled them and poked the folded end into the clay. When it was all placed, she would use razor-sharp scissors to trim it to the quarter-inch length of Jared's natural hair.

It was repetitive work. Her hands developed a rhythm; the room settled, and then disappeared as she folded and poked and folded and poked.

The rattle of the door handle stabbed her ears. She jerked. The tweezers drove a narrow trough into Jared's head. "Shit!" she said as Davis skidded to a stop halfway through the door.

"I made you jump," he said. "I am so sorry."

A brisk October breeze flowed in around him, brought her the smell of fresh dirt and mint.

She put the scissors down, shoved away from the table and smiled. "No worries. I'll fix it later."

With his hair tossed and twisted and a dirt smudge on his cheek, he looked like a little boy who'd played outside all day. Until you got to his shoulders. He still had a post-summer golden tan that lit fire in his hazel eyes. His quick grin drove deep dimples into his cheeks.

His gaze lifted from her to the baby beside her.

"Is that the child you had in here earlier? The one with the head that—"

"Yes."

"Damn, you're good," he said. "I'll bet not one reconstructionist in a thousand can do what you do," he said over his shoulder on his way to the sink.

"There probably aren't a thousand of us combined," she said. "But thanks. I am proud of this one."

He poured enough soap in his right palm to wash a cow, added water and attacked the dirt.

"Any sign of rain?" she asked, her daily question. Nashville had received none for the past six weeks. The grass died long ago. Trees

suffered in near-audible pain. The mighty Cumberland River was
still hanging in there, but without rain upriver, there would soon be
water restrictions that could turn the two hundred and fifty acre
active cemetery part of their five hundred acre funeral business into
a grassless desert.

"No," Davis said without turning. "By the way, I left the
backhoe in the cemetery."

As he worked on his hands, which were doubtless operating-
room clean a good two minutes ago, his big shoulder muscles
bunched and relaxed. Always a fascinating display of manhood,
right now with her mind numb from so many hours of intense focus,
it was hypnotizing to the point that Neva lost herself. Gray was a boy
when he died, all long limbs and growing muscle. At thirty, four
years older than Neva, Davis was a man, solid, toned, buff. The only
man she'd ever dated, the only man she'd ever wanted to date. When
he finally deemed them clean, he rubbed the towel over his hands,
carefully drying each finger, then the backs. Neva's half-dream
evaporated as she thought how gentle those hands were on her
breasts.

"Think that's all right?" he continued, raising his voice enough
to drive through her thoughts. "It'll be easier to open the baby's
grave Monday."

She cleared the lust from her throat, forced herself to focus,
barely remembering his earlier words. "It's as safe there as it is in
that old shed. Lock's been broken for ten years." To distract herself,
she touched the underside of Jared's new ear. Hard and dry. "How'd
it go today?"

He hesitated and her heart skipped a couple of beats. He insisted
on putting himself through the rough therapy of exposing himself to
caskets, funeral homes and, above all, graves in the hope that
familiarity with those things would end the awful nightmares he'd
endured since his younger brother, Stephen, disappeared thirteen
years ago, along with two other boys his age.

The nightmares began two weeks later and were always the
same: locked in a casket, can't get out.

The missing boys were never found.

Neither was the kidnapper.

Davis's shrink thought familiarity with the death business would
ease his fear. So, at least three times a week most weeks, Davis's

hands, those same hands that designed towering structures in New York and San Francisco, wielded a shovel in Oakley's cemetery. He'd started out as a bad gravedigger and was now a passable one, but his tenure as Oakley's least expensive employee might be ending soon. His latest project would turn four blocks of downtown Nashville into a pedestrian plaza and was demanding most of his time.

Just as she became convinced he wasn't going to answer her question, he said, "Pretty good." He hung the towel on the rack beside the sink, came near and put a warm hand on her shoulder. "I don't ever dream when you sleep over."

Without looking up, she said, "Too worn out."

"Was that a compliment?" he asked.

"Shameless self-promotion."

"Damn well-deserved." His hand was calloused now from his work with the shovel. It scraped her neck a bit as he kneaded her tired muscles. But despite the roughness, his touch was welcome. "Ran into your dad earlier. He didn't look happy."

"Houston Drennon is driving him crazy."

"So I've gathered. What's his deal?"

"Nobody knows. He offered to buy this place. Dad said no. He bought the old Drake place, refurbished it, dropped his prices to nearly nothing. He's driving us out of business. Us and every other funeral home in Nashville. Dad's tried to talk to him. He doesn't want to talk. He wants Oakley's. Period." She glanced at Jared's half-covered head, then at her watch. "I'd better get back to it if we're going to have any time tonight."

When he said nothing, she glanced up into his strained face. Her heart sank. Only one thing could take him from her tonight. "Ah, I see. Your detective found another lead on Stephen."

Davis nodded.

"Promising?"

Stephen would be twenty-five now. Davis believed he was alive and unable or unwilling to make contact. That seemed about as probable to her as his being struck by lightning. Davis had been completely supportive of her obsession with Gray, her never-ending yet useless drive to determine why a happy sixteen-year-old blew his brains out. She struggled for something supportive to say. Trouble was, she suffered with him as each lead fizzled. She wanted him to accept that Stephen was much more likely dead than alive. Even more importantly, accept that if he was alive, he was *choosing* not to contact his family.

As she waited for his answer, a knot grew in her stomach.

"Max is pretty sure Stephen's dealing drugs," Davis said finally. "Which isn't all that surprising, I guess. But it does kinda destroy my fantasy that he was kidnapped by a nice childless family and forgot his real name."

"That's quite a fantasy," Neva said. *Shut up, shut up, shut up*! But the knot was in control now, driving words she didn't want to say through her clenched teeth. "He was twelve, Davis. Not two." She stabbed the tweezers deep into the angora, then pulled them out so loaded, the tangled hair tore loose.

She watched it drift to the floor, Davis silent by her side.

"Damn stuff is like lint," she muttered, struggling for control.

Davis scooped up the angora, laid it carefully in her outstretched hand.

The air stretched, grew heavy.

Tell him you're sorry! She cleared her throat.

Davis turned slightly away.

She bit her lip, took a deep breath. A rewind. They needed a rewind. "What's the clue?"

He hesitated, took a breath of his own before he said, "Supposed to be a deal tonight behind the donut shop."

"*Our* donut shop?" The surprise she'd been unable to edit from her voice said everything she was thinking. Oakley's neighborhood once consisted of gracious homes marching in lofty serenity toward Nashville's ever-expanding downtown. But Nashville had moved on, left this area behind to be occupied by a myriad of semi-failing businesses, including restaurants, tax preparers and fortunetellers. The donut shop across Gallatin Road was a raveling eyesore populated with people so interesting, even the cops didn't hang out there. It wasn't her business to edit him, but she couldn't help worrying.

Davis nodded.

She shook her head. "It's too dangerous."

"Only if they see me."

"They're *going* to see you. It's a damned dope deal, Davis, not late-night poker. Let me call Uncle Rex."

His gaze snapped to hers. "So he can bust my brother in the middle of a dope deal? I'm trying to find him, not get him sent to jail."

"I'm worried about *you*."

"I appreciate that. But you have to let me do it my way. This isn't my first try, you know. I've got a pretty good handle on where to be and where not to be. I don't put myself in danger."

A dull rumble from the other side of the wall stopped Neva from saying something else she might regret. "Ice," she said. "At last."

She and Davis gazed silently at the door that led from the low-ceilinged basement prep room into the huge vaulted garage. Oakley's hearses filled the first two bays. They left the one nearest the prep room empty for Ice's deliveries.

His long, thin form came through the door.

"So nice of you to show up," Neva said, her voice sharp.

He jumped as if she'd poked him. An uncharacteristic flash of irritation hit his eyes. She was working to soften her tone when he finally grinned and said, "Bitch, bitch, bitch."

"If you'd keep regular hours, I wouldn't have to bitch."

"You'd bitch anyway. It's in your ovaries. Lucky for you, I got me a hot woman waiting, so your crap don't bother me in the least. All I wanna do is load these stiffs and get outta here."

He loved to push her buttons.

"Do not call them *stiffs*," Neva said as always. "They're people." The knot in her stomach relaxed as they moved into their usual banter.

"Yeah, yeah, yeah. They're people. Stiff people," Ice said. He glanced at Davis. "How the hell do you stand this woman, dude? I mean, does she rag your ass like she does mine?"

"You don't really expect me to get in the middle of this, do you?"

"Guess not," Ice said. With ease of practice, he pulled two gurneys from the far wall, shoved one ahead and dragged one behind. As always, Neva had the door open by the time he got there. "She'd probably cut your nose off with one of them sharp knives she likes to play with," he finished with an eyebrow waggle at Neva.

As Neva went back to her stool, Davis raised *his* eyebrow.

"What?" she said. "He was trying to include you."

"Jerry does try; I'll give him that. He just can't quite pull it off. I'm telling you, he's got the hots for you."

The air stretched again and tightened as it often did when she was with both Ice and Davis. Davis didn't trust Ice. Neva literally trusted him with her life. "He'll like you even less if he hears you call him Jerry," she said. "You're wrong. He's fifteen years older, thinks I'm his baby sister." She shrugged. "Besides, I'm not his type. He likes slutty blondes with big boobs."

"Me, I prefer neat little redheads," Davis said, and once again the tension bled from the air. He nibbled the back of her neck, which brought her over-heated libido roaring through her like lava. She reached back, hooked her arm around his neck. "*Petite*, dear. Not little. Petite and don't start something you're not willing to finish." She let him go as Ice came back. "Are you taking your 'hot' woman to that stupid redneck bar?"

Ice glanced up. "Paddy's?"

"Whatever."

"Paddy's is for beer, pool and woman-watchin'. I'm taking her to a nice place."

Neva snorted. "Where they bring a glass with the beer?" Sparring with Ice was a way of life, but when Davis was around, it usually served the additional function of keeping her firmly between the two of them.

Ice shook his head. "Listen to that," he said to Davis, speaking directly to him for a second time before turning back to Neva. "I am taking her to a restaurant with white tablecloths and a special waiter for the water. She's a real nice lady."

"Then try to hang on to her. You know how you are," she said with an exaggerated sigh. He dated often, first dates, maybe a second, but that was usually it. The look on his face tonight said this one was different, perhaps one he would really like to keep. Maybe at forty-one he was finally ready to settle down, marry, have children.

The thought of his having a wife gave her no grief, but the thought of children made her squirm a bit. After her mother disappeared into depression and then again when she lost Gray to suicide, Ice had made her happiness his special project, worked for it even when her own depression drew her blankets over her head and kept her down for days at a time. Silently, she laughed at herself. Twenty-six was too old for these thoughts. Gray's death and the trauma it caused were ten years old. She had a father, a wonderful father. Ice should have a child, maybe six of them. And when he did, she'd try to be as good to them as he'd been to her.

"I know how I am," he said with a sad shake of his head. "If I were a woman, I wouldn't have me, either." A smile spread across his face and drove the sadness from his eyes—blue eyes so pale they would have appeared colorless had it not been for the deep blue ring around the pupil. He held her gaze for a moment, then raised a hand and said, "Have a good night, kids. See you tomorrow."

When the garage door closed behind him, Davis said, "See what I mean? That wasn't a big brother look."

"Yes, it was. You're seeing brotherly love."

"Like hell." Davis gazed at her for a moment, shook his head slightly and said, "I'd better go, too." He reached for her face, then stopped. "Oh. Before I forget, you left a makeup case at my house last week."

"Oh, yeah," she said with a grin. "Thanks again. You made a lovely woman."

A blush crawled from beneath his collar. "After I let you practice on me? You're gonna rag me about it forever, aren't you?"

"Not forever. Someday I'll be old and senile and won't remember," she said with another grin. "But I do appreciate it. I'd never tried changing a man into a woman before."

She'd had a customer who wanted to look like a woman in his casket. Davis had agreed to be her model. She'd had no idea where to start. Beards and heavy bones did not lend themselves to the female face. Davis allowed her to scrape his face until it glowed, thin his chin line with darker makeup and put half an inch of mascara on his long, already lush eyelashes. Based on her success with him, she'd given Mr. Gainer a try.

"How'd it turn out?" Davis asked.

"Mr. Gainer's partner was happy. His mother took a shock, but even she had to admit he made a lovely woman." She slid off her stool and put her hands on his cheeks. "I'm sorry about before. I know you can handle yourself, but will you promise to be careful tonight?"

He covered her hands with his. "I'm a terrible coward, as unflattering as that is to say." He moved his hands to span her waist. "First sign of trouble, I'll run and scream like a little girl."

"I would love to see that," she said.

"No, you wouldn't." His hazel eyes softened. "I'm really sorry about tonight," he said. "If it weren't a good lead, I'd never—"

"I understand," she said. She searched his eyes again for sore spots, afraid her sharp words had cut into his ego, but they were clear and full of warmth. She tiptoed, kissed his lips.

He pulled her sharply against him.

His body was rock hard, his arms warm. He smelled like wind and dirt and something minty. Holding her gaze with his, he lowered his lips to hers, driving passion ahead of his touch, then slid his hands up her rib cage and cupped her breasts in a move that surprised her even as it rekindled the fire she'd doused earlier. They'd always been rather sedate in their lovemaking, always in the privacy of his bedroom. But he was leaving tomorrow for a week.

"Not in here," she managed as she nodded toward the room next door.

He lifted her. She locked her legs around his waist, let him walk them both through the casket room and into the into the small storage room behind it. Still holding her, he locked the door, then leaned her against it, letting his hands explore.

"Oh, my God," she breathed, drowning in sweetness so deep it hurt.

As if she weighed nothing, he set her on the long, wooden table against the wall. She skinned out of her T-shirt and lacy bra, barely getting the latter off before his mouth found her nipple, then trailed fire down her belly while he slid her out of her jeans.

Manipulating her with nips and touches, he had her quivering when he entered her with a powerful stoke that made her gasp. He held a moment before he plunged, then retreated and plunged again, moving hard and fast, seemingly out of control.

But she knew better.

When she was at the brink, he stopped, let her catch her breath, then began again. Time after time, he brought her tantalizingly near release until she wrapped her legs around his, taking control, driving his passion with hers, refusing to let him stop until his cry joined hers.

CHAPTER THREE

Davis had been gone for two hours or so, but she still quivered with the after-effects of their lovemaking. Quivering hadn't slowed her down, however, and now the new side of Jared's head was covered with quarter-inch-long fine hair. It was, as she'd predicted, slow-going, tedious work.

Neva arched and massaged her back. She was also rag-doll, spot-seeing exhausted. She wanted her four-poster bed with the down comforter and about nine hours of sleep.

Jared's face was liberally dusted with bits and pieces of angora. She chose a soft-bristled brush and was flicking the tiny flyaway pieces to the floor when her cell phone broke into "Evil Woman." Moya's ringtone.

"Hey, cookie," Neva said. Her shoulders ached. She lifted them, let them fall, laid the brush on the table and flexed her fingers, grimacing at their length, their thinness. Artist's hands, her mother called them. Long ugly sticks, Neva called them.

"Helloooo?" Moya's voice said in her ear. "Are you there?"

"Sorry. I'm so tired I can barely stay awake. You were saying?"

"I said, are you in the prep room?"

"Why, yes, as a matter of fact, I am."

"Why?"

"Beecauuuse I work here?"

"Why are you not at Davis's?"

"Oh, of course. That would make sense. This is his last night in the States for a week. But, alas, he's off chasing invisible butterflies. I'll be sleeping in my own bed alone. Is that where you are?"

"In your bed?"

Neva could almost see Moya's wicked grin. "No, stupid, at the house."

"I'm in your parking lot," Moya said.

"Really?"

"Car was running just fine when I left the grocery," Moya said. Her tone morphed into disgust. "Now it sounds like a kid with whooping cough. I saw the lights and your car, figured I could catch a ride home." There was a second-long pause and then, "I'm sorry about Davis, granny. He'll be gone a week, right?"

"Seven days, one hundred sixty-eight hours, one thousand eighty minutes, six hundred four thousand eight hundred seconds. Not that I'm counting. And clearly neither is he. Come on in. I'll unlock the door."

"You sure? I don't want to interrupt the great artiste."

"The great artiste is nearly through."

Like Jared's face, Neva's clothes were covered with bits and pieces of angora. She'd ignored them while she was in the zone, but as she moved, the tiny hairs dug in and began to itch as if a billion ants had moved into her clothes. She unzipped her jeans and was struggling out of them when Moya danced through the door, a vision in a pair of form-fitting designer jeans, long, leather high-heeled boots and a frilly blouse. She'd piled her ebony curls on her head and woven sparkles among them. Her dark, dark eyes had a thousand-watt shine. She closed the door, locked it, glanced pointedly at Neva's panties-covered butt and said, "Um, not my style, granny, but don't let me slow you down."

"Kiss my ass," Neva said as she kicked the jeans away and ran for the shower room, clawing her legs with both hands.

"I could, I guess," Moya said. "There's enough of it showing."

Neva stuck her head around the door and said through teeth clenched against the itch, "Stay away from the angora, smarty, or you'll wind up in here with me. I'll be right back."

She dropped the rest of her clothes in the farthest corner, leapt under the water, used her hands to squeegee the hair down, then slung it onto the shower floor. In seconds, the drain clogged. She cleared it, dumped the hair into the trashcan in the corner, then padded back, leaving wet footprints along the concrete.

When the hair was nearly all gone and the maddening itch subsided, she toweled her skin until it glowed, which removed the rest, and pulled on a pair of old jeans and a T-shirt that said, "Keep Smoking. Your Undertaker Needs the Business."

When she returned, Moya was sitting on a padded chair at the old red and white Formica table in the far corner. "Tell me," Neva said as she ran her hands through her curls and tried to tame them into something resembling a style, "what did you do tonight that's got your eyes all shiny?"

"I smoked grass."

Neva stopped in mid-step. "You did not!"

"No," Moya admitted with a grin, "I just love to make you look like that."

"Like what?"

"All prudy-faced. I went out with Ken Stasher."

"*The* Ken Stasher?" Moya and Ken, both registered nurses, worked together for a home health agency. For months, Moya's daily conversations had included at least one reference to Ken Stasher.

"The one and only. Is that Larissa's baby?"

"Yes. God, Moya, she's so trashed she can hardly talk."

"I can imagine," Moya said. "I didn't know her well in high school."

"None of us did."

"To lose your kid like that. It must be awful." Moya moved to the prep table, circled the child. "The newspaper said his head was—"

"It was. He never had a chance."

"He's perfect. I knew you were good, but this is just spooky."

"Been telling you I'm a freakin' genius."

"More like just a freak. Listen, you know how I thought Ken was gay?"

Neva had long since learned to follow Moya's hopscotch mind, which, when she was excited, seemed unable to focus on one thing for long. "Because he was neat?"

"Yeah, well, he's nice, too, polite, holds the door."

"So, naturally, he *must* be gay."

Moya slitted her eyes. "Stop it. Thing is, he's not."

"And we know this how?"

"We kissed him."

Neva grinned. "Wow! On the first date? Mama Rosita would be horrified."

"You're in top form tonight, granny. Something good happen to *you*?"

Amazing what sex could do for a girl, or maybe it was the elixir of Moya, the wonderful and intoxicating energy that flowed off her best friend. "I'm just glad to see you."

"I guess so!" Moya said with a teasing smile. "You spend all your time with that Pratt guy."

"Davis is gone for a week."

"One hundred and sixty-eight little hours," Moya sang to the tune of "What a Difference a Day Makes," forcing the extra words to fit.

"Point is, we should be able to get in some quality girl time, find a few adult beverages."

"Yeah, but when he's back, I get dumped." She was teasing, but it hit Neva hard.

"I don't mean to do that. It's just that—" She broke off. What was it that made her choose Davis over Moya? Sex? Yes, but not just sex. It wasn't that she was more comfortable with Davis. With Moya, she could be herself, say anything she liked. That wasn't true with Davis, not yet anyway, although she'd certainly done a bang-up job of saying what she thought earlier tonight. She would never want to be without Moya no matter how often she married or how many children she had. But when Davis was around, she wanted to be with just him.

Oh hell, maybe it *was* sex.

"You know I love you," she finished. "Besides, you're gonna be spending all your time with Ken."

"Whoa, granny. First date. I may never hear from him again. You know how *that* goes."

"He'll be back, sweetie." Neva put her chair back under the table. An ominous ache was creeping ever nearer the middle of her forehead. Probably fatigue backed by hunger. "You gonna leave your car here?"

"Yep. I'll have the garage pick it up in the morning. Speaking of tomorrow, can I drop you off and drive your car to work?"

"Sure. Oh, before I forget, Zanna called. She'll be in Tuesday. Think you'll have your car back by then?"

A couple of frown lines appeared above Moya's pert nose. "I guess so. Depends on what's wrong with it."

Neva shrugged. "If you don't, we'll borrow Dad's car."

"Cousin Zanna. Your misplaced twin sister."

"We really don't look that much alike."

"The hell you don't."

"Her eyes are dark; mine are—"

"—sapphire glories," Moya said. "She's taller. I've heard all this. From a distance and even up close if your hair is cut like hers, she could double for you."

"Well, anyway," Neva said, "we have to leave my car at the airport for her Tuesday. I'll park in the short-term parking lot, take the shuttle to the airport, text you when I get there. You pick me up outside."

"Okey dokey. Count me in."

Rozanna did have the same dark auburn hair as Neva. Her face was long, too, with the characteristic Needham cleft chin, but that was where the resemblance ended. Neva's face was thinner at the high cheekbones they both shared. Her ears were smaller, too. Zan had elephant ears. Neva'd made all kinds of fun of those ears when they were young, but Zan forgave her...finally.

Zan was precious to Neva. Neither she nor her cousin had so far inherited their mothers' depression. Which was good for them both, but better for Zan than for Neva. Aunt Ann swallowed a fatal bottleful of pills when both girls were six years old.

Always good to see the talented Zan, whose song lyrics—country, country-Western and crossover—lived on albums by people like Deana Carter and, just recently, Gabe Dixon. She went where the work was, but right now, she was popular enough to write her own ticket. Being a smart girl, she divided her year evenly between L.A. and Nashville.

"Davis has never met Zan," Neva said.

"Ken has," Moya pointed out.

"I think they had maybe one date forever ago. Not jealous are you?"

"Of Zan? Just because she's tall and perfectly made and has this incredible curly auburn hair and enough talent for six people? Who, me? Jealous? Don't be silly."

"Oh, shut up," Neva said. "You don't have to worry about any woman, girl. And you know it." Neva took a step. A wave of vertigo swept her like an angry tide. She clutched the table edge.

Moya grabbed her arm. "You okay?"

"Just tired. And hungry. Let me put some makeup on Jared, and we'll be outta here."

She'd figured out the right makeup for the child while she worked on him. Ivory with just a tiny dot of chestnut. For one so young, Jared had dark skin. When the overall makeup was perfect, she mixed pink with the same ivory, then hovered over the boy's cheeks while she decided how to put the color down. Cheek color could and often did ruin a good restoration.

For a baby, it was particularly important.

Holding her breath, she smoothed on a gossamer film of color, then stepped back to view it from a distance. "I think that's right," she said.

"He looks like he's sleeping," Moya said.

It was after midnight when Neva pulled the door closed behind them, yearning for a glass of wine, a little cheese and her bed, mostly her bed.

The night air had developed a bite for the first time this fall, a harbinger of the cold to follow in late November or December. The cold air cleared Neva's head. Automatically, she glanced at Oakley's cemetery, which ranged along the tall hill behind the funeral home itself. On the side nearest the funeral home were tall, ancient stones. On the far side, the grave markers were flat rectangles, easier to maintain because they could be mowed over instead of around.

But it was the brush-covered wild part of the cemetery that caught her attention. Normally that tangle of brush and overgrown trees was thick enough to keep kids from playing in the cemetery itself. But in October, they couldn't resist holding séances among the gravestones. A coven of local witches also liked to hold their festivals there, which was fine with everyone until Neva's dad found their fire still smoldering one year. With all the brush on the hill, the fact that October was Nashville's driest month and the current drought situation, an unattended fire could burn through the entire neighborhood.

Since then, they'd checked the hillside every night in October for any signs of intrusion. So far this October, there had been none, but now a steady glow way up on the hillside in the uncleared section caught Neva's gaze.

Standing under the huge streetlights that ringed the parking lot, she couldn't be sure. She tripped down the slope that eventually led into a deep, concrete drainage ditch behind the funeral home until she was outside the reach of the lights. There it was. Steady for sure, not flickering, which was strange for a fire, but definitely behind the cemetery in the brush.

"What the hell?" Moya said.

"Kids or witches. Damn it. I'm too tired for this shit." When the state instituted mandated sentencing so criminal trespassing carried a five hundred dollar fine and thirteen months in jail, Neva and her dad decided they would never call the police on the kids who sneaked into the cemetery. Neva would have to personally explain to the little dears that they couldn't hold their séance there, no matter how eager they might think the dead were to rise again. Or, if it was the witches, remind them to douse their fire.

Either way, it wouldn't take long.

If she were not totally exhausted, it would be no big deal.

CHAPTER FOUR

"You'd think the word would be out that kids weren't allowed in Oakley's cemetery," Neva said, maneuvering the first and sharpest of the three curves that led to the top of the hill and the end of the road.

"Probably *is* out," Moya said. She'd propped her boots on the dashboard, moved them when Neva made her belt up, then scooted down and put them back. "Thing is, kids grow up, leave the neighborhood. New kids don't believe the old stories. And there you are."

"Out at midnight when I am so terribly wine-deprived and sleepy."

"Mostly wine-deprived?" Moya asked.

"Yes. Although I am also sleepy. Hungry, too."

"If only you needed to pee, you'd be in total misery."

Neva glanced at Moya. "That would be a good thing?"

"Not so much."

Neva hit the next curve a bit fast. The rear end slid. She steered into it. The car obediently fell into line.

"Slow down, granny," Moya said. "This road is a snake."

"To keep people from using it like a racetrack."

"Doesn't keep *you* from using it like a racetrack. Slow down!"

Neva sighed and took the final two curves like the granny Moya called her. Just before the pavement ended, she turned right, bumped over the low asphalt curbing and onto the carefully maintained sod.

Her headlights cut tunnels through the blackness. A white van loomed in the darkness, parked just outside the tall monuments, its lights off, interior dark.

"These 'kids' are old enough to drive," Moya said. She rummaged in her purse.

"Getting your piece, Annie Oakley?"

"Damn right." Moya carried a Glock. She had a permit. She was trained and a good shot. Since Gray's death, Neva was not comfortable around guns. It wasn't that she blamed the gun for Gray's death, but she'd seen its destructive power in that single second, didn't ever want to see it again.

She was waiting for another smart-assed comment from Moya when shadowy images developed just beyond her headlights. Two figures, she thought. One short and stocky. The other a waif, thin, petite, a woman from the length of her hair.

As the light intensified on the couple, the woman twisted and clawed his hand, which was clamped around her upper arm. Her back was familiar, someone Neva had seen recently. Moya dropped her feet to the floor and leaned forward with her gun in her hand. "What the—"

The man's body went rigid as if the light burned him. He whirled into the light, bringing the woman with him; his expression dared Neva to come closer. He raised his middle finger into the air.

But Neva's attention was riveted on the woman.

Moya sucked in a sudden, sharp breath. "Is that...that's Larissa Dudin!" She grabbed the dashboard. "What's he doing?"

Reacting beneath a layer of shock, Neva accelerated with a half-formed plan to knock him out of the way, save Larissa. He jerked a revolver from behind his back, aimed it while Larissa twisted and jerked in his grip, a frenzied marionette.

His shot exploded.

Something shrieked across the top of the car.

Neva threw both hands over her ears and slumped in an effort to get her head below the windshield.

"Goddamn!" Moya spat. "Stop, granny!"

Neva stomped the brake. The car shuddered to a stop.

Moya leapt out, squatted behind the open door.

He shot again, missed.

Moya's answer missed, but it sent him to the ground. Larissa, jerked down with him, beat at him with her fists.

He slammed the gun into her head in a vicious blow.

Larissa went still.

Neva tried to assess her options. Get much closer, he'd put a bullet between her eyes.

Moya shot again.

He twisted, laid his weapon along the ground. Larissa slammed her fists onto his gun hand, knocked the weapon free. He lunged forward to grab it. She boxed his ear, leapt to her feet, kicked him twice and ran like hell for the car.

Moya's Glock erupted into thunderous shots that kept him diving for the safety of the ground every time he tried to get his feet under him.

Larissa pounded down the hillside.

Her assailant cowered against the earth with his arms over his head.

"One hit," Moya said between gritted teeth. "Just one." She shot twice more before he grabbed his arm, rolled to his side.

Neva kept her gaze on Larissa, mentally running with her, whispering encouraging words Larissa couldn't hear. The glaring headlights showed the huge bruise on Larissa's face where he'd hit her with the gun. Her lips were smashed and torn. Blood covered her chin.

If Neva could get her hands on the son of a bitch, she'd tear off his balls and stuff them down his stupid throat. "Stay with me, Moya."

She rolled the car forward. Moya ran beside it, bent over beneath the window.

Larissa was closer now, her eyes wide. Terror stretched her face.

"Come on!" Neva yelled. "Run, Larissa!"

Larissa's assailant rolled to his stomach, winced, laid his arms along the ground, the gun between his hands.

"Moya!" But Moya had fallen enough behind so she couldn't simply drill the bastard.

Neva hit the brakes.

Moya slid to her knees, peeped around the door, gasped and drew a bead.

A gun boomed.

Moya's?

Larissa arched as if someone had kicked her.

Her eyes widened.

Her mouth opened. Her head snapped back.

She fell prone just beyond the car's front bumper.

Moya tore another clip from her pocket and slammed it home, pulled the slide back and fired.

The dark man leapt to his feet, ran crouched for the bushes, his arm hanging useless by his side while Moya's bullets tore up the ground inches behind him.

Neva raced to Larissa.

Moya met her there.

Blood covered the back of Larissa's blouse where it had spurted from the bullet wound.

There was no bleeding now.

Larissa no longer had a beating heart.

Neva dropped to her knees. If she'd moved faster, if she'd seen them earlier, if she'd—

A bullet whistled over her head.

Moya whirled, sent a shot into the tall monuments behind them, ran for the car and called over her shoulder. "Get in the fucking car, granny. Get us the hell outta here."

Neva backed the car around.

Her side-view mirror exploded. Fragments blasted against her window like the tiny fragments of skull that hit her face once long ago. She twisted away from the image, tried to focus on now, struggled and lost. "No. Oh God, no. No!"

"Shut up, granny!" Moya yelled. "Shut the fuck up and drive!"

Fresh tears burst from Neva's eyes, but she managed to stomp the gas.

The Mustang leapt forward. Neva bit the inside of her jaw and let the pain clear her head.

Larissa, Larissa, Larissa.

The drumbeat of regret and anguish stopped abruptly as another shot rammed into the back fender like a pile driver.

"Faster!" Moya begged.

CHAPTER FIVE

The second shooter unleashed a volley against the back of Neva's car. Two bullets slammed into the trunk.

One skidded across the top.

Moya popped out of the window, squeezed off a shot, dropped back, saying, "I've got 911 on the phone. There's this huge wreck on I-65. Most of East Precinct is up there. She's called downtown, but it'll take them longer. In the meantime, she says—"

"You tell her there is no 'in the meantime.' She doesn't get somebody up here now, we'll be dead." Neva could breathe again and the sludge that had covered her brain was bleeding off. She talked herself down while she maneuvered the car across the grass. Smart was what they needed right now.

Smart. Not crazy.

Sudden movement from the bottom of the hill caught her eye. Davis's red pickup truck burst from behind the curve of the hill like a jet plane from a cloud. Neva's heart leapt. He must have heard the gunshots from the donut shop across the street and—

The pickup raced past the curve, hit the straight section and slid onto Gallatin Road, leaving Neva speechless.

"What the hell was that all— Granny, look!"

Neva tore her gaze from the road and turned to follow Moya's. A low-slung sports car was tucked in the brush to her right. The word *CORVETTE* sparkled in her headlights. The tailpipe sprayed mist. The shadow of a man's head showed through the back window.

She could outrun a van.

Not a 'Vette.

She forced Davis from her mind and said, without taking her gaze off the car, "What did 911 say?"

"Said she would do what she could."

Already moving much too fast, Neva asked for even more speed. The 'Stang bounced over the asphalt curb, hit the road sideways. Neva tapped the accelerator. The rear end caught.

The car straightened.

Behind her, the Corvette's engine roared.

He'd been waiting for them.

The land dropped away on Moya's side in a sharp grade that ended in the deep concrete ditch behind the funeral home.

Neva flew through the short, straight section, hit the brakes momentarily as she went into the first curve, a long, sweeping, easy thing that the 'Stang took without breaking stride.

The 'Vette's lights glowed behind the curve. She had some distance on him, but not enough.

Second curve coming up.

Very sharp.

'Vette scooting out of the first one.

She hit the curve with her tires shrieking. The acrid smell of burning rubber choked her. The Mustang sloughed toward the outside, slid through, broke a little as it exited, then grabbed asphalt and shot forward.

No time before the third curve. She had to be through it before he left the second. She twisted through the curve's preamble too fast, had to correct.

Her headlights touched the tall monuments looming to her left. The back wheels broke loose, threw the car into a sideways slide directly at the steep slope.

Old car had no airbags.

If they slid off that grade, they would likely die.

Her mother's face, the one she wore before depression stole her life, rose in Neva's mind. Deep blue eyes filled with love.

The outside back wheel caught against the low curb, slid shrieking for a long moment before it flung the car forward. Neva wrestled the wheel, tried to stay on the road, but it was a bumper-car steering wheel with no control.

The front tires hit the low curb on the other side.

The Mustang went airborne.

Neva's stomach rocketed with it, then fell as the car thudded down with a jar that ran from her tailbone to the top of her head. It was now a four-thousand-pound sled careening across her father's expensive sod, ripping it, shredding it, sucking the remnants into the tire grooves, eradicating any traction they might have gained.

A family plot rushed toward them, its towering spire a solid five thousand pounds of stop-you-in-a-heartbeat concrete surrounded by another low curb. The front tires caught, slung the car sideways, again screamed as they tore along the asphalt.

Neva jerked the wheel.

The car whirled like a carnival ride.

Trees, monuments and dark sky blurred past them. Neva's gaze fastened on the rapidly approaching ten-ton angel, circa 1801. Balanced precariously on one slender foot in the middle of its pediment, the angel would topple with one solid blow.

She gave into instinct, wrenched the wheel to the right with all her strength. They would fare better in a roll than beneath the angel's weight. The 'Stang rose onto two wheels, hovered, dropped to the ground with another heavy jolt and stopped.

With her gaze tight on the angel's face, Neva watched it dissolve into relief, then settle back into the concrete mask it had worn for more than two centuries.

Odd what terror could do to a person.

She turned to find Moya's dark eyes so wide the whites showed. "Oh, dear God, Neva, don't *ever* do that again."

"Right," Neva said. Her voice shook like a woman's three times her age. "Never again." She glanced over her shoulder.

The Corvette was halfway around the hairpin curve. All that sliding and spinning had taken practically no time. They still had a chance, but no way in hell could she get back to the road before he was on her.

"Hang on," she said as she backed the car around. "We're going graveside." Nobody knew this cemetery better than she. She didn't need no stinking road to outrun these bozos.

The 'Stang flew across the cemetery, dipping, swerving, weaving among the stones like a gazelle. "Tell me where he is, Moya. Give me the blow by blow."

"Coming around that sharp curve now. God, he's got speed. And maneuverability. It's a *great* car."

"No commercials. Where is he?"

"Sorry. Hitting the straight section now. Next curve in about thirty seconds."

Neva tapped the accelerator. The Mustang responded like a car just off the assembly line. She tapped the pedal again.

It would be close. Too damned close.

"Granny, he's moving fast."

That he was.

Awful fast.

The last section of tall monuments lay ahead, a small family plot bought forever ago. The family grew; people died; the spaces between the graves were narrowed to make room for the next batch.

Neva measured with her eye. Her fenders wouldn't make it.

She swerved hard, flew between the family plot and the monument beside it. The car hit a hole, dipped; then they were running hard.

The 'Vette's lights were still in the curve when the 'Stang bounced onto the road, tires spraying dirt in clods against the undercarriage, throwing it out behind them like a wheat thrasher. "Stay with me, baby!" Neva yelled as the back wheels slid. "Stay with me."

The 'Vette's lights hit her back window.

Her car straightened.

"Go, granny, go!" Moya yelled.

He roared up behind her, wove to her right. She moved with him, then moved back as he tried to move up on her left.

The back window exploded into a thousand cracks. Moya got on her knees, leaned so far out of the window, Neva thought she might fall. Her gun roared.

The 'Vette swerved off the road, its tires squalling, careened wildly toward the deep ditch. If he hit at that speed, he was a goner.

"Got him!" Moya said as she hauled herself back inside.

At the last second, he turned. The car stopped perpendicular to the ditch. He leapt from it as Neva flew past the edge of the building and lost sight of him.

She roared out into wide, empty Gallatin Road. Tomorrow, it would be wall-to-wall cars plodding their slow, congested way toward downtown, but right now it was her own personal racetrack with all traffic lights flashing yellow.

His buds would come after her in their van, but she'd easily beat them to East Precinct.

Where Neva would send someone back for Larissa, make sure she got to rest beside her child.

CHAPTER SIX

The boss leaned back in his enormous leather chair and allowed his fingers to caress the rosewood desktop before him. The heavy brass drawer pulls were made to his specification by an artist who prefaced his work with no fewer than ten sketches, each offering a differing slant, so many, in fact, the boss had asked for a full day to decide from among them.

An icon to wealth, the desk was his latest acquisition, placed in this office in contrast to the barbaric things about his business he couldn't always avoid.

One of his top employees, a tall man with fair hair and eyes, sat in a smaller leather chair across the desk. His ashen face was ghostly against the dark red leather. Sweat covered his forehead. His hands were clasped so tightly in his lap the knuckles glowed white.

The boss's organization had few rules and many rewards. The most important rule, however, was that failure was not an option.

The knobs on the boss's hands where his little fingers had been were reminders of his own failures. Both of them. His own boss had positioned the bolt cutters for a clean cut to minimize the pain. The resultant pain had nonetheless sent him begging for street drugs, anything to stop it.

Not all his pain had been physical.

He prided himself on being careful, checking behind him, taking no chances. Yet he'd failed twice. First, to complete the job to specifications. Second, to realize the punishment he would doubtless receive in time to stop it.

Less than a year later, he'd twisted the garrote and watched the life light fade from his boss's old, rheumy eyes.

He wriggled his remaining fingers slightly now. Amazing how the little ones itched and ached even after thirty years.

His employee shifted, uncrossed and recrossed his legs. The boss lifted his gaze to the man's thin face. "Tell me what happened last night. All of it. Even the parts that will make me angry."

"We took that woman—"

"Larissa." He knew the names of his employees, even the women. Other people had harsh, ugly names for the roles the ladies played in his business, but they were humans with individual names.

Most of his ladies came from foreign countries, but he'd found Larissa practically in his own backyard. A loner, she'd given him her virginity eagerly, as if it were a life-long burden she couldn't wait to lay down. He kept her with him for a long time, but business was business. Eventually, Larissa took her place among the other ladies, dry-eyed, her face the suffering mask he'd first encountered.

When she disappeared a year and a half ago, he'd felt an odd pride that she alone had managed to escape them and sent no one to find her. In fact, if Sam had not seen her standing on a street corner with her baby in her arms, she and her child would be happy and free today. Sam, clearly motivated by frustration that she'd outwitted him and managed to escape, had been overzealous, killing her child. Feeling he had no other real choice, the boss had subsequently ordered her found and punished.

"We took Larissa to the woods," the employee continued. "Sam, he'd already slapped her around a little but, you know, sir." He spread his hands. Long fingers. Doubtless strong, too, like a musician's hands. Did he play an instrument? "Sam and I, we've been seeing some cockiness among the women. We think it's because of her. She escaped. So they think maybe they can, too." He raised an eyebrow as if he'd said something clever.

"Yes," the boss said. "Go on."

"Figured we'd give her a work over, put her down, take pics, show them to the gir—women, let them see what happens to runners."

"Exactly the right course to take," the boss said with a mirthless smile. "How'd we get where we are?"

The employee again uncrossed and recrossed his legs. "Sam was bringing Larissa up. That cop and I had just put his car in the brush so nobody could see it when this Mustang comes driving up the road. Sam was high-tailin' it up the hill with Larissa. Mistake he made was when the lights hit him, he turns around, drags Larissa with him, so the broads in the 'Stang are staring right in their faces. Larissa 'bout breaks his ribs and runs for the car. He's trying to get a shot at her, but this broad is firing, and he's on the ground trying not to take a bullet."

He went on to describe a scene that was no surprise to the boss, a cluster of missed opportunities and stupid decisions that nearly ended with the cop nose down in a huge ditch behind a privately owned business. He wasn't worried about the cop. Smart man. More than smart. He'd take care of things. Sam was another matter.

"Where is Sam?" the boss asked, interrupting the narrative. He'd heard all he needed.

"I put his ass on a plane for Miami this morning." The employee checked his watch. "He should be there. He'll be mopping decks for a gunrunner on its way to Colombia. We won't see him for a while."

There were no records to tie Sam to the boss. There were no records to tie any of them to him.

He'd learned from the very best. The boss blinked away the image of those old, rheumy eyes.

"Ronnie said there was this guy, too," the employee said.

There'd been no mention of a man. Just the two women.

"Ronnie said the dude was a real nut, sir, thought he knew Ronnie, kept calling him Stephen or something. Ronnie told him to get the fuck outta there, pulled his gun. The guy took off like a shot. Ronnie chased him all the way to the river, got there just as the dude drove off, said he tried to get the tires but missed."

"Do you know who he is?"

"No." The head shook from side to side. "Ronnie was so busy trying to hit the tires, he didn't look at the license number."

"Do we know what he looks like?"

The employee spread his long fingers. "It was dark, sir. I don't think Ronnie got a good look."

The boss clenched and unclenched his mutilated hands. "Do you play a musical instrument?"

The man jerked up, staring as if he could read something in the boss's face. "No, sir. I...well, as a kid, I played the saxophone, but I haven't touched it in years."

"Good." The boss rose. "Are you left-handed?"

"No, sir. Right."

"Please stand up and give me your left hand."

The little blood remaining in the man's face drained out. For a long second, the boss thought he would faint, but he managed to get to his feet.

"Put your left hand in mine please."

With his eyes bulging, he laid it palm up in the boss's outstretched left hand. Sweat trickled down his cheeks. "I swear, sir.

It was a cluster, I realize that, but we did the best we could. Those women, they were—"

Barely hearing him, the boss separated the little finger from the rest, tested its sideways motion. Removing a man's fingers was not necessary. What was necessary was to get his attention, leave him with enough pain to prevent another failure. His employee's body was now so stiff it looked made of wood. "Failure is not an option," the boss said. "I think you were aware of that." He lifted his gaze to the man's blue one and held it, then twisted the little finger to the side.

It broke with a satisfying snap.

The employee cried out, jerked his hand back and doubled down over the pain.

"Make up a story and go to the hospital. They'll set it, give you drugs." The boss disapproved of the man's drama. One broken finger was nothing compared to two severed ones.

"Find those women. Bring them to me."

His employee stumbled from the room in silence.

The boss swiveled to stare through the glass window behind him. The setting sun had painted the sky behind the capitol into a mirage of crimson and orange. Let other people ooh and ah over a tropical sunset. He never tired of watching a Tennessee sun set behind its highest seat of power.

A seat he hoped to occupy some day.

CHAPTER SEVEN

Claudia Yates moved down Church Street with the shuffling gait of a woman twenty years older. Her filthy clothes stank so she could barely stand herself. Itchy fleabites covered her ankles and calves, which were streaked with blood where she'd clawed them.

The contacts that changed her sapphire eyes into muddy brown ones were old and dry and needed replacing. She had one more package of rolled cotton to stuff her cheeks to change the shape of her face, as her niece Neva had taught her.

She'd been on the streets for three long years. Too long. For this rotation, however, she only had one more day to masquerade as Cee the homeless woman. Usually, she'd be looking forward to a month of being herself, but lately a month wasn't enough. Seemed she barely got home before it was time to come back.

Today was her fifty-second birthday. She'd celebrated it by walking the pain out of her sciatic nerves, pain driven there from sleeping on a hard sidewalk all night. She dreamed these days of soft mattresses and nice clothes, shoes that had heels no matter how low, and tea, hot, fragrant tea with cream and sugar. Some people spent their summers on forty-foot yachts. Her greatest desire was a cup of real tea.

It was as pitiful as it sounded.

Another thing. The Gucci blouse in her closet. Glorious grays swirled with amazing blues, just the thing to set her eyes on fire. She'd meant to wear it out, go somewhere nice for a long dinner and drinks. Maybe invite Rex. But she'd been called back to the streets a week early, and so it still hung, tags and all, in her closet, a summer blouse she wouldn't get to wear for another six months.

Arthritis bit her every morning. Her knees ached even in the sunshine. Her feet stayed tired.

Something stung her leg. Claudia clawed at it, felt blood dribble as she stopped. She was doing nothing more than feeding the tiny vampires.

Winter was coming and with it the ache in her bum knee and the old gunshot wound in her right shoulder. Didn't hurt so bad in front of a fire in her living room. Particularly if she also had a glass of wine.

She gazed at the tall buildings, as familiar to her as her own home. Nashville gangs were reaching for its jugular as they'd done in Chicago. Did she regret volunteering for this assignment? She'd pointed officials in the direction of no fewer than four groups, two of which were imports from other states, there to establish gangs and take a cut of their profits. Could someone with lesser experience take up where she left off?

For the hundredth time since ten a.m., she checked her surroundings. Halfway down the block, the sun glinted on the highly polished surface of Stan's Gibson guitar as he played Brenda Lee's "I'm Sorry." He'd shoved his cowboy hat back on his dark head; leather boots covered his feet. From here, she couldn't see his battered guitar case, but most days it held a spattering of bills and change dropped in by passersby. That money would be donated to the Nashville Rescue Mission at the end of the month.

Working undercover meant paying attention to detail. Stan's back was against the outside wall of the old Kress Building, which hid the service revolver tucked in the small of his back. The tiny transmitter in his ear was designed to look like a hearing aid.

Claudia could handle herself, but carrying a weapon didn't fit her cover.

This might be a good time to bow out. Her circle of homeless friends was changing with the weather. In winter, they moved south like birds, filled southern cities to the breaking point.

They knew which cities had programs. They liked non-religious programs. Most of them believed if there was a god of any kind anywhere, they wouldn't be living on the streets.

Claudia moved past Stan and across Church Street without a glance, watching for signs of trouble. Blood drops on the sidewalk were a hugely bad sign.

Right now the sidewalks were clean.

Cee's cover included a sister in Manchester, Tennessee, a town small enough and far enough away from Nashville that the chances any of her homeless friends knew of it were small. Every three months or some variation thereof, the sister sent Cee a bus ticket, which she picked up at the post office in the arcade.

"Cee?" Lisa stood in the shadow of an awning, peering through dark eyes. Her hair had probably been light brown at one time but was now a brownish gray tangle. She was overweight and wore the usual eclectic homeless outfit: two jackets, one a screeching neon green and the other made of worn and frayed leather. Her six blouses were piled beneath the jackets; her four skirts hung in separate lengths with the longest next to her body.

Based on Lisa's mood swings, Claudia believed she was bipolar. Lisa trusted old Cee and was extremely observant. Right now, however, she seemed anxious. "That man." Her words slapped out in rapid-fire. "He put her in the dumpster. The dogs—"

Claudia bit back the more normal questions such as what woman and what man. "Where?"

Lisa jerked a grubby thumb over her shoulder toward the alley. Claudia stepped to the side, easily saw the broken cooler at the edge. She lifted her gaze toward the old, rusted dumpster, caught sight of the powerfully built man running toward the other end of the alley.

As if he felt her behind him, he slowed, turned. She jerked back behind the wall, unsure whether he'd seen her.

No way in hell was she going in that alley, draw some crazy banger after her. She'd cue Stan. He could get somebody out here to look at the girl, do what needed doing. What difference did it make whether the body was found now or in half an hour?

She damn near ran over Lisa, then staggered, caught off balance both for real and in the sense that she had no idea how to explain why she wasn't going into the alley. "Man down there," she finally said.

Lisa grabbed Cee's shoulders, dug in her fingers. "You gotta get her. She ain't dead."

"Ain't dead?"

"She was alive. I seen her move. I did." Lisa's voice dropped to a whisper.

Damn, damn, damn, damn!

Claudia moved down the sidewalk into Stan's line of sight, leaned against the brick wall of an abandoned clothing store and put her head in her hands. Stan hit a heavy chord in the middle of "Behind Closed Doors." Message received.

What she should do now was go to the mission and leave whatever had happened in that alley in the alley. Good, able-bodied, armed police persons would do what was needed.

Without getting stabbed or shot.

If the girl was alive, every second counted. Claudia whirled to face Lisa. "I'm tellin' you now, I get hurt, I'm whippin' your ass."

Lisa shrank back into the shadows. "She was movin', Cee. She was."

Wasn't Lisa's fault. Claudia shouldn't be mean to her.

Her heart pounded like it wanted to escape her chest while she waited for Stan to move down the sidewalk. He'd sit where he could see the alley, but if he managed to see anything more than shapes in the quickly deepening shadows, it would be a miracle.

Nonetheless, she waited until he got in place to step into the alley.

The man was gone, but two emaciated stray dogs pawed at the dumpster, a sign the girl was dead. Dogs wouldn't paw after a living body. Something in there was broadcasting a yummy-smelling invitation for canines and rats. Another issue: how to get rid of them without getting bit.

The back door of the Cross Keys Restaurant flew open. A young boy in a filthy apron dropped a disposable pie plate full of ham scraps on the ground. The dogs fell on the ham, filling the air with snarls and growls.

Claudia scooted past them.

The dumpster's top was open, but even at five-six, she was too short to see inside. The side doors were bent and rusted. If she couldn't get them open, she'd have to give it up. The sickly sweet smell of decaying flesh was choking her.

She grabbed the door.

It dug into her hand.

She gritted her teeth and threw herself into the effort, praying the thin metal didn't cut her. A cut filled with rust would require a trip to the hospital.

She hated hospitals.

Finally, screaming like a cat in heat, the door tore along its track. She'd never get it all the way open, but she managed to wrestle it enough to see what was inside. Panting like she'd run a mile, she dug the little flashlight from between her breasts.

Judging from the wild placement of the woman's arms and legs, he'd tossed her over the top. Claudia flipped her hand at the buzz of flies on the woman's face. They lifted as one and then fell into fifty individual buzzing pests and gave her the first glance at the woman's injuries. She sucked in a quick breath, tasted putrefaction, stepped back, rage boiling through her.

They'd beaten her, messed up her face.

Claudia swallowed again, leaned back in.

She moved the light back up the girl's torso. A hole in the middle of her chest, its edges raised. An exit wound. The brownish blood around the hole said she'd been dead a while. Lisa must have seen her limbs sway as the man carried her, thought she was moving.

How many women were beaten to death, shot, knifed by people they trusted? How many were slowly dying of abuse right now? If she had her way, every woman would carry a gun. Couple of these bastards got their balls blown off, maybe the rest would think twice.

The back of her neck prickled.

He was at the far mouth of the alley, opposite where Lisa waited. He was the same height and general build as the one she'd seen earlier. She couldn't see his eyes, didn't know whether he was peering at her as she was at him.

A shiver wracked her.

Old Cee hobbled, so Claudia was forced to hobble also, hoping Stan was still across the street, hoping he would hear her if she had to scream, hoping the man behind her was gone.

Heavy footsteps moved toward her, running fast.

She broke into a trot. Keeping Cee's cover wasn't as important as keeping her life.

He sped up.

She had nothing to fight with, not even a rock.

She hobbled around the building at her end of the alley, scooped up the old cooler, flattened herself against the wall.

Movement caught her eye.

Large George, so called because he was seven feet tall and weighed at least 350 pounds, raced down the sidewalk like a man running for a bus. He whizzed past her as if she didn't exist, full-out running so the ground shook with his steps.

Claudia opened her mouth to tell him to be careful, but before she could speak, she heard a muted "uhnnnn." Something heavy hit the pavement hard. She could almost see her pursuer slamming into George's chest. Must have been like slamming into the nose of an oncoming locomotive.

Large George burst from the alley, grabbed her hand and took off at a dead run.

No way she could match his stride, let alone his speed, so she took refuge in old Cee's limp. George tugged at her hand. "He's down now, Cee, but he ain't gonna stay down long. We gotta hurry."

"Doin' the best I can, George," she said, but a sudden sound behind them sent her flying and diminished old Cee's limp considerably.

CHAPTER EIGHT

At the mission, George dragged the glass door open and shoved Claudia through. She whirled back, but the darkness had already swallowed him.

Big man moved like a cat.

The mission was full of people. If the son of a bitch who'd chased her from the alley followed her here, a lot of people could get hurt. Automatically, she reached behind her, but the service revolver she'd carried in the small of her back for years wasn't there. Despite the dangers of living on the street, old Cee didn't carry a weapon. Didn't fit the character, but right now, Claudia would have given a year's pay for the comforting feel of steel in her hand.

She stayed near the door with her mouth dry, and peered through the heavy glass. She'd not seen him well enough to recognize him, but she had his general shape: a short, squat, powerful man, a man who could wring your neck without breathing hard.

As the minutes ticked by and she began to calm, she thought of the dead woman, wondered who she'd been. Was there a husband, maybe some children walking the floors waiting for her to come home? Or was she just another working girl whose death would go unnoticed and unavenged?

Had it not been for Large George, Claudia might be beside the dead woman in the dumpster. Claudia could handle herself, was better trained than most women, kept in shape, practiced, made Neva practice, too, just in case. But a woman went into any fight with a man already at least one point down. Her muscle mass was lighter, her body less dense, more easily broken. Women won bare-knuckle fights with men by using the muscles between their ears.

She knew every trick in the book, but, still, she blessed George for moving in when he did.

Between the powerful lights on the mission's roof and the streetlights, she had a good view of the sidewalk. Down the street, lower Broadway was rocking and rolling. Street bands played on the banks of the river. The restaurants were so crowded people were forced to wait on the sidewalk. Place like that, lots of people, lots of noise, a perfect place to hide, just blend into the crowd and move with it.

Thirty minutes later, when nobody had approached the mission, Claudia began to wonder if she'd imagined his pursuit. Maybe the poor man was in a hurry to get home, running not after her but toward the last bus of the night.

Besides, the mission was serving roast beef and gravy from the room behind her, and the smells had her mouth running with water. She took one last look down the street and then turned for the big room. She'd eat, get a shower and then gather Cee's few things.

Because tomorrow, she went home.

She'd taken two steps when Scott called her name. He was in the shadows just beyond the cafeteria's glass doors. His hair looked like he'd tried to pull it all out. His eyes were dark with worry.

"Can I speak with you?" he asked.

"Sure."

"In my office."

Scott's office was down the hall, one of many that housed the people who kept the mission going. He held his door open for her, gestured at the overstuffed chair in front of his metal desk. Scott's office would have embarrassed a janitor, yet it seemed to make him, chairman of the executive board, extremely happy.

Claudia sank into the chair, conscious as always of the fleas that were doubtless leaping under the desk after Scott's ankles.

"I got a call just a few minutes ago," Scott said. He leaned sideways suddenly and scratched his ankle.

She shifted. "Okay."

"A man. He wouldn't identify himself. He asked if you were sleeping here. I told him I didn't give out that kind of information. He said he would come and see for himself." Scott put his elbows on the desk and clasped his hands. "Did something happen tonight?"

"Yes." She filled him in.

When she'd finished, he said with a shake of his head, "No way you're sleeping on the streets, and it's too dangerous to the others for you to stay here tonight. I'll call Rex for you."

"Thanks."

Scott ran a tight ship, but in a 14,000-square-foot facility, safety was illusory at best. The front doors were locked at midnight, but fire codes required they be locked only on the outside. A man wanting in simply knocked.

Claudia was no chicken, didn't run anytime somebody crooked a finger, but Scott was exactly right. This wasn't a street grudge. If her pursuer thought she'd seen him, she wouldn't stand a chance.

She left Scott's office to find Lisa waiting for her in the hallway.

"You comin' back tonight?" Lisa asked.

"My sister's sick and my brother-in-law's on his way."

"You be back?"

Claudia gave Lisa an eye roll. "Ain't I always?"

"Yeah," Lisa said. "But lately, Cee, I dunno. Somethin's different. You sick? You got that stuff makes people die?"

"Cancer? No, Lisa, I don't have cancer. I'm just old and tired and wish I had a nice soft place to sleep, like at my sister's house. She said she might let me stay sometime. I mean, really stay, you know? Like live there. Now that she's sick, well," she said with a slight smile, "maybe I can."

"You come back, Cee," Lisa said. Her lower lip hung in a pout. Anger filled her eyes. "You come right back. Just like you always do."

"Okay, Lisa," she said with a pat to the woman's fleshy back. "I'll be back just like always. Meanwhile, you take care of things."

"Like what, Cee?"

"Like Bobby," Claudia said, speaking of the youngest of the three children on the streets right now. Little tow-headed, green-eyed kid. His head reached barely to his mother's thigh. Good woman. Hard-working, good to the boy when she had the time. But she worked twelve hours a day at a dry cleaner that paid her slave wages. Their home was an ancient car that Metro police ignored instead of dragged away. There were no babysitters on the streets, so Bobby was left to take care of himself while she worked.

Most of the people on the streets protected Bobby and his mom, hiding Bobby from the do-gooders from Child Protective Services, who would snatch him into a foster home in a heartbeat. Bobby didn't need a foster home. He needed a home for himself and the good woman who loved him.

She made a note to talk to Rex about the kid. There *were* decent people who would take the homeless into their homes, give them six safe months to get things under control. If Bobby's mother could have half a chance, she'd make it work.

Slinging Cee's backpack over her shoulder, Claudia shoved through the door.

Music and garbled crowd noise wafted from the tourist area. Bright lights and crowds stoked economies, but she missed the old Broad Street. She and her dad had often stopped by the old Acme Farm Supply down there, then moved on to the hardware place. A sunny Saturday morning spent moving from store to store until they had food for her mother's chickens and enough nails to fix the shed roof.

All that was gone, replaced by the jiggle and jump that drew tourists.

Up the street, just past the Mason's Lodge, a taillight blinked. Three blinks. Stop. Three more. Claudia hefted her backpack, adjusted the strap and headed up. She watched every cranny and crack on the way, scanning for deep shadows or shadows that moved, anything out of the ordinary.

Finally, she opened the passenger-side door of the dark sedan, threw her backpack into the back, slid inside, closed and locked the door.

"Thanks for coming," she said, smiling into Rex Mason's darkly tanned face. His blue jeans, red-checked shirt and cowboy boots told her he'd been at home when Scott called. His Sig lay on the console between them.

The snotty little skinny kid who'd followed her younger brother, Robert, around when they were kids had managed to grow into a handsome man. First a handsome young man, then a handsome husband and now a handsome widower.

"You okay?" he asked as he pulled away from the curb.

"Fine. Scott got a bit spooked."

"So he said. Stan said they got that woman's body out of the dumpster."

"They find any unconscious men on the ground nearby?" Claudia asked and then shook her head at Rex's puzzled look. "Long story. I'll tell you tomorrow." She fastened her seatbelt and moved as far away from him as the belt would allow. He wouldn't comment on her stench no matter how bad it was, but if she was nearly choking on it, he was bound to smell it, too.

Besides, there were the fleas.

"We know who she is," Rex said.

Claudia jerked around to stare at him. "Who? That woman?"

"Yes. We know who she is, think we know who killed her. Or at least the organization that killed her. One of two."

"Who?"

"Got two traffickers working the area," he said and then shrugged. "Well, hell, we've probably got a hundred, but two big ones, two that matter. She escaped from one of them about a year, maybe year and a half back. They found her this week, killed her baby."

"As punishment?" she asked, a picture of infant Neva in her mind. Babies should be off limits to violence, protected by a common taboo. The penalties for harming them should be torture, not death, torture as barbaric and wrong as it was to harm a helpless innocent.

"Looks like the kid was dropped. Like maybe it went down wrong."

Claudia remembered the woman's face, wished these men a slow and painful death.

"You going home?" Rex asked as the light at Ninth changed to green.

"Yes."

"Don't recommend it."

"When I say I'm going home, I mean eventually. Right now, you should take me to the big-box store on Nolensville Road. I'll go in as Cee and come out me, only still filthy and stinky, pick up my car and drive home." Scott had doubtless filled Rex in on the man who'd chased her down the alley. If she got home tonight, she'd have to fight Rex to do it.

She loved his protective nature, appreciated that he cared what happened to her. But she was far from helpless. Three guns—one a brand-new Beretta Nano, the other two Glocks—were scattered in strategic places around her house. They were loaded and ready to fire.

Her doors and windows were alarmed, and while she had no illusions that someone who wanted in could get in, she'd made it as hard as she possibly could. She even had a tape of a deep-voiced

German shepherd that would activate the minute a door or window was jiggled.

Sleeping on the streets had taught her to sleep with one eye practically open, so she heard even the slightest rustle, had to hear it to survive out there.

Besides, there was no rule that people had to be snatched from their beds. They could pick her up outside East Precinct if they wanted her badly enough.

There was no safe place.

Rex took I-65 South, headed for I-440, which would lead them to I-24 and eventually Nolensville Road.

"I don't like it, Claudie," he said, using the nickname he and Robert used when they were too young to say her name right.

"I'll be okay. You know I will."

"I know no such thing and neither do—"

The sedan went airborne, all four wheels off the pavement. Steel shrieked as a huge force from behind shoved them forward.

"Mother of God!" Rex yelled, his gaze in the rearview mirror, eyes wide, his face pale.

The sedan bucked, twisted again. Claudia managed to get a glimpse of the rear window. A truck's grill filled it top to bottom and side to side.

Rex slammed his foot on the brakes. The tires joined the steel in full-throated protest.

He gave up on the brakes and accelerated, pushed the speedometer up to 90. When he let off, the big rig pushed him to 100. The needle pegged out and still the force behind them shoved them on, driving them inexorably forward. Metal shrieked as bolts popped and screws let go.

"Damn it! I'm afraid to turn the wheel," Rex said. "We get sideways of the son of a bitch, he'll T-bone us." His face was greenish with fear.

He stomped the brakes, threw himself against the seat, stiffened his leg, but the brakes were helpless against the truck's weight and power.

Her mind whirling so fast she could barely think, Claudia grabbed the Glock.

Metal clanged onto the pavement as pieces of the rear end began to lose their grip on the frame.

The sedan couldn't take much more.

She thrust her head through the lowered window. Wind battered the back of her head like soft rocks, lifted the tightly glued wig and sent it flying. She gritted her teeth and peered through her own hair, which flew around her face like a cloud of moths.

The truck's windshield was high above the car's roof. No way to get a bullet into the driver.

Another hunk of metal tore from the rear end, clanged to the pavement and screeched its way under the truck.

Her hands shook. The wind tried to snatch the gun.

She drew a bead on the front tire, the only real target available, sighted to the best of her ability, stiffened her arms and squeezed the trigger.

The Glock kicked back.

The truck wobbled, swerved right, its front bumper screaming across the back of Rex's sedan, forcing the vehicle toward the guardrail.

Rex again slammed on the brakes, stiffened his leg and shoved back again until the seat bowed out with the pressure, fought the wheel around.

The truck swerved across the other lane toward that guardrail. The tire Claudia hit shredded under the pressure and threw huge hunks of rubber across the road.

"Hold on!" Rex yelled.

Claudia shoved herself back in her seat in her turn. The sedan was on a collision course with the guardrail. They wouldn't die, but at this speed, it wouldn't be gentle.

The brakes caught. The car slowed.

Rex fought it to a stop.

"If it'll run," Claudia said, her words panting with her shuddering breath, "keep going. God knows what he'll do."

Rex pulled back onto the pavement, tested the brakes and the wheel.

"It's wolly-gaggling," he said. "Rear end's probably way out of line. I can't get much speed, but it runs." He remained occupied with keeping the car on the road until they hit the straight section on I-440. "Claudie, did you talk to anybody tonight? Did anybody else know about the woman you found?"

Large George knew.

Rex distrusted George. They'd found two private detectives in Homeless Town years ago. Gangland-style killing, bullets through the forehead. But Rex had focused on George, suspected him of the murders.

Claudia had pointed out how little proof he had.

He'd pointed out that George beat his wife to death.

She pointed out that at the time, his wife was beating their two-year-old son with a skillet.

Rex pointed out that George hit her fifteen times, hit her long after she was dead. "That's rage, Claudia," he'd snapped. "I'm watching George, and you should, too."

She *had* watched George, seen his gentleness, seen him accused of ridiculous things. Being a big man, George said, made you an easy target. For all his lack of education, George had a rough kind of wisdom that could benefit more highly educated people.

If she mentioned George, Rex would haul him into East Station, scare him half to death.

"Just Scott," she said.

Rex gave her a quick glance. "See our friend anywhere back there?"

They'd rounded the inner loop and were now poking down I-24.

Claudia scanned the vehicles around them. "I don't," she said.

"Good. I want you to stay at my house tonight."

Her neck and back hurt from the blow they'd taken. She remembered those hard heels in the alley, not to mention the bizarre and sudden attack they'd just endured.

Rex's place was comfy. He'd be working during the day, perhaps at night. Wasn't like they didn't know one another well enough to be roommates for a while.

"Okay," she said, and then tried to lighten their heavy mood with, "But I get dibs on the TV."

He shot her a grin. "As long as we don't have to watch that girlie shit."

"What girlie shit?" she asked. "I watch only high-brow programming, stay exclusively on the public broadcast channels with a few forays into English productions."

Rex barked a short laugh. "Umm hummm."

Claudia settled back against the seat with her hand on her neck. They'd stirred a nest of vipers.

The important thing now was to stay out of their way.

CHAPTER NINE

When she came off the streets, Claudia's first act usually was to purchase a pair of jeans and a top, panties, bra and a new backpack from the big box. She then used their restroom to sponge off and change her identity, leaving the place as a somewhat dingy, but reasonably acceptable tall woman with silver-gray hair and sapphire blue eyes.

Tonight, she'd purchased three pair of jeans, panties and an equal number of tops, two bras, makeup and a pair of shoes in addition to the new, non-flea-infested backpack because Rex was now arguing she should stay with him for a week or two.

"I can't live with you," she'd said in the midst of the argument.

"I don't know why not." His angry gaze swept her like a saber. "It's a nice house."

"Yes, Rex, but it's not *my* house. I could stay a day or two, but I have to live my life."

"A day or two, then," he'd finally agreed, but she knew him well. He'd circle back to demanding a week, keep at it to wear her resistance down. He insisted on coming inside with her, where he remained so totally glued to her hip, she barely talked him out of going with her into the bathroom.

"I think there's an ordinance against that," she'd said. "Wait here." She loved that he cared, couldn't imagine a better friend, but geez Louise, his laser focus sometimes made her feel trapped. She stopped in the middle of that thought, remembering the times Neva had cried out at her for just such a laser focus.

It would be good to see her niece. She and Moya and that wild Zanna girl. Claudia called them the three Mouseketeers when they were young. There wasn't much difference now. Unless Zanna was in California, if you saw one of them, you saw all three. Maybe she'd take the girls out to dinner while she was—

She broke that thought. She might not just be off. She might be done. Rex certainly wanted her off the streets, but was she ready? She was slower than when she was young, a natural part of aging that could get her killed on the streets. Was she *too* slow? Or had she just been a blazing fighting machine at twenty-five?

She'd been okay, good enough to do the job, get a few commendations and climb the ladder of success far higher than any other woman on the force, particularly those who'd started when she did.

Back when all women could do was get coffee for the guys.

She wanted to leave at her peak, not at the end of her usefulness, never wanted to see pity in the eyes of her coworkers, absolutely would not stay on the streets when she couldn't hold her own or was a danger to others.

She locked the stall door behind her, slid Cee's filthy clothes off, stuffed them in the plastic bag she carried in the backpack.

"Die, you little shits," she said to the fleas.

She'd not had time for that shower at the mission, and now she wanted one with the same hunger a starving woman would want food, but that would have to wait. She ran her hands through her hair and scratched deeply into her scalp. She soaped up her hair twice a week at the mission if it was safe, but it needed a good shampoo.

The old, dry contacts and that horrid wig were already gone, so no need to worry over them.

She slipped on a bra and panties, slid on the jeans and carried the blouse to the sink where she soaped her arms and hands and dried with paper towels, then slipped the blouse over her head.

It was well past ten. No one interrupted her. She could have probably taken a sponge bath all over, but neither she nor Rex knew whether they'd been followed. Didn't think so, saw nobody, but the truck had come out of nowhere.

Drug dealers and slavers had all kinds of eyes parked everywhere. The guy in the black Brooks Brothers suit on a downtown street was as likely to be a slaver as the blue-jean-clad Hispanic. Stuff made big bucks, and big bucks bought big power.

The blouse was green and lit fire in her eyes. She pushed her hair back and took just one second to inspect her face. High cheekbones, rounded chin. She was dark like her brother, both of them having taken after their father, whose own father had been Cherokee. She'd always been glad she got the old Indian skin. It wore well, never burned in the sun, and mosquitoes hated it.

It would wrinkle soon and badly, she guessed, based on the map of her father's life that was etched in his face by the time he was sixty. But wrinkles were a part of living.

And living was good.

The whisper of soft soles across concrete flooring stopped her thoughts. A cold shiver ran through her. Nerves. Understandable, but this was a public restroom. People used it.

The shiver returned.

Rex was outside because she'd made him stay out there.

Stupid woman.

She whisked her makeup into the new backpack, tiptoed to the wall nearest the entrance, flattened against it. The backpack wouldn't make much of a weapon, but it was all she had.

The footsteps faltered as if their owner was aware of the threat behind the wall. A slight sigh filled the anteroom. One step. Then another. Without loosening her grip on the backpack, Claudia slid nearer the door.

She'd have a single second to decide whether to swing. She wanted a good look.

The steps resumed in a sudden flurry. Almost before Claudia could take another breath, a tiny figure scurried through the door.

Reflex brought the backpack halfway up before she saw that the woman's small hands were on the waistband of her blue jeans.

Claudia froze.

Broken zipper. Thus the sigh and the faltering steps. She was holding the jeans together with both hands.

Claudia softly exhaled. The woman whirled, took in the backpack, paled. Her eyes rounded.

"It's okay," Claudia said. "I'm leaving. Sorry about your pants." She hefted the bag, dropped Cee's clothes and the old backpack into the trash. She left the bathroom sagging with releasing tension.

* * * *

Rex stopped at the end of his driveway, waved Claudia around him. By the time she reached the garage, he'd activated the door. She drove inside, pulled as close to the wall as she could and doused the engine. Behind her, the garage door groaned as it descended.

It was about halfway down when Rex ducked under.

"You okay?" he asked.

"Fine. You?"

"Yeah. I've called downtown. They're sending somebody out." He pulled his keys from his pocket. When the door was open, she stepped through and said over her shoulder, "I can't stand this dirt another minute."

"You know where the guest bath is. If they get here before you get out, I'll stall them."

She turned back, put a quick hand on his arm and squeezed. "Thank you."

"For what?"

"Picking me up, giving me a place to stay. I wasn't very nice about it."

"You're never nice when I try to take care of you," he said with a grin, but he put his hand over hers and squeezed in his turn. "God, woman, you smell like a hog. Get a shower."

CHAPTER TEN

"Okay, Ice. I get it."

It was Sunday near noon. Still exhausted from Friday night, already irritated she'd had to work today, Neva was in no mood for Ice's parenting.

He tossed his hands into the air. "Don't think you do, little girl. Midnight. Not the right time to play in the woods. We've had this conversation before."

"Kids and witches," she said. "They're in that cemetery every year. You've helped me run them out. What's got your panties in such a twist?" Ice's anger was a seldom thing, but today, he'd shoved his gurneys against the wall hard enough to make them clang, then whirled on her as if she'd kidnapped his oldest child.

"My 'panties' are twisted because you nearly got your stupid self killed. Do you understand that?"

"I was there. My car's got more holes in it than a colander. Had it not been for Moya, we'd be toast. Larissa Nelson is dead. Hell yes, I understand. Fully and completely. Without a doubt." She hadn't realized she was shouting until he flinched.

She lowered her voice. "I know you're trying to help me. I appreciate it. I will be ultra, completely and totally careful. There's a cop driving by this parking lot every two hours, one parked outside my house all night. I am the niece and goddaughter, respectively, of not one but two Nashville detectives."

She pointed at the high shelf. "See the gun? Betcha never thought I'd have one of those. Moya wouldn't let me come to work without it. She wants me to go to the range, learn how to shoot."

"And will you?"

Neva opened her mouth, then closed it. She'd managed to bring that one in from the car by wrapping it in a towel so she didn't have to touch it. There'd been guns in the Oakley house as long as she could remember. One of her earliest trainings at her father's hand was how to handle the weapon, what to touch and what not to touch. He'd kept his guns locked away, but he'd been smart enough to prepare her in case she found one that wasn't.

She'd gone to the range with him when she was older, learned how to shoot, learned how not to shoot. She'd been as comfortable with a gun as she was with a makeup kit.

Until Gray's death.

After, she'd fought her way out of near catatonia to near normalcy. She'd work on liking guns again someday.

Just not *this* day. This day, the thought of touching it made her shudder.

"That's what I thought," Ice said.

"Moya and I blundered into something dangerous, I admit that. But it's over. I've already told the cops what the guy looked like. They've found Larissa's body. Why would these people want me?"

He put his hands on her shoulders. "I don't know, sweetie. I just know it makes me sick to think of them—"

"They won't," she said, unwilling to hear the rest. The police thought she and Moya had interrupted a group of human traffickers, although the cops had been reluctant to guess what the traffickers were doing in the cemetery, maintaining that would take investigation. Neva knew little about such people beyond the fact that they were ruthless flesh peddlers who coerced and forced innocent women and children into a hellish life. Ice didn't have to warn her to be careful. Her neck prickled every time she walked through a door. She continued, knowing the sincerity in her voice was quite genuine. "I'll watch every step, Ice, check the car before I get in. Moya and I have agreed not to go out alone. We're as scared as you are. Believe me."

"I wish you'd learn how to use that gun."

"I *know* how to use it, Ice. I just can't—"

"—touch it," he finished for her.

She nodded.

He hung around for another few minutes, but they'd both said all they had to say. He left shaking his head and warning her again to be careful.

Ten minutes later, Neva's phone played "Wouldn't It Be Nice."

"Hey," Davis said, his voice warm and friendly, sounding like he was in the next room instead of four thousand miles away. "Thought I'd check in before I have to leave again. Everything okay there?"

Not even. "Pretty good. Did you have a good flight?" Until that second, she hadn't known how she would deal with Davis. He'd been in the cemetery Friday night, but "in the cemetery" covered a lot of land. No way he didn't hear the gunshots, but if he'd been on the backside of the hill, which seemed likely judging from where he'd emerged, he might not have realized how close they were. In any case, if he wanted her to know what he'd done that night, it was up to him to tell her, not for her to drag it from him.

"Delayed in Chicago for an hour, which meant it was nearly midnight London time when we landed. I went right to bed. It's six p.m. here. Noon there?"

"Yep."

"Weather is typical: cold, cloudy and wet. I toured around earlier with an old buddy of Dad's, which means I was regaled with the British equivalent of 'I knew you when you pooped in your pants' stories, but he's a good egg."

They talked for ten minutes. She told him about Moya and Ken. They laughed together over Moya's assessment of Ken's sexual preference.

"So, attractive, neat and polite means gay," Davis said with a chuckle.

"Apparently."

"Listen," he said, "about Friday night…" He hesitated.

Neva held her breath.

"You don't feel like I talked you into something your father wouldn't approve of, do you?"

What the hell? Oh. He was talking about… "Are you kidding me?" she said, laughing as much at the unexpected turn of the conversation as at the idea he'd coerced her into sex. "I wasn't just a willing partner in our mutual crime, buddy. I was enthusiastic, eager. In other words, if you hadn't jumped my bones, I would have jumped yours."

"If he'd come in—" Davis began.

"He almost never comes back that late," Neva said, realizing as she spoke that there was no reason he *couldn't* come back that late. She'd allowed her overheated libido and disappointment to turn her into a teenager. "We'll be grownups from now on. But your only guilt here is that you are too damned sexy to resist. How'd it go with

Stephen?" She mentally bit her lip. She'd meant to let him tell her, but her curiosity had driven her elsewhere.

"You're pretty irresistible yourself," Davis said. "As for Stephen, I did see a man who looked like him. Might even have *been* him. I tried to make contact, but that didn't work out. I guess I should have expected he wouldn't know me. The last time he saw me, I was a skinny kid with a mouthful of braces."

"But you do think it might have been Stephen?"

He hesitated. "Might have been," he said finally. "He looks just like the picture you aged, but it was dark. He didn't exactly throw his arms around my neck in welcome. I could be wrong."

A sudden alarm cut through Neva's ear. She jerked the phone away, but kept it close enough to hear him say, "Oh, sorry." The noise stopped. "That means I have to go. Having dinner at a men's club with Charles, and I'm not dressed."

"Sounds interesting."

"Wish you were here," he said.

"Me, too. Talk to you tomorrow?"

"Yep. Tell Moya I said hey."

When he clicked off, she gazed at the phone for a long minute, trying to read his mind. From his description of Friday night's encounter with Stephen, you'd think it was a cakewalk. Hadn't looked like a walk of any kind. More like a wild run.

Was he spinning the truth so she wouldn't worry? Or was there a darker reason he played it down?

She turned with a shrug toward the five bodies waiting against the wall. He'd told her what he wanted to tell her. He didn't have to do more.

CHAPTER ELEVEN

It was well after dark when Neva stepped from Oakley's shower, dried off, pulled on an old sweatshirt and her most comfortable blue jeans.

Her phone played the rumba she'd chosen for anonymous phone calls.

"Neva," John Pratt's deep voice said when she answered, "is my errant offspring with you?"

Confused by his question, she answered automatically. "No, he's not. I talked to him around noon. Is he not answering?"

"No," John said. "At least he *didn't* answer. I've only called him once. Probably shouldn't be so impatient. We have a client who needs some help. Since he was to leave for England tomorrow, I'd hoped he could meet with her tonight."

Struggling to keep the shock from her voice, Neva said, "Are you sure of the date? I thought he left yesterday morning."

There was a moment's silence. "I could be confused, Neva." Another short interlude. "In fact, now that I think about it, I am confused. He did leave yesterday. You're exactly right. My memory isn't as good as it once was."

"No problem." She didn't know Davis's dad well, but his voice sounded tight, uncomfortable.

"Since he's out of the country, I'll need to handle this myself. I hope all is well with you."

"Just fine. And you?"

"Couldn't be better. Busy, but that's a good thing."

When he clicked off, she tucked the phone in her pocket, then leaned over her prep table and stared at the far wall.

Was Davis in England? Of course. He said he'd toured with one of his dad's old buddies, said he'd slept well, said it was six p.m. He hadn't *said* he was in England, but, really, why would he?

She shook her head. No reason to doubt Davis. His dad probably did have memory issues. Most people did from time to time.

She forced her gaze and her thoughts to the one body against the wall that wasn't ready, a woman, blonde but with the dark skin of a brunette. The makeup to match her skin was at Davis's.

She needed it. That was true. If it also gave her a chance to check his suitcases, well, that was just fine.

Her cell phone played the theme from *Lawman*.

"Hey, Uncle Rex."

"What's wrong?"

"Nothing. I'm just tired."

"You going home now?"

"Yes, but I need to stop by Davis's first. I left some makeup over there. I will need it tomorrow."

"I'll be outside his house, follow you home. There's a black and white at your place. They can stay one more night."

She glanced at the gun on the shelf as she reached for the doorknob. Ice's concern had landed on fertile soil. She'd seen Larissa's face.

Evil, vicious men who used and abused women as they saw fit.

She should take the thing with her.

She got her fingers nearly to its towel before her stomach twisted.

She pulled back, flexed her fingers and went for the door.

Uncle Rex was meeting her.

She'd be fine.

Outside, she peeped under the rental car, checked the back seat and then slid inside.

Lights flickered through the woods at the top of the hill like oversized fireflies.

Cops. Been up there all day.

"You guys should go on home," she said as if they could hear her. "No way you can really see anything."

A huge hunter's moon, deep orange like a pumpkin, dominated the eastern sky. In its strange light, clouds scudded, driven by a brisk wind that made the trees rattle. A night for witches, warlocks and the things that make little girls hide under the covers and pray for morning.

Neva parked her rental car under the streetlight near Davis's sidewalk. Uncle Rex's sedan sat on the other side of the street facing her.

She turned her left-turn signal on, then off.

He blinked his in response.

Outside, she allowed her gaze to follow the massive brick structure upward past its second story. It was the most visited home on the annual Nashville Historic Trek, a testament to Davis's skill and creativity. She'd never before seen it dark, which must be why it usually filled her with warmth and good feelings, and tonight felt cold and a little frightening.

Her new key felt stiff. The lock was stubborn so she wondered if perhaps it wasn't going to open. Finally, with a distinct click, it did. She swept the street with her gaze, stepped inside, closed the door.

The streetlight gave the room enough illumination so she could move around. Too dark to see details, but she knew this foyer quite well. Davis had removed its ceiling, then hung a single slab of rose-colored marble along the sixteen-foot-high back wall and set a narrow, lighted pool at its base. The fountain pumped water up the back of the marble and allowed gravity to pull it down in a soft whisper.

She reached for the light switch, then stopped, suddenly shy at being here without Davis. If his neighbors saw the lights on, they'd likely tell Davis. She'd have to explain why, which she could certainly do, but if she left them off, used the small flashlight she had in her pocket, the issue wouldn't arise.

Not that she felt guilty.

Exactly.

Her flashlight beam fell on the long, narrow table. She moved it to Stephen's picture. Dark-haired where Davis was light, Stephen was shorter, clearly a child produced by a different mix of his parents' genes. On the right of the picture, Davis kept a stack of colorful flyers that said he would pay for any information leading to his brother, dead or alive. A year ago, she'd used FaceGen, the software that helped her restore faces, to generate a picture of him as he would look now.

She studied it.

Can you possibly still be living and not contact your family?

From what Claudia said, living on the streets folded layers of stiff indifference over the soul and heart.

Maybe Davis was right to keep looking.

He spent most of his time in his den, a repurposed bedroom at the far end of the long, narrow hallway. She stopped at its door, caught as always by the beauty within. The cut-glass window Davis had designed himself filtered the light outside so it filled the room with prisms that floated through the darkness. She spent several moments filling herself with its beauty before noticing the deep shadows near his antique desk.

She pointed her flashlight at them.

The lower drawer hung open. Papers littered the floor. Her makeup case, which had been under the desk, was shoved to one side.

She dropped to her knees, peered in the drawer at a gray metal box. She knew better than to touch it. If someone else had been in here, fingerprints would be important. She snatched a pair of scissors from the middle drawer and slid their tips under the edge of the box, flipped it open.

The deep molds where his gun and its clips should have been were empty.

She sat back on her heels, staring at the papers on the floor around the desk. It made sense he'd want to be armed to watch a drug deal, but this mess around her—that was so not Davis. She tidied the papers, felt something thick in their middle, pulled out an envelope.

A strange envelope, stretched in the middle as if someone had forced something too large into it. She laid it on the desk. The rectangular stretch was dollar-size.

An envelope full of money.

And a gun.

Her first thought was to call Uncle Rex. But then she remembered her phone conversation with Davis, how normal and comfortable he'd sounded. If he was in trouble, he hid it well.

She gazed again at the objects.

His gun, *his* money.

His business.

She reached for the papers, then rocked back on her heels as Davis's wild rush from the cemetery rose in her mind. What if this mess wasn't Davis's? What if the slavers had tossed the house looking for clues to his whereabouts.

She'd call Uncle Rex's cell phone as she drove home, tell him what she'd found here, let him check it out tomorrow. She rose. She'd spent too much time in here already. Uncle Rex deserved his dinner and a soft place on his couch.

* * * *

Rex Mason tried to keep his eyes open.

No sleep last night and none so far today.

Getting older, dude. Can't do these marathons anymore.

After he saw Neva home, he'd sack in for twelve hours. He'd already exceeded his hours this week.

Metro didn't like to pay overtime.

He barely caught sight of the bum before the crazy old coot slammed his hands against Rex's window and babbled something around a wad of tobacco.

Poor old soul. Probably cold and hungry.

Rex slid his gun into his right hand, lowered the window. "Whassup, old timer?"

"Officah, I need some whiskey."

"What you need is sleep, old buddy. You got a place?"

"Yessah, but first I need some whiskey."

"Go on, now," Rex said, his attention snagged by what might have been movement near Davis's front door. "Step aside for me, buddy." He peered around the man's shoulder. Davis's front door was closed. If Neva didn't get her ass out here pretty soon, he'd go after her.

"Whiskey," the bum said again.

"Tell you what," Rex said, "I got no whiskey." He held up the handcuffs. "But I can put these on you, take you downtown for the night. Won't be any whiskey, but you can have a warm bed. Whaddya say?"

A slow smile crossed the bum's face. "Nah," he said, eyeing Rex as if he knew a secret he wouldn't share. "I'll be goin' on, officah. You have a good night, now."

He backed away from the car with that strange smile on his face.

Rex checked his watch. Five more minutes and he was going after her.

* * * *

She grabbed the makeup case, headed for the door, stopped as Davis's drafting table caught her gaze. Davis's scissors were still in her hand. She dropped down on the stool behind the table, put them down, ran a hand softly down the yellowed blueprints clipped to the board.

Who else would try to change four blocks of downtown Nashville into a pedestrian mall? Four blocks of restaurants, bars, honky-tonks and gift shops.

He'd fought his way through architectural peer reviews and scathing newspaper articles, determined to prove what none of them believed: that you could create a network of subterranean tunnels beneath Nashville's downtown to deliver goods to the restaurants and stores in those four blocks.

The half-mile-deep pile of rocks beneath that part of Nashville spoke against him. Then Frank Gorman, Pratt Architecture's principal architect, showed up with these old plans. Davis said Frank'd had them in his attic forever. They were hard to read, Davis said, but they clearly showed a network of hand-hewn tunnels beneath Nashville's lower downtown area, exactly where Davis needed them.

Davis said there were no other copies of the prints anywhere, no record of the tunnels he could find. He'd keep them secret until he could decide what to do with them. Last week, he brought the drawings to Oakley's, explained they could form the nucleus of his delivery tunnels.

The idea of these forgotten tubes built beneath Nashville's streets had mesmerized Neva. Even Ice seemed enthralled, stopped in the middle of his delivery to take a look, asked about a specific building.

"That's the old Elk's Lodge," Davis said. "It's made of stern stuff. I could blast half of Nashville down before that one would jiggle."

"Do the Elks still meet in that place?" Ice asked.

"Been defunct for years," Davis said. "They rent it out for parties and the like, I understand."

A board creaked in the hallway.

CHAPTER TWELVE

Neva flattened herself against the wall.

Uncle Rex was outside.

There was nothing to worry about.

Then she remembered that Davis had soundproofed his walls during the renovation, saying the houses here were so close his neighbor could hear a half-hearted fart.

She'd thought it funny at the time.

A rush of adrenaline sent her heart galloping.

You are such a coward. There's nobody in here.

Unless it was Davis.

Davis, who was not in England, who came home to find someone in his house and noises from his sanctuary. In which case the gun was in his hand.

She should call out.

If it wasn't Davis, she'd lose any chance at surprise.

She turned the scissors so the sharp end was poised to stab. One thing for sure now, the creaking was no random noise, not old boards shrinking or new boards drying. They groaned with each heavy step.

His breathing said he was a big man. The streetlight sparkled only as far as the middle of the room. He'd be a shadow when he entered, but the dark also hid her.

"I just know it makes me sick to think of them," Ice's ghostly voice whispered in her ear.

She crossed her legs against a sudden urge to pee.

He stopped outside the door. She inched back, held her breath.

He slowly stepped in, shorter than she'd expected, but a powerful shadow whose outstretched arms turned from one corner of the room to the other, scanning with his dark weapon.

His shadow slid across her.

Her lungs begged for air.

He moved deeper into the room, one careful step after another. The shimmering diamonds fell on his face, making a Matisse-like image. But beneath its fractures, she managed to see that he was swarthy, beefy.

Spots swam in her eyes. Her body screaming, she waited until he breathed out and breathed with him.

If she could get to the front door, Uncle Rex would see her.

She had two choices.

Stand here and wait for Uncle Rex to find her.

Or take care of herself.

She sucked in a slow breath.

He'd turned again to the far corner, his back to her.

She gripped the scissors with both hands, tried not to think of how it would feel to shove them into human flesh, tiptoed up behind him, willed her mind to go blank. The scissors flashed in the fractured light, a sudden gleam bounced back to the window.

He whirled.

Too late for her to stop.

The scissors ripped through his side with a sound that turned Neva's stomach upside down.

He cried out, swung for her head.

She ducked. The scissors pulled free.

He twisted down over the pain, gun still in his hand.

She raced through the door, screaming at the top of her lungs, "Help! Help! Uncle Rex! Help!" She pounded down the hall, her arms already reaching for the front door. If she could get outside—

He grabbed her collar, jerked her off her feet.

She landed hard, saw stars, rolled and buried the scissors in his foot.

"You fucking cunt!" He grabbed her arm in a steel-like grip, jerked her up.

Her feet dangled in the air.

She clawed for his eyes, missed.

His fist cocked back.

She drew in a lungful of air.

His blow stopped her scream before it was born.

* * * *

Neva climbed slowly from a dark hole into a wave of pain and the stench of stale cigarette smoke.

Her face felt like she'd fallen out of a two-story window.

She was looking at the side wall of a van, stretched out on its filthy carpet. She remembered Larissa's beaten face, the fear in her eyes.

Neva's flesh shriveled.

Moving in slow motion, she lifted her head, listened for sounds from the front seat.

Her head whirled. She lay down again.

The seats were down. She had a clear path to the front.

His breathing was harsh. She'd hurt him pretty badly.

Good.

Should make it hard for him to chase her. If she got the chance to run.

Did he know she was awake? She kept her breathing full and soft, slowly pulled her feet apart. No restraints. Her hands were also free.

Two more good things.

The windows were dark.

A lighter scraped. Cigarette smoke wafted to her.

She wanted to believe the cops were right behind them. Common sense told her this van had been parked behind Davis's house, that Uncle Rex never saw it.

He knew she was gone by now, had seen the blood on the den floor, the scissors she'd dropped.

He got the gist.

If he managed to find her, it would be dumb luck.

This was up to her.

Her throat tightened. She forced a breath through it and talked herself down.

You'll find a way. You will. Just wait for it. You'll know it when it comes. It'll be all right. Just stay calm and watch.

The turn signal's tick-tick filled the van. He slowed, angled down a ramp. She fought her breath back into rhythm.

Left turn onto gravel. He crunched around in a circle and stopped. From outside, country music battered the windows, "Islands in the Stream."

Country music and a gravel parking lot. Could it be Paddy's, watering hole of the Ice Man?

The smoke stench faded.

He opened the door. Cold air flowed over the front seats. Country music poured in at a volume that made her ears ring.

She breathed deeply, stayed still.

The door closed. The music stopped reverberating in her chest.

Neva pulled deep into her body, concentrated on her breathing. Yoga breathing. Deep, live-giving, asshole-fooling breathing.

Relax, relax, relax.

The back doors sprang open. Cold air covered her.

"Fucking bitch." He shook her. "Hey! Hey!"

Pain knifed down her neck. She let it go, stayed loose. With a grunt, he slammed the doors and set the alarm with a ping.

She counted to ten before she scrambled up. The building was behind the van, a squat concrete-block affair with "PADDY'S PLACE" glowing in red neon letters above its metal roof.

She considered her options. Run inside screaming like a crazy woman that someone had tried to kill her, let the good ole boys come to her rescue?

Or run like hell and hope she could find a place to hide before he came back?

If Ice was in Paddy's, she would be safe. If he was not, if the men in there were best buddies with her abductor—worse, if some of them were working with or for him…

Too many unknowns.

She slid between the seats into the still-warm driver's seat, peered through the windshield at the row of houses on the other side.

A fifties neighborhood. Low, ranch-style houses, far apart. A sense of passing time made her decision for her. She flung the door open. The horn blared, then blared again as she leapt out. Her feet churned in the loose gravel. The world tilted; then the cold air snapped it into place.

Neva sprinted across the road, slid behind the first house.

Too far out in the boonies for streetlights, this yard didn't get any of the light from Paddy's parking lot.

It was totally dark.

The house blocked the musical high notes, but the base pounded against her chest like jungle drums. She peered into the darkness, frantically trying to force her irises to open so she could see a place to hide.

The music stopped. Just like that. No trail away, no final chord. Pounding base. Then nothing.

Except the whisper of tennis shoes on asphalt.

She imagined more than saw that these houses were built on a single plot of cleared land. The yards would flow from one house to another with no break. What she couldn't see was whether there were any outbuildings, barns or basements in which to hide.

She listened.

He moved far faster than she would have thought possible with a wound in his foot.

She had nothing with which to fight.

It was time to run like hell and pray.

CHAPTER THIRTEEN

Neva raced across open yard, gazing wildly at the windows as she sped past, hoping for one that was open. They were not only tightly closed, they were hidden behind storm windows.

The music was rolling again, this time a slow song, just as loud as the others. Still, she heard him pant behind her. She glanced over her shoulder. He was taller than she'd remembered.

He ran like a gazelle.

Her right foot caught under something hard, threw her to the ground.

He loomed from the darkness running right at her. Too close. Way too close. She leapt up, waited for him.

When she could smell him, she whirled away. He rushed on past, leaving a breeze to brush her face.

She lit out the way she'd come.

"Neva!"

She pivoted in mid-stride, turned even before she had convinced herself it was he.

"Ice?"

"We don't have much time."

"How did you—"

"Tell you later."

He grabbed her hand, whirled her around. She stumbled in the wake of his long, long legs, tried to watch the ground for more traps, tried not to slow him down, tried to breathe, listened for the slightest sounds of a pursuer.

They raced across two yards before Ice stopped her at a steep bank, then plunged down. Her shoes slid on the leaves. Ice grabbed her upper arm with strong, steely fingers and dragged her with him.

Water sloshed below, a miracle in this drought.

He stopped at the creek's edge, held her steady while he whispered in her ear. "Water's cold, but there's a culvert down a ways." He looked over his shoulder. "It's the only place around here to hide." He paused. "From the way you lammed it out of the parking lot, I'm taking a wild guess somebody's after you?"

"Correct," she said. The center of her back prickled.

"Come on, then," he said. "I think he saw me follow you."

The icy water drove a gasp from her as it filled her tennis shoes. In seconds, her toes ached.

Ice slogged along like the creek was filled with bathwater, showing no sign of discomfort, but his hand grew cold.

An owl called, its voice low and spooky.

She could see Ice and little else, but way down the creek, a solid blackness stood like a barrier between her and all that followed.

When they finally reached it, he dropped her hand. She stood where he left her, watched him move in a strange dance at the mouth of the culvert, which she could now see was nothing more than a big round pipe fitted inside a square concrete structure.

"What are you doing?" she whispered.

"Entrance is blocked. Stay still."

The pain in her feet and legs was unbearable, but she stayed where she was. Ice moved what looked like a year's debris from the creek to the bank. The heavier stuff hit the water with a splash that made her jump.

Finally, when she thought she could not stand the cold for one more second, he grabbed her hand.

"There's a sidewalk on the left side," he whispered. "Say nothing. Do not let my hand go no matter what."

The water deepened as they stepped inside the pipe, deepened and moved more swiftly now that the entrance was open. He held her hand tightly, his fingers icy, his body shaking with cold.

The culvert smelled like hay and rotten grass and something sickly sweet. Ice led her to the left until her toes painfully struck something hard.

He helped her onto the narrow ledge, just wide enough for them to stand on. The cold air was freezing the drops of water on her feet into crystals.

Ice drew her back against him, wrapped his arms around her, then touched her lips with a single finger.

Stay silent.

He was sharing the scant body warmth he had left. She snuggled in his arms and regretted every time she'd been nasty to him, every smart-assed word. If they got out of this alive, she'd make it up to him.

His body was warming her back, but did nothing for her feet.

How long would they have to stay here?

Water flowed through the culvert with a liquid slap and "He Stopped Loving Her Today" flowed from Paddy's. Combined, they covered any lesser sound.

Her mind expanded outside the culvert, searching like a raptor for any sign of life, trying to feel his presence, prepare for his arrival.

Something slid down the bank behind them.

But did not splash into the creek.

Ice tightened his arms around her, again put his finger against her lips.

A flashlight beam stabbed through the pipe, its scope wide, its power weak.

The beam swept from side to side and up and down, but came no farther into the culvert. As it played from side to side, Neva saw the brilliance in the way Ice had positioned them. The light could not reach the left side of the culvert unless their stalker stepped into the freezing water.

Ice had bet their lives he would not.

Finally, the beam withdrew.

She sagged with relief.

Ice put his finger against her lips again. They stood in frozen agony for what seemed forever before the flashlight beam stabbed from the other side of the culvert, the unblocked side, where no debris could screen them. He flashed it around, even checked the ceiling, then angled and stabbed it directly at them.

Neva swallowed a gasp as the light came within a hair of her feet. Ice shrank against the wall, took her with him. They stood frozen in every sense of the word, waiting for the beam to touch them, to find her toes or legs, to betray them.

It pulled back.

He cursed as he scrambled up the bank. Heavy footsteps padded across the culvert, then faded as he went toward Paddy's.

Ice held her still until she could hear the man no longer.

"I think it's safe," he said.

They sloshed through the water only as far as the opposite bank, and then scrambled up to the road. As soon as she reached the pavement, Ice put his jacket around her shoulders.

"No, Ice," she said as she handed it back, "you need this."

"Put it on. I don't like the way you look."

"There's not enough light for you to tell how I look. Keep your jacket." He shook his head, hung the jacket on her shoulders again. With a sigh, she shoved her arms into the sleeves, still warm from his body. She *was* freezing, but so was he.

They needed to get to warmth fast.

They hobbled on frozen feet across the culvert, then ducked into the yards, making the rest of the slow, painful journey behind the houses. Directly across from Paddy's, they surveyed the parking lot, nearly full now with pickup trucks and utility vehicles, but no vans. Finally, Ice said, "He's gone."

The Ice Wagon was parked at the other end of the parking lot. Teeth chattering, he helped Neva in, then started the engine and flipped the heater to high. The air inside was nearly as cold as that outside. She ripped off her soggy tennis shoes and socks and tucked her blue, aching feet under her. Ice whirled the truck around in the parking lot. "Who was that guy? Where's Pratt? And what the hell are you doing out here?"

"I don't know who he is. Davis is in Europe, I think. I'm out here because the son of a bitch cold-cocked me and dragged me out here."

Ice's gaze shifted to her face. His twisted in a look of fury so hot it actually scared her. "Son of a bitch! I'll kill him."

"He's armed, Ice."

"Ain't we all? Tell me what happened."

"First, you tell me how you popped up like a rabbit out of a hole."

"I'd just pulled in when you hit the gravel, left that van's horn blowing like a New York cabbie. I saw that guy looking out of the window, figured you were in trouble and took off. Now your turn."

She told him about her trip to Davis's house.

Ice listened without a word, but his face grew grimmer and his mouth flattened into a straight line.

She'd argued with him that she was safe.

She'd been very wrong.

Would she ever be safe?

Would they try again? Maybe snatch her from her own bedroom the way Polly Klass's murderer did?

She shuddered.

Ice put a hand on her arm. "Steady, old girl. We'll get through this. Go on."

When she finished, he said, "I don't guess you got his license number?"

"I was unconscious when he put me in the van," she said. "I've really not seen him, either, couldn't describe him, but he's got a rip in his left side and a hole in his foot."

"That's why he didn't catch me, then."

As the heater warmed and they drove farther away from Paddy's Place, she realized there were tears draining down her face even though she wasn't *consciously* crying.

Ice pulled a packet of tissue out of the console. "Here," he said.

She dried her eyes.

"You are totally useless," he said with a grin. "Some guy kidnaps you. You don't have his license number. You can't identify him. You're *useless*. I'll bet you didn't get a single license number from the assholes in the cemetery, either, did you? Come on, admit it. Not a single digit."

She admitted it, then said, "Can I borrow your cell phone? I need to call Moya."

"Better call your dad. He's worried. Something about you were at Davis's but they didn't know how you left. Your uncle is upset." He fished his phone from the holder on his belt and handed it to her. "Be sure to say I told you he called." When she didn't respond, he cut a sideways glance at her. "What? It doesn't hurt for him to think well of me."

"He's always thought well of you. He just wishes you'd be on time once in a while."

"Bitch, bitch, bitch."

Her dad's cell phone rang four times. When it went to voice mail, she pulled it from her ear and stared at it, wanting to believe she'd dialed the wrong number. But her dad's rich baritone had been on the voice mail. Dad's cell was the business phone, the lifeblood of the business. It was *always* answered by the third ring, so much so that she'd laughed at him when he added the voice mail message.

She tried the Oakley home phone, which also went to voice mail, but that only meant Miss Sylvia, as she thought of her mother, was under the covers. She tried Claudia. No answer.

"Get 'em?" Ice asked.

"They're not answering."

"None of them?"

"No."

He glanced at her. "What do you want to do?"

"Get to the funeral home. Fast."

CHAPTER FOURTEEN

Neva clung to her seatbelt as the Ice Wagon slid around sharp curves and blasted down the straight sections. Cell phone communication was iffy, she tried to comfort herself. Her father might be distracted. Her entire family might be distracted.

Rigghhhhtttt!

Her dad's cell phone had never before failed.

Not once.

Ever.

Neither had his landline before he got a cell phone.

Ice slowed for his turn into the road beside Oakley's, glanced into the side-view mirror and said, "Shit! Cops!"

The patrol car was right behind them, blues flashing. Ice had driven like a wild man. Doing it for her.

"I'll pay the ticket," she said.

"Don't worry about it," he said, but his face was grim. He had a DUI less than a year ago. If he lost his license, he'd lose his business. He hit his turn indicator. The cops followed him.

Ice pulled into the parking lot looking completely miserable.

Neva was digging through her brain for something encouraging to say when the flashing blues went right past them and continued up the cemetery road.

The hillside glowed in near daylight, impossible at this time of night. Six cop cars were already parked nose to ass in a straight line pointing up the hill.

"What the hell?" Ice said.

"Dunno. They were up there when I left tonight."

"With those lights?"

"No," she admitted. "They had lights, but not like that."

"They've found something," he said. He backed the Ice Wagon around, headed up the hill, parked off the road beside the last car in line and was out of the truck before she could get the door open. She struggled to get her still-wet socks and shoes on, then leapt from the truck, realizing much too late that landing on her half-frozen feet was gonna hurt a lot.

Ice was halfway up the hill by the time she reached the sod.

She glanced down the line of cars. Except for her father's car, all the vehicles were cop cars. There was no sign of Uncle Rex's sedan.

Cop's convention, maybe. A place to share war stories and talk about their wives.

Except that they wouldn't light the hillside like a UFO landing site for that, and nothing about it would draw her father or keep him from answering his phone.

Far above, Ice ducked under the crime-scene tape and kept going.

Neva followed him.

The powerful light backlit the branches and sent the trees lunging at her like skeletons.

She hugged herself.

In her worst times, she'd sat beside Gray's grave and talked things out with him. Not once, except for Friday night, had she ever been afraid in this place. Now, the shadows among the tall tombstones hid dark and troubling spaces where the worst of the world could hide.

Even the bones along the hill seemed restless.

She shook herself hard, bit the inside of her lip.

There's nothing different here but you.

And about eight cops.

Who are up the hill while you are down here alone.

She sprinted after Ice.

Her father was in the clearing with the officers. His face was flushed, his arms crossed over his chest.

"I don't know," he was saying as she slipped up beside him. "These are unauthorized graves. They may have been dug with my backhoe. I can't really speak to that. It stays in a shed with a bad lock. Anybody could have used it. But I can speak to the rest of what you're trying to say. Oakley Funeral Home did not, let me repeat that for you, did *not* dig these graves. Neither did it bury whatever or whoever is in them. I have no knowledge of them. None!"

Neva touched his elbow. He swung around, sagged as he saw her, then grabbed her to him and held tight. She felt his chest hitch against her and wondered if the tears he battled were ones of relief she was safe, or of panic over what the police had shown him. He thrust her back, brushed her hair from her face and recoiled. "Who hit you?"

"Tell you later. What's going on up here?" she asked, batting her eyelashes against her own tears. His embrace had made a small child of her, but from the looks on the cops' faces, this was no place for small children.

"Before you answer that, Mr. Oakley," the officer beside him said, "I'd like a chance to talk to Miss Oakley alone."

"Sure," her dad said. "You take her right over there and talk to your heart's content. Just one thing"—he held up his forefinger—"she does not leave my sight. Got it?"

The officer nodded. "If you don't mind, Miss Oakley."

With a quick look at her father, she followed the policeman to the far edge of the clearing.

"Thank you," he began.

"Look, I don't know any more about this than Dad. If there are graves up here, they're not ours."

"That's good to hear." He pulled out a long, narrow notebook, poised a ballpoint pen over it and began to ask questions. At first, they were her name, birth date, where she went to school—dumb personal questions. "Now," he said, finally, "where were you tonight?"

"I'm sorry? Am I under suspicion?"

"Everybody's under suspicion right now, Miss Oakley. Where were you? Your father didn't seem to know. He seemed quite concerned."

Neva felt her face begin twist in a wry smile. Pain bloomed along her injured cheekbone, and she dropped the smile. "My family is a little overprotective where I'm concerned. I had a bad experience ten years ago, didn't handle it well. I was going to file a report with you guys about where I was." She filled him in on her night while he jotted notes and prompted her for information. In the end, he flipped the notebook closed.

"Okay. Thank you." He turned.

"Wait!"

He turned back, looked expectant. "You don't seriously think my father had anything to do with this?"

"I think you and your father are fine people, Miss Oakley. But so far we have found fifteen graves in this area. We began investigating one. That's when we found a half-decomposed body—a man who apparently tried to dig his way out. We're assuming he was buried alive. That's not just murder, ma'am. That's the kind of crime that makes decent people sick. We're going to find those responsible. If we have to make good people uncomfortable in the process, I'd say it's worth it, wouldn't you?"

The passion in his voice rocked her back. She nodded her agreement, then gazed out over the clearing. Some of the largest bushes were shoved back, their roots hanging in the air beside tall piles of dirt.

Fifteen graves! Fifteen. Given how often she checked the hillside before she left for the day, especially in the fall, how had she not seen the people who dragged these victims up the hillside, murdered them, or worse, buried them alive?

Finding no answer to her question, she walked back toward the group.

She needed a cell phone to call Uncle Rex.

CHAPTER FIFTEEN

"Thank you, Charles." Davis turned in the soft leather seat and held out his hand to the silver-haired gentleman beside him. "This was great."

"I hope you will find it helpful, Davis. I'll come for you at eight tomorrow morning."

The chauffer opened Davis's door and touched the brim of his hat. Davis smiled as he stepped onto the sidewalk, then turned to wave at Charles as the chauffer pulled the gleaming Rolls Royce into traffic.

As remarkable as Sunday had been, Monday was even better. Davis had expected his father's old friend to be a good architect but had not been prepared for the warmth of the Charles's camaraderie, the depth of his knowledge or his unexpected willingness to tiptoe into the unknown. The fledgling drilling process Davis discovered online had actually been used more than once for similar projects, perhaps none as deep as Davis would need to go, but thanks to Charles's experience and friendships with other noted European architects, Davis now had a portfolio of such processes from which he should be able to devise the right one for Nashville. Weariness swept over him, the result of jet lag and two long days trying to keep up with Charles both physically and mentally.

Davis nodded at the doorman and stepped through the heavy brass door of the exclusive men's club at which Charles insisted Davis stay, and for which Charles refused to allow either Davis or the firm to pay. The elevator was lined in solid oak and carried the faint smell of cigar smoke. England banned smoking in all buildings in 2007, but this building, permeated for more than a century with cigar and cigarette smoke, would forever carry the smell. Davis leaned his head against the hard wood while the lift rose to the fourth floor, the penthouse, where his suite waited. He allowed his thoughts to turn to Neva. Despite his delight and fascination with Charles and the information they'd gleaned, the decisions they'd made together, yesterday's conversation with Neva had left him uneasy all day. He'd not lied, exactly. Davis prided himself on being honest. But he'd not told her the entire truth about Friday night. He'd mentioned seeing Stephen but not being in the cemetery practically nose-to-nose with his brother, nor had he mentioned Stephen's hostility or Davis's run for his life. He'd not wanted to frighten her.

He now realized what a perfect place the cemetery was for illicit business. Isolated, dark and lonely, its nature prevented most people from visiting at night. Neva, however, having been raised among death, sometimes climbed that hill to talk to Gray in the dead of the night. He had to warn her.

Something in her voice yesterday bothered him. Not unease, exactly, more a hesitation, as if she was waiting for him to answer a question she wasn't willing to ask. He'd wrongly assumed he'd overstepped by making love to her in the funeral home. She'd laughed that off, but something wasn't right between them.

Or was he being paranoid? A lover apart worrying over every inflection in his woman's voice?

The lift bounced to a stop. Its brass doors rattled open to show a bottle in a silver wine cooler on the mahogany table in the foyer. Davis didn't have to check the label to know the wine was a Bordeaux from France—and expensive. He glanced at the clock. It was nearly midnight. He should wait until morning, get some rest. He shook his head at that thought, poured himself a glass of wine, sank onto the plush leather sofa and hit speed dial for Neva's number.

"Hello?"

The sound of her velvet voice made him long to see her. "Hey, beautiful."

"Hey yourself, handsome… How's merry old England?"

Again, that hesitation in her voice.

"Cold and wet, as always, but I've learned a lot. Miss you."

"Miss you," she said. "Where are you staying?"

He gave her the name of the club and described it for her. "Amazing place. All thanks to Charles." Feeling compelled to give her a detailed accounting, he spent ten minutes taking her through the streets of London, the offices of Charles's venerable firm and the research they'd completed.

"Well," she said when he finished, "sounds like you had a busy day." She was silent for a second and then, "We had a bit of excitement here yesterday."

He listened in horror as she told her story of torture and murder. When she told him the police had now found multiple illicit graves, the glass stem snapped in his hand, tore a tiny slice from his thumb and drove him to his feet.

The minor pain in his thumb was nothing compared to the pain of realizing he'd become an accessory after the fact to murder because he'd not reported what he'd seen Friday night to the police. His head spun slightly. What would she think of him? While she continued her dark and macabre story, he poured the wine into a crystal tumbler, dropped the broken glass into the trash and wrapped a paper napkin around his bleeding thumb.

Davis barely made it back to the couch before she said, "There's more."

He held his breath. She launched into a story of her abduction and battery. With great effort, he forced his hand to relax around the tumbler before he crushed it.

When she completed her story, he sat in stunned silence.

"Davis? Are you there?"

"I'm here," he acknowledged. "Did the police find the son of a bitch?"

In the stupor after she regained consciousness, she'd failed to garner any information that could lead to the man's arrest. Davis prided himself on being civilized, somewhat British in the way he dealt with others, his father said. But what burned its way up his throat could in no way be considered civilized. He set the glass on the table beside him. His hands clenched around the imaginary throat of the man who'd dared harm Neva. Davis wanted to throttle the life from that man, something he could do without regret.

The savagery of the image shocked him back to himself as he again heard Neva ask, "Davis?"

"I'll come home," he said. "Catch the first plane out tomorrow. But first I have to tell you something."

She tried to interrupt, but if he allowed her to stop him, he'd never get rolling again. He talked over her until she went silent.

"The dope deal we discussed didn't go down at the donut shop, although they did pull in there for a second or two. I followed them up the cemetery road, parked my truck at the bottom of the hill near the river and climbed up to a grave with a hedge around it."

"Gray's grave," she said, sounding surprised.

"I didn't know," he said, wondering if this could get any more bizarre. That he should choose to hide beside Gray, his rival for her affections even though the boy had been dead for ten years, was nothing short of weird. Davis shook the thought away and continued, "I was hoping to catch Stephen alone. I hid behind the hedge, waiting for a chance to speak to him. He and the others were higher up the hill. I knew I'd have to leave the shelter of the hedge eventually, but I hesitated. I told you I am a terrible coward."

"I don't believe that," she said.

He warmed at her words. He'd never had any reason to test his courage. Private schools and colleges did not expose one to the usual warfare between growing boys. He'd never struck another in anger, never shot at anyone, never been in a situation where he needed to flex his muscles. He wanted to believe he would rise to the occasion, as the saying went, but without experience, he had no real way of knowing. "Well, anyway," he continued, "I was peering through the branches. Damned bushes are thick as horsehair. I could barely make out anything. I had moved back to think when a man stepped around the hedge. Even in the semi-darkness, I could tell he looked like Stephen. He did a double take, and for this one amazing moment, we stared at one another without moving. I thought he'd recognized me as I had him."

Davis swallowed to loosen his throat. He could have touched his brother, pulled him into his arms. The magical moment had emboldened Davis so he'd whispered, "Stephen," but the other man jerked back. His face twisted as he pawed for the weapon behind his back. Davis related all this to Neva in a matter-of-fact tone that completely belied the pain in his heart.

"He reached for his weapon, and I ran," Davis said. "Ran like a scared rabbit to my truck and drove away. He shot at me, I think. I heard several shots. I barely remember what happened after that. I didn't report any of this to the police, Neva."

She was silent for a moment and then she said, "Thank you, Davis."

"For what?"

"Telling me the truth."

Davis knew then she'd seen him that night, and when he asked, she said he was correct. The thing in her voice must have been hope that he would think enough of her to tell the truth. She'd tested him. He shuddered to think how close he came to failing. "I'm sorry," he said. "I should have told you from the beginning. I had some stupid idea I was protecting you."

"I know," she said. "It's all right. But don't come home now, Davis. Not because I don't want you here, but because you need to be there. I'm okay. Uncle Rex has his men watching me and Moya. Moya's making me carry a gun. I'll be fine. You'll be home Friday. Stay and learn what you can. Moya and I reported everything to the police, so you don't have to worry about that, either."

"I want you to stay out of the cemetery." Davis regretted the words the second they left his mouth, driven by a picture of her in the hands of the sex slavers she said the police believed had been in the cemetery. Whatever his motivation, he had no right to tell her what to do. He scooted down a bit in his seat as he waited for her next words.

"I understand. Ice has read my title clear already. Dad's joined in as well. You all have my best interests at heart. I won't go up there, not alone, anyway."

"How did you escape that man?" he asked, realizing she'd left that part out of her narrative.

"Ice rescued me," she said and left Davis feeling like the most useless man alive.

CHAPTER SIXTEEN

Tuesday afternoon, Rozanna Clark reactivated her cell phone. They'd made good time from Los Angeles, were on the ground ten minutes sooner than scheduled. The man beside her shifted and glanced pointedly at her left leg. For the third time in as many minutes, she forced it to stop bouncing. She was excited to be in Nashville, her home no matter that she lived six months in L.A. She was eager to see Neva and Moya. She was tired of sitting.

She glanced through her seatmate's window. Indian summer, a gift to those in the Southland, happened in the midst of ever-colder days with an unnatural but oh-so-welcome warmth and blinding sunshine. She watched the parched grass on the edges of the asphalt runway slide by. Nashville's airport could never compete with LAX, but that was what she loved about it. Big enough to have all the amenities, small enough so it didn't even require an internal people-mover system.

Zan used her tennis-shoe-shod feet to slide the cat carrier from beneath the forward seat. Ginger's little pink nose shoved against the mesh below her reddish-golden eyes. She traveled well, a good thing since she swapped houses along with Zan. Thirteen pounds of red and white Maine coon tabby, she was Zan's main squeeze.

"Almost, sweetie," Zan crooned. "Almost out of here."

Her cell phone said two thirty p.m. Plenty of time to pick up steaks, three bakers, a loaf of French bread, maybe a salad, a couple of bottles of Cab, and have dinner ready when Neva and Moya got home. With her backpack over her shoulder and Ginger's carrier in her hand, Zan followed the crowd as it wheeled as a single organism toward baggage claim. She had only one: a purple bag with large orange polka dots. Easy to spot. It held the things the airlines wouldn't let her carry on, including her boots.

It was the first bag onto the belt. She grabbed it, swung into the restroom, stripped off her tennis shoes and pulled on the boots.

Rozanna Clark could not be seen trucking around Nashville in tennies. Not even. Besides, the heel of her right boot was removable. Embedded in it was a sharp knife. She'd never needed it, remembered it only when she traveled, but was glad to have it just in case.

The long-term-parking bus waited at the curb. She swung onto it humming a snatch of a tune that wafted into her dream last night. Just a few notes that could ultimately go anywhere, or nowhere, but intriguing little fellows, nonetheless. She popped the backpack and the bag on the luggage rack and took the first seat.

In her lap, Ginger shifted and mewed. Zan put her fingers against the mesh. Ginger shoved her face against them.

Nashville International's parking lots sprawled for acres on the airport's northern side. The long-term-parking bus was more than half-empty, but to accommodate departing passengers, the driver was required to stop at each loading zone. Unfortunately, Section 135, where Neva's rental car waited, was as far away from the terminal as was possible. Neva's text hadn't explained why there would be a rental car, just gave the license plate number, description and parking place. A Ford, of course. The Oakley's were Ford people, unlike Zan's dad, who wouldn't allow a "Fix Or Repair Daily" into his garage. A 2013 bright red Ford Fusion shouldn't be too hard to find, especially since she had the license number in her phone.

The bus finally rolled to a stop at Section 135. Zanna hefted her backpack onto her shoulder, grabbed the suitcase and stepped off. Ginger danced a real jitterbug. The carrier dipped and twisted.

"Hang in," Zanna said. She spotted the red Fusion immediately, verified the license number.

She set Ginger on the ground and felt for the magnetic box Neva said would be against the wheel well behind the right front tire. The key was inside.

Using the driver's-side controls to unlock the remaining doors, Zan hefted her bag into the trunk and tossed her backpack over the seat. "Now, sweetie pie," she said, "just another minute."

The carrier was as large as the airlines would allow, but still small for the cat. Zan would let Ginger run free inside the car, stretch her legs after the long flight. She slid Ginger into the front passenger seat and was headed for that side when hard heels rang on the pavement behind her.

"Excuse me."

She turned, automatically put her hand on her mother's necklace, the glowing amber ball with a bug inside that never left her neck, not even when she bathed.

But from the looks of him, she didn't need the comfort of her talisman.

He was tall, dressed in a pair of khakis and a soft white pullover. He carried a pure leather briefcase so highly polished it glowed in the warm afternoon sun. His brown eyes were worried, his face taut. He looked innocent and honest and worried, but, still, she twisted the key between her first two fingers. *The better to rake your eyes with if you are not as nice as you look, my dear.* "Yes?"

"I wonder if you could help me." He gestured at the parking aisle. "My brother was to leave a car here for me. I have the keys." He held up a key ring with a fob much like the one in Zanna's hand. "But he's been in a terrible wreck. Summit Hospital. I think that's right. Summit?"

Zan nodded. "It's just up the road."

He took a huge gulp of air, worked visibly to control his face. "They want me to come right now." His eyes filled. "They said I should hurry."

Zan hesitated.

"This is my driver's license." He held out his wallet with his right hand. The left was clenched so tightly around the briefcase, the knuckles were white. His name was Andrew Haile. He was forty-one, lived in Jackson, Tennessee. He was smiling in the pic, and his brown eyes were soft.

"Okay," she said. "Let me get my cat out of your way." She glanced up at him. "You're not allergic to cats, are you?"

"No," he said. "Please hurry."

CHAPTER SEVENTEEN

"Heard from Zan?" Moya asked as Neva slid into the front bucket seat of Moya's little Honda.

"No. Bet she's got steaks and salad and huge baked potatoes already cooking."

"Mmm," Moya said, licking her lips. "I'm starving. There's our escort."

The cruiser circled the parking lot and followed them out.

"Wine, too. Sounds like a feast."

Moya swept across the sparse downtown-bound traffic and into the endless out-of-town stream. "I have a date tomorrow night."

"Yeah? Big Ken?"

"The same," Moya said.

"Try not to be so excited about it."

"I *am* excited. I just don't want to sound like a teenager."

"Because I won't love you anymore?"

"Because I'll feel like an idiot." Moya turned to the window. "I hate this time of year. The pretty leaves are gone; the flowers are all dead. It's dark when we get home."

"Me, too," Neva said. The flowers and leaves would return. Her thoughts were in the brushy mess behind the cemetery. The FBI was now on the scene because it was believed that some of the interred were from other states. Twenty shallow graves, they said, one of the few facts about their investigation they'd deigned to share. They'd moved in to the hillside with their crime-scene tape and vans full of technicians.

The news media moved in with them, offered nightly updates on the "grizzly find in Oakley's cemetery." No amount of pleading would get them to call it what it was: empty, unused land *behind* the cemetery. Oakley's business, already dismal, dropped to nearly nothing. If it weren't for her father's share of her fees and the little he made from Ice's bodies, he'd have no income.

Something had to go their way pretty soon or they'd all be looking for work.

Moya turned right onto Kenwood Avenue, another once-prosperous area Nashville had left behind. Their rented house was at the end of the street, a modest three-bedroom, but it had a small in-ground pool in the extremely private backyard. They'd splurged on a hot tub, given it to one another, Zan included, for Christmas their first year in the house.

"Don't see Zan's car," Moya said as she pulled into the turnaround behind the three-car garage.

"Probably gone to the store," Neva said. She checked her texts and found none. "She could have let us know, though."

"Independent gals. That's us," Moya said.

By the time Neva gathered her things, Moya was inside. "Call her," she said as Neva stepped into the kitchen. "Ask her to pick up some ketchup."

"She'll have a tantrum." Neva put her left hand on her hip and said in a reasonable approximation of Zan's breathy voice, "Only an uneducated redneck would put ketchup on a fine steak."

"Yeah, yeah, yeah. This *educated* redneck wants ketchup. Call her."

"How about I text?"

"You chicken shit." Moya tossed her hands in the air as she went down the hall toward her bedroom. "If that's the best you can do."

Neva texted, "Hey, how come you didn't call when you got in? The ignorant redneck wants ketchup. No point in arguing. Just get the large bottle!"

She headed for her bedroom, where a pair of soft lounging pants and pullover shirt sans bra called her. She tossed the phone on the bed while she shed her workaday clothing. Zan's tantrum could wait until Neva was comfy.

It would be great to have Zan back. Davis and Ken would complicate matters a bit. Zan didn't have a Nashville guy of the moment. 'Course that might change at any time. Girl drew men like flowers drew hummers. They'd manage, though, to find plenty of time for one another.

Neva was proud of her cousin. Zan had always been talented, had a voice, too. In fact, that was how she started. Writing songs and singing them at church and then at a few honky-tonks, which had made her dad chew his lips. But she'd stuck to it, even cut a couple of records that didn't do badly.

She also pitched songs to other artists and found she had much more success there. Now, she sang for family and friends. She spent her time banging out songs on her keyboards, one of which had residence in Zan's Nashville bedroom.

After the dinner dishes were loaded in the dishwasher, the three of them would adjourn to the hot tub with at least one bottle of Cab. They'd continue whatever conversation they'd begun at dinner.

"What'd she say?" Moya had drawn her curls onto the top of her head and secured them with a gleaming silver barrette. She, too, had opted for soft clothing. Nobody in this household wore a bra unless there were men involved or their parents were visiting.

"Dunno," Neva said. She collected her discarded phone, glanced at the tiny screen, expecting to see something smart-assed. The screen was clear. "Nothing," Neva said, looking up at Moya. Moya frowned. Neva said, "I guess you pissed her off royally, girl."

Moya grabbed the phone from Neva's hand. Soon, her thumbs were flying over the keys.

"Make sure she knows that's you and not me," Neva said after a minute.

"First thing I said. She'll respond now," she said with a smirk. "She'll take my head off."

Moya had texted, "Listen up. I don't give a rat's ass how good your steaks are, they're better with ketchup. So get over yourself and buy the stuff. And text back so we'll know you aren't the imaginary product of one too many glasses of Cab. Uh, you *did* get the Cab, right?"

Neva watched for the little dialog bubble that showed when a friend was typing. When it did not appear, she glanced at Moya again.

"Nothing?" Moya asked.

"Nothing."

"You're kidding me? You don't think I really made her mad, do you?"

Neva punched in Zanna's cell phone number. "One way to find out," she said. Four rings later, the voice mail invited her to leave a message. "Look, kid. You're beginning to worry us. Call me." As she clicked off, she said, "Probably paying for the groceries. She'll call in a minute."

"Listen!" Moya said. She turned toward the front door.

At first, Neva heard nothing, but then a tiny cry, a mew.

"A cat," Moya said with a twist of her mouth. "We are not feeding it."

The cat cried again, a mournful, pitiful sound that ran through Neva like a spike. "I can't just leave it out there."

"Of course you can. Cats live outside. They eat filthy things like rats. They do not belong in the house."

Neva rocked back in mock astonishment. "I don't believe my ears. You've been hiding this distaste from Zan all these years. What do you do when Ginger's here? Hold your breath?"

"Ginger's different. She's a nice cat, stays in the house, sleeps. Doesn't eat live things." Moya's nose wrinkled. "If you let that animal in here, you have to take it to the shelter in the morning."

"Deal!"

The cat cried again and then, as Neva neared the door, went completely silent. *Scared but too hungry not to ask for help.* She opened the door, expecting to see the cat's bottom as it pranced down the stairs.

"What the—" The cat was in a carrier, the same kind of carrier Zan used when she flew with Ginger. "Now, why would anybody leave a cat in a carrier—" She stopped as the animal poked its nose against the mesh, its reddish-gold eyes wide with fear. Neva dropped to one knee, put her hand on the mesh. Ginger rubbed her face against it, marking Neva as the cat always did when she first arrived. Relief spread though Neva and let her know just how worried she'd been about Zan.

"It's Ginger," she called to Moya. She stepped onto the porch, glanced down the empty driveway, then back at the cat. Zan wouldn't leave Ginger out here unless she was coming right in. Neva left the cat where she was, which made Ginger howl, a sound Neva had never before heard from the big cat. She ran down the driveway and around the house.

The turnaround was as empty as the driveway.

So where was Zan? No way in hell she'd have left Ginger on the porch alone unless she planned to be right back.

Neva picked Ginger up on her way back, set her inside and locked the door, then opened the carrier. Ginger raced down the hall toward Zan's bathroom, where they kept her litter box.

"She coming in?" Moya asked.

"Zan's not out there."

"What?" Moya's eyes widened. "She left the cat?"

"I guess," Neva said. "This is getting pretty dumb."

She once again called her cousin, once again left a voice mail message, this one a bit more pointed and a good deal less hearty.

If Zan was playing some sort of trick, it was not funny.

CHAPTER EIGHTEEN

Mike Floyd glanced at his longtime partner, Dale Sims. Sims was a clueless, happy little pig of a man who bounced through life without putting too much stress on his brain. Floyd picked Dale up about twenty minutes ago after they'd finished a twelve-hour shift during which absolutely nothing worth talking about happened.

Those were the bad days as far as Floyd was concerned, but Sims thought riding around eating donuts was just about a perfect way to spool out a shift. The clock on Floyd's dash, the clock that graced the dashboard of every Corvette until 1968, the clock he'd paid a ton of money to have installed in his new one, said ten. Two hours before midnight. The partners had to be on duty again at eight the next morning.

He shifted his massive shoulders, the product of many hours at the gym, and said, "We're going to drive it away." This in answer to Sims's question, "What the hell are we supposed to do with it," which was itself in answer to Floyd's statement that they were to pick up a car at Summit Hospital.

Hanging with Sims often felt like crawling down an interstate highway. No matter how hard you tried, you couldn't get up any speed.

For this reason as well as a few others, Floyd kept Sims away from the boss. From what he'd said, Sims had this picture of Floyd speaking directly into the big man's ear. Sims seemed pitifully grateful he wasn't required to attend those meetings. In fact, Floyd spoke only to J., who was the boss's man in the field. He'd never laid eyes on the boss, hoped he never would. Chatter was the dude liked to break fingers. It was said he could snap a bone in half in less than ten seconds.

Floyd shuddered. He could take a beating as well as the next man, but the thought of torture made him nauseous. Fuckup like Sims could cost a man three broken fingers in one night.

"You know how to hotwire a car, Sims?"

"Yeah," Sims said. "Why?"

"'Cause when we find this red Ford, you're gonna hotwire it." Floyd pulled a folded piece of paper from his pocket, held it out. "This is the license of the Ford and the addy where you should take it. There's a phone number—" He broke off as Sims's head rotated toward the side window. "Are you listening?"

"Yes, Floyd, dammit, I'm listening."

"Take the paper, Sims."

Sims snatched it from Floyd's hand. "I can't read in the dark."

"You can read it when you get in the Ford. Jeesh, you can be such an idiot sometimes."

Sims said nothing.

Floyd went on. "Buddy of mine lives there. You call the phone number on that piece of paper. He will open the garage door. Drive the car inside."

"Then what?"

"You cut off the engine and walk out."

"How do I get home?"

"I'll pick you up, stupid. I'm going to follow you."

What he didn't tell Sims was that Floyd's buddy worked with a small group out of rural Cannon County, south of Murfreesboro. Within twenty-four hours, the Ford's parts would be selling to people in California, Montana, Texas and maybe twenty other states. They'd file the VIN off the engine. Nobody would ever find this car no matter how hard they looked.

They found the Ford parked at the back edge of the parking lot. Sims took the locksmith's unlock tool with him.

"Check the door before you use that," Floyd said as Sims left the car.

Indeed, the car was unlocked.

Floyd followed the Ford into the subdivision that led back to the river behind the mammoth Spring Hill Funeral Home and Cemetery. Lakewood was the last road in the subdivision, backed right up to the river. A great place to live except that the river was a good twenty to thirty feet below the houses.

Just as Sims pulled into the driveway, Floyd's cell phone rang. "Get him outta my driveway," Don said. His voice was high and breathy, as if he'd been running a while.

"Whassup?"

"Got Fed troubles, my man. Get the son of a bitch outta here!"

"Shit!" Floyd said.

In a typical Sims move, the Ford was sitting with its nose practically touching the garage door. Not only could the door not open, but because Sims was so far down the driveway, Floyd had to run its full length to speak to him.

Sims lowered the window. "Why don't he open up?"

"Get outta here, Sims. Just back out."

"And do what? I'm not drivin' this hot car much longer, Floyd. I got a career to protect here."

Funny thing, dumbo didn't appear worried about his job every Friday when Floyd popped a grand into his hand. Ten hundreds. Every single week.

Sims never mentioned how he might lose his badge.

Floyd jerked his thumb over his shoulder. "Follow me."

By the time Floyd got back to his car, Sims was in the street again.

Sims was right about one thing. They had to get rid of the car.

Floyd's hands tightened on the wheel.

Failure was not an option.

Lakewood became Brush Hill after it passed under Briley Parkway. He'd run with a councilman for a while, little short dude, loved to fish and hunt. Lived on Brush Hill.

Man was dead now. With a jolt, Floyd remembered that the guy's house, hell everything he owned, was tied up in court. Kids fighting over who got what. If that was still true, if he could remember where the thing was, its backyard ended at the cliff above the river.

Shove that Ford over fast enough, it would disappear forever.

Floyd slowed, watched Sims's headlights run up behind him, stop just before they would have crashed into the Corvette's ass. That councilman's house was a log cabin, the old kind, chinked with mud. Its low roof and long front porch would give it a distinctive outline. On the left side of the road, backed up to the river.

The houses began to look familiar, even in the dark. Floyd slowed again. Not far now. Maybe the next one. No. The next? Damn. Okay, gotta be the—

There it was. The driveway had disappeared beneath vines, but because of the drought, they fell apart as he turned in and continued to part like the waters of the Red Sea as he drove to the house with Sims right on his ass.

"That's right, little piggy," Floyd said under his breath. "Stay close so you won't get lost in the driveway."

He turned behind the house, pulled the 'Vette against the garage door, killed the engine. He'd wait until dumb-ass parked the car before he left his. Be just like the idiot to run over him.

Sims pulled the Ford behind the house and stopped. Floyd met him as he opened the car door.

"Here's the deal," he said, barely able to see Sims's little piggy eyes, it was so dark. "You're gonna drive that car down that way." Floyd pointed toward the eastern horizon, where the harvest moon was just rising. "Stop about halfway down. We gotta figure how to get this thing running so it soars off the cliff. I want it in the middle of the river."

Sims gazed over the top of the car. "Long way back there, Floyd. Dark, too."

"Yes, Sims, it's dark. That happens sometimes when the sun goes down." Floyd stopped. Would do him no good to piss Sims off. He put a hand on the other man's meaty shoulder. "Sorry, partner. I'm jazzed."

"Yeah, me too," Sims said.

"You go on down there. I'll look for something to hold the accelerator down."

"Need a rope to fix the steering wheel, too, Floyd. It'll turn if you don't. Damned thing'll go in circles, maybe come after us."

"Right," Floyd said, thinking how Sims that was. Dumb as a wooden fence, every now and then he popped up with something you'd forgotten and saved the day.

Maybe that was why Floyd kept him around.

CHAPTER NINETEEN

Rex Mason crept softly to the corner of the tall, clapboard house and peeked around, still not sure he'd made the right call when he followed Sims. He'd been in position for his part in the FBI bust, there early because that's how he liked doing business.

He'd seen the red Ford drive in, seen the door open, recognized both Sims and Floyd, the golden children of East Precinct.

There was a curve in Rex's thoughts where those two were concerned. Until now, he'd put it down to jealousy.

Most of East Precinct had done some pretty amazing things that went unrecognized. Amazing things went unrecognized for most cops.

Except Floyd and Sims.

Their behavior tonight screamed covert action, and yet, they were supposedly the best cops on the force.

When Floyd and Sims drove away together, Rex called the agent-in-charge, told him what he was seeing without naming names, received permission to begin pursuit, but not permission to engage. That had been made extremely clear.

No permission to engage.

Rex never argued with people smarter than he. The Feebs had all at one time or another assured him they were much smarter than he.

So, no engagement.

He waited until both cars were out of sight to go after them, saw the Ford's taillights ahead, fell into line, staying far enough back so his pursuit wouldn't be noticed, but near enough to see if they turned.

When Floyd pulled into the driveway beside the old log cabin, Sims the Brilliant put on his turn signal. Rex laughed out loud.

Rex pulled over while they drove to the back of the house, sneaked down the driveway next door, flattened himself against the outside wall and listened long enough to know any conversation they'd had was over.

They were implementing.

He inched down the wall, moving his feet carefully so as not to rustle the gravel, until he could slide his head around the corner. The moon was rising fast, but the giant cedar behind the house was between Rex and its light for the moment.

That wouldn't last long.

They'd driven the car far down the yard, parked it among trees whose leaves were gone, so Rex could see pretty well.

Sims knelt beside the car, fiddling with something inside. Floyd was going back and forth carrying heavy bags that required both hands. When he threw one into the trunk, the car bounced.

Bags of car parts, stored here and then moved out later?

Maybe. Sims slid into the driver's seat. They'd disabled the interior light, but Rex could see Sims wrapping a rope around the steering wheel and tying it off somewhere in the middle.

Immobilizing the steering wheel so once the car was in gear, it could go only one direction.

They were disposing of it. Sending it over the cliff into the river.

Because they were tipped off about the Feebs?

Maybe.

No, they would have ditched the car, then driven it somewhere safe when the heat was off.

He peered around the corner again, checked the car's silhouette. What make was Neva's rental car? Fusion. A 2014 red Ford Fusion.

His Google app brought up the picture in a heartbeat. The Fusion was long and boxy.

Rex stuffed his iPhone back in his pocket, his mouth drying as he did.

Neva had called him earlier, worried that Zanna hadn't arrived. He'd pretty much blown her off. Zan was a songwriter, a creative nut. She likely decided to spend the night with a guy she met on the plane.

She'd call tomorrow.

The cousins would duke it out, then make up.

No need to call out the troops.

If he was wrong, if Neva's fears were justified, the thing Floyd was covering in that trunk could be Zan. If she was still alive, the fall to the river would kill her.

Do not engage.

Fuck that shit.

He was halfway around the corner when the car engine roared.

Its back wheels spun.

It leapt forward like a bull out of the gate, rocketed down the yard toward the bluff. Rex pulled his Glock and took aim at its back tires. Too late. It sailed off the cliff, hovered in mid-air for a long second, then dropped from sight.

Rex raced to his car, roared back down Brush Hill. Zan could hold her breath for two minutes. Then she'd breathe water, her lungs would fill and she would die.

Two minutes.

The speed limit along Lakewood Drive was thirty miles per hour. Rex was doing twice that when he hit the first curve, screamed by the suspect's house, where at least a dozen people milled about in the front yard and bright lights turned the night into day.

He hit the barrier that blocked the driveway to the river, sent it spinning in three pieces and blessed the drought as he flew down the thin gravel without sliding once.

"Hold on, Zanna girl. Hold on."

His headlights picked up the car, its nose smashed against the rocks that in normal times would be considerably below the water level. Its back tires were slightly raised and unmoving. The impact must have killed the engine.

If she survived the fall, he'd have her out of there in a minute. He should have given Neva's instincts more credence instead of mouthing platitudes and company policy. If that girl was dead, Rex would never forgive himself.

He pulled up beside the wreck, leapt from his car. A quick check of the front and back seats and the floorboards told him Zanna was not there, but he snatched a backpack from the back seat and carried it with him to the trunk.

Now the heavy bags Floyd loaded seemed ominous. Their weight could suffocate her even though the car remained above water. Ignoring everything he knew about crime scenes, Rex grabbed a rock from the rubble, slammed it up under the lip of the trunk until it opened. Bags of mulch popped into view.

Rex grabbed the first one, slung it behind the car, continued hauling them out until the only thing left in the trunk was a suitcase, its orange polka dots staring into the darkness. Rex dragged the case onto the rocks and dropped the backpack beside it.

She wasn't there.

He dropped down onto the rocks, wiped the sweat off his face, feeling the grit on his hand roughen his cheek.

She wasn't in the trunk, but unless he missed his guess, the suitcase and backpack were hers. She was in deep trouble, and he'd wasted almost an entire day because he'd been an arrogant dickhead.

Rex pulled his cell phone from his pocket, sat with his fingers hovering over the keys for a long time. Floyd and Sims were dirty. Floyd practically lived with the captain. A case of carefully crafted wool over the captain's eyes, or were they working together?

On the other hand, Rex had incredibly important evidence in the suitcase and backpack. Fingerprints, DNA, hairs, all kinds of evidence could be clinging to those articles as well as the inside of the car. He could hardly take them home and hide them in his closet.

He could call the FBI agent-in-charge, but the agent would go straight to the captain.

Finally, he typed in the phone number of a man he trusted literally with his life, told him where he was, asked him to come. He clicked off, reported to the agent-in-charge that his chase had been a case of mistaken identity. He apologized, accepted the agent's forgiving grunt and clicked off just as the headlights he'd hoped to see rounded the curve.

CHAPTER TWENTY

The persistent pinch in her elbow forced Zan's heavy eyelids open. Somewhere deep in her brain alarm bells clanged and cymbals crashed, but the meaning of all this noise was swallowed beneath a heavy sludge that covered not only her mind, but her limbs. Her arm weighed almost too much to lift, but she managed to jerk the needle from her vein. Needle. She'd had surgery, then. Tonsils? No, she had those out when she was five.

Oh well. Something else. She dropped the needle behind her and rolled to her side, asleep before she finished the motion.

She dreamed of betrayal and tragedy, the stuff songs can be made of if they're not too dark. Nobody wants to listen to musical horror. The feet that shuffled outside her door became an ancient Roman guard with whom she marched, nestled between their bodies. The cloaks they wore were thin and the weather was cold. Her sandaled feet were filthy and her legs already so tired, she could barely move them. This dream made no sense. The ancient Romans had been dead for centuries. Her feet were cold, tucked as close to her body as she could get them. She lay on a hard surface.

She forced her eyes open with her finger and thumb. Where was she?

How did she get here?

Andrew Haile.

He'd reached across the seat to pat her arm, thank her, she'd thought.

Then the sting of a needle. She'd shoved her way out of the car, but the drug slowed her. He'd snatched the back of her T-shirt before she took more than two steps. Her last memory was grasping after her necklace as it flew from her neck.

Panic upped her respiration by two hundred percent. She dragged herself up, took a deep breath, exhaled it slowly, listened carefully to the sounds outside, assessing as much as she could with her brain twisting inside her skull like a terrified rabbit.

The breathing calmed her. Her brain-rabbit stayed vigilant but stopped twisting.

People were moving outside, some barefooted, others shod in heavy boots. There was no noise save the plop of bare feet, the ring of shoes and the rustle of clothing. People, lots of people, all moving without a word.

Her throat closed. She forced it open with another breath. Her head spun. She leaned forward, let the blood run to her brain, concentrated on keeping herself stable, broke out in a cold sweat.

This would not do.

The sound of feet seemed to move away from her door. She waited until a sudden vertigo ended to raise her head. When it steadied, she scooted to the nearest wall, gathered herself and rose, holding to the wall in case she became dizzy again.

The room was twilight dark thanks to a slice of bright light that managed to shove through the crack beside the door. It was small, empty except for herself and the IV stand. When she stepped back, her foot slid into a puddle where the needle she'd snatched from her arm had continued to pour forth its mind-numbing drug.

Zan picked it up, kinked the tube, tied it and hung the whole thing back on the rack with the needle stabbed into the line, taking a moment's refuge in that simple housekeeping move, but the second it was done, her mind leapt. *OhmyGod, ohmyGod, ohmyGod where am I and what do they want from me?*

She fought the panic down again, but in the dark recesses of her mind, she agreed with the panic. Nothing good could come from this.

Still holding the wall, she slid toward the crack. There were two cracks, actually, but the one on the left side of the door was so small its light was useless. The other offered a thin view of the room outside.

Still working on throwing off the effects of the drug, Zanna moved carefully, soundlessly, one foot at a time, testing each step for creaks or groans, although the floor was smooth and warm, marble, she thought from the little she could see of it. Not likely to creak *or* groan.

At the crack, she saw the banquet-sized room with, as she'd guessed, marble floors, dark blue with shots of gold. The same substance covered the walls. She looked up to find the ceiling equally covered, at least twenty feet high. The room was crisscrossed with ropes hung six, maybe seven feet off the floor. Hanging on these were bed sheets, some more white than others. Zanna lowered her gaze to the floor beneath the sheets and saw the wheels of rolling beds. Beside each was a base atop a circle of wheels, IV stands.

Beds, drugs and bare feet.

Her blood went cold. She squatted, hugged herself, stood again as she heard voices coming her way.

"No rough stuff, you got that?" The voice was gravel-filled, wheezy, the voice of a long-term smoker.

"Yeah, I got it." This one was smooth, younger, quivering with eagerness.

They came into view, one short and swarthy with curly black hair, Hispanic. The other was tall and slender, not bad looking. The short one lifted a curtain.

Zanna got her first look at her future.

An emaciated woman lay on the bed wearing a short gown made of nylon netting that covered nothing. A long tube, identical to the one Zan found in her vein, was connected to the woman's elbow, secured there with duct tape. As the man stepped in, the woman managed a death-head grin, doubtless the best she could do. The guard watched her for a second before he dropped the curtain and walked away.

With the flesh between her legs shriveling, Zanna watched the man's feet disappear, heard the creak as his weight bore on the cot. The poor woman sighed, a heart-breaking and lonely sound. Acceptance of the unacceptable, acknowledgment that the time had come to endure.

Zan's eyes filled.

In seconds, the man's heavy grunt signaled his release. His feet reappeared.

There was no sound from the woman.

After that, the line of men never ended. Zanna sensed more than saw that the sheet-shrouded cubicles stretched back across that immense room, from side to side and front to back.

Most of the interaction between the rapists and their victims was brief, but at least twice, a woman cried out. Both times, hard-soled shoes came running at the cry.

None of those cries happened where Zan could see. She had no way to tell whether the woman was protected or punished. She suspected, however, that except in cases of extreme cruelty, the guards' job was to make the customers happy.

Having learned what she could by watching, she turned back to her room. Her gaze landed on the IV. They thought she was drugged, might not check on her for a while. If she was going to escape, now was the time, the only time.

With the hair on her neck standing straight up, she inched her way along the walls. She forced herself to move deliberately, touch every surface, tug every crack. She found nothing until she got to the middle of the back wall.

Until now, the marble panels had been narrow. This one was at least three times the width of the others.

Where the others ran from the ceiling to the floor, this one stopped in the middle. The patch she'd sewn on her living room curtains where Ginger had torn them in an inexplicable frenzied hysteria last winter came to mind. They'd patched this part of the wall.

Why?

When she pulled, the panel lifted. When she turned it loose, it settled against the wall.

Her second, harder pull lifted it halfway, but made it creak.

Whirling toward the door, she waited a breathless second.

Now, now, now! Do it now!

Lifting the panel in small increments, she got it far enough back so she could get her head under it.

Musty, long-contained air filled her nose. Her hands curled around the edge of the opening.

Holding on with one, she shoved her other hand through.

Nothing.

Whoa.

A window.

In a closet.

What the hell?

She swung both arms around through the hole. Her fingers hit a rope. She snatched it, poked around some more, found another.

Something banged against the wall far below the window.

She stopped. Held her breath.

Again moving in increments, she used the rope to bring the thing toward her, grabbed it when she could.

A flat board with the ropes woven around it, outdoor-swing style. A picture clicked in her head. She'd seen this at Thomas Jefferson's house.

A dumbwaiter.

This one was much larger, likely ancient, probably hadn't been used forever. Would likely break and send her to the bottom of the shaft. Which might be only eight feet down.

Or a hundred.

Her chest tightened. If she stayed here, she knew what waited for her.

She took a deep breath.

Now, for the hard part: getting herself onto the platform without killing herself or alerting the others.

CHAPTER TWENTY-ONE

Ginger was curled in the chair she preferred, the only non-leather one in the living room.

Neva had filled Uncle Rex in on Ginger's surprise arrival. He said he'd stop by later today, that she should put the carrier in the closet and not touch it again. Said they'd likely want to take samples of Ginger's hair and maybe her DNA. He would bring the right people.

She'd read recently about several women who escaped after ten years of rape, abuse, imprisonment. Ten years. Abuse, abasement, captivity, beatings, miscarriages, forced pregnancies.

Ten years.

Neva set Ginger in her lap, stroked the cat's silky fur, scratched under her chin when she raised it. Never, ever would Zan have left her. Or Neva didn't think she would have. Zan had a quirky streak, had been known to detour from the straight and narrow path. In fact, where Zan was concerned, there pretty much wasn't a straight and narrow path.

But to drop Ginger off without a word? Not happening.

No need to jump to conclusions. There could be a lot of explanations, despite the fact that Neva could think of none.

Zan was strong, resourceful, a powerful woman. She'd be a hard one to lure into a bad situation and woe unto any man who tried to keep her where she didn't want to be.

Uncle Rex wasn't taking it too seriously, either, from their conversation yesterday. He'd even said Zan was a bit flighty.

It was remotely believable she'd met some hunk on the plane and decided to spend the night with him. Remotely. Like it would be believable if Neva suddenly quit her job and ran to New York.

In short, it wasn't very damned likely.

If Zan had done something stupid, Ginger would be with her.

The cat rumbled. Neva scratched behind her ears and then set her back on her chair.

Zan was a musician. Maybe she'd tried to smuggle in pot and—Sheeeeeshhhhh.

Neva grabbed her iPod, stuffed the buds in her ears, turned the music up loud to drown out her thoughts. But even with AC/DC booming through her head, she couldn't stop thinking.

She conjured up a picture of Dr. Novak, Miss Sylvia's doctor since Neva's sixth birthday. Twenty years Novak had pumped Neva's mother full of drugs, then blamed Neva and her father for Miss Sylvia's lack of improvement.

Words, ugly words, words her mother did not want her to speak, struggled against Neva's clenched teeth at every one of these quarterly meetings like the one scheduled for two p.m. today. How could it not be apparent to Novak that the drugs were too strong, put Miss Sylvia down so far she couldn't struggle up even to wash her hair? After all, it was Novak who prescribed the med that woke her up enough to participate in the quarterly bashing of her family.

Neva had beaten Moya's ears off with her anger, rage and frustration, because she couldn't talk to anybody else. Her father looked through her when she tried to talk to him, and her mother was comatose.

Sometimes, like now, anger spread through Neva like acid. It was anger at Novak, but it also encompassed her parents. If their plumber screwed up the water pipes as badly as Novak screwed up her mother, they would sue him.

Night after night when she lived with her parents, Neva had come home to find her father sitting in the dark house, alone, his hands over his eyes, trapped by his decency in a lonely, cold marriage as completely as if he were chained to the wall.

Her mother had disappeared from his life.

Like Zanna. And just like that, her worry about Zan was back in full force. She dropped the iPod on the table and headed for the shower. Maybe the water could drown out her worries.

The noonday sun tried to force cheer into the sky, but without periodic rain, Nashville's airborne filth had melded with the natural particles to turn the normal vivid blue to a depressing muddy yellow.

Summit's parking lot was nearly full. Neva pulled all the way to the back before she managed to find an unoccupied space.

She slid from the Mustang, which she'd retrieved from the auto body shop on her way. It looked new: no bullet holes; new side mirrors; a new windshield, back window, passenger side window;

and a bright new paint job. The car looked so good, it seemed the whole affair in the cemetery might have been a dream.

Her thoughts finally off of Zan and on the drubbing to come, she grabbed her bottle of water without checking the top. As she cleared the seat with it, the top wobbled and fell.

"Crap!" No time for this stuff, but no way in hell she was going in there without the bottle. When she could not keep her mouth shut any other way, she filled it with water.

She reached under the edge of the car, hit the cap with the side of her hand and sent it skittering. "Damn, damn, double damn," she muttered. Setting the bottle out of harm's way, she lay on the asphalt, trying not to think of the oil and filth beneath her, and peered into the deep gloom under the car. Took a minute for her eyes to adjust, but when they did, she saw the round pillow that was the bottle cap, but also another object, a ball with a tail running from it toward the back of the car.

Necklace. Probably a kid's from a bubblegum machine.

With one swipe, she collected everything, then stopped to make sure the bottle cap was pinched tightly between her finger and thumb. The ball had rolled into the center of her palm, leaving its tail hanging.

Scooting her knees under her, she brought both objects into the light, dusted her clothes and screwed the cap securely onto the bottle, then tossed the necklace into the driver's seat. She'd throw it away when she got home. It arced high. The weak sunlight drove fire through the ball and stopped her cold.

She knew that necklace, had seen it a jillion times. Neva shook her head. Couldn't be. Zan never took the damn thing off.

N-e-v-e-r.

Novak was going to kill her. She glanced at the hospital. If she left right now and ran, she might make it on time.

But it looked just like…

With shaking fingers, she pulled the globe from the seat, held it to the sunlight, unable to deny, now, that it was a completely round piece of amber, rare as unicorn hooves. Zan's had a bug, a mosquito, she said, inside, a mosquito with a missing leg. As rare as round amber was, bugs in amber were even more rare, and as far as Zan could find out, she had the one and only piece with a five-legged bug.

The bug was embedded deep in the center of the thing. Neva turned it slowly, counting legs as she did, holding her breath until she had completed a rotation.

Five legs.

The sixth, one of the back ones, was not there.

She clutched it to her chest and leaned down with a sharp pain that, had she not recognized it as fear, would have felt like a heart attack. Zan's necklace on the ground with its chain—she opened her hand—torn as if someone had jerked it from her neck, someone who was trying to keep her from running away, someone who was fighting for his own life. Because Rozanna Clark would never have gone willingly.

"Oh, no," Neva whispered. She slumped against the car and tried to force her frozen brain to think. Ginger on her front porch alone, this necklace in this parking lot.

What to do, what to do, what to do, what to do. She slapped her hand down hard on the car's roof, let the shock and pain center her thoughts, fished a small plastic bag out of the console, dropped the necklace into it.

All thoughts of good Doctor Novak erased from her mind, she punched in Uncle Rex's number. When he didn't answer, she left voice mail, asked him to call her the minute he got the message.

She glanced at her watch.

Ten minutes late.

She slid the necklace into her pocket, then took off at a run up the tall hill, slid to a halt at the information desk.

"Do you have…have…have anybody who's not been identified?" She was breathless from the run.

The elderly lady behind the desk raised crystal green eyes. "Not identified?"

"You know, somebody, a woman, who was brought in unconscious and hasn't waked yet? Or maybe a head-trauma victim with amnesia? Or someone in a coma?" Neva sucked in a deep breath. "My cousin is missing."

Understanding flooded the green crystal. "Ah," she said, her petite fingers flying over the keys. "I think I can answer that. Let me see." She broke off, peering into the screen. "Yes… No." She chuckled briefly and said, "Let me try that again. We did have a patient with a head trauma, but he was discharged a week ago."

"My cousin is a woman."

"He's the only one," the lady said. Her greens softened. "Has she been missing long?"

The concern in her voice brought tears to Neva's eyes, but she said, "No, but she's not that person. You know? She wouldn't make us worry." She stopped, aware she sounded disjointed, then said, "She would have called if she could."

"I am so sorry," crystal green said. "I hope you find her soon."

Novak's inner office was decorated in soft earth tones. The carpet was so cushioned, it felt like a sponge. Three plush leather chairs faced the desk, which was a piece of antique art with hand-carved edges and a solid cherry top large enough to land a plane on.

Miss Sylvia sat in the chair farthest from the door. Robert Oakley glanced at Neva with a quick smile, but his face was drawn and pale. Apparently, Novak had already started her regular beating.

Neva's hands curled.

Novak's ferret face darkened. Her mouth twisted. She shoved herself up in her chair and said, "Nice of you to join us, Miss Oakley. I've been talking for"—she consulted her Rolex—"eighteen minutes. I'll recap."

"Please don't bother, doctor. I'll catch up as you go along." Neva slid into the chair beside her father, laid her hands on its arms. He covered her left hand with his right. Neva took a deep, deep breath and tried to focus on Novak instead of the necklace that shoved against her leg.

Behind the desk, Novak pursed her thin lips. "We were discussing your mother's drugs." She tented her fingers under her chin and launched into a plodding, detailed account of those drugs. She used every acronym and Latin name in the lexicon, obviously much more intent on impressing than informing. She finished with, "Your father tells me, however, that there has been no change in your mother's condition."

"You think, Dad?" Neva asked in surprise. "I thought she was sleeping more often, like she sleeps continuously. Don't you?"

"She does sleep a lot—" Neva's dad managed before Novak interrupted.

"She sleeps because she has no reason to be awake." The tone was smug, the smile condescending. "If either of you was there to stimulate her," she continued, "she'd be awake more often. You, in particular, Neva. I understand you have your own life to live, but I would think you'd take more interest in your mother."

Neva's teeth found the soft tissue of her right jaw. She sank them in, clutched her water. "I'm not sure how you know what my activities are, Dr. Novak—"

"I know because your mother has told me you are never there."

"I visit Mom at least twice a week. She thinks I'm not there, Dr. Novak, because the drugs you give her make her sleep continuously."

Keep it together. Don't lose your temper. Have a drink of water.

"I don't believe you have any medical training," Dr. Novak spat. "I can assure you her sleeping has nothing to do with the drugs. It's because she has nothing better to do."

"You're comparing my mother to a cat," Neva said. She heard the anger in her voice, knew she should stop, but like the night she'd challenged Davis, the knot in her stomach wasn't going to let her stop. "Cats sleep when they have nothing to do. She's a human being. She's sleeping because she's drugged to the hilt."

"Now, Geneva," Sylvia's sleep-slowed voice drawled. "Don't be rude to the doctor."

Neva looked at her father, who caught her glance and held it. Did she read a desperate request in that gaze or was he trying to stop her? The amber again shoved into her leg. The thing Zan focused on to remind her of Aunt Anne. If someone had taken a stand, demanded the right doctor, the right drugs, would Aunt Anne still be alive?

"I'm sorry, Mom, but somebody's got to do this." She squeezed her dad's hand, let it go, turned to face Novak squarely. "The drugs aren't making her better. They're giving her permission to do nothing. They should be a stopgap. I don't need a medical degree to see that."

Novak opened her mouth. Neva raised a hand. "I've listened to you for many years, doctor. You can listen for a change. If your drugs were going to make her better, she would be better. She isn't. She's worse." Neva leaned out so she could see her mother. Sylvia's eyes blinked, the expression on her face pretty much, "What is happening here?"

"Mom, if you want to get better, you'll have to do it yourself. Throw the drugs in the trash, get out of that bed, take a bath, get your hair done, go grocery shopping, whatever. But *do* something. I love you, but it's time somebody told you the truth. Find a new doctor, one who's interested in curing you, not redecorating her office with your fees."

Novak sucked in a furious lungful.

Sylvia's mouth was open, but her gaze was tight on Neva's face. She might be drugged, but she was listening.

For once.

"Dad and I love you. We'll wipe your butt and wash your hair as long as you make us, but it's not fun. Not for either of us. We want you back. We want you alive. We want you well."

"Miss Oakley—"

Suddenly, Neva was weary. She wiped a hand over her face while Novak watched her with hawk-like attention.

"Dr. Novak, I've let you beat the hell out of me and my father for many years. Dad can do as he likes, but I won't be back here." She leaned out again, captured her mother's gaze. "Do something, Mom. Take a stand. Make a move. Help us help you."

The receptionist jerked up as Neva breezed past, but her high-pitched "Miss Oakley?" was left in the air as the door closed behind Neva.

She leaned against the wall, tried to calm herself. She'd said what needed saying, but there was no way to tell how Miss Sylvia would react. If she reacted badly, grabbed a handful of pills and joined her poor sister in death—

She turned back for the door, then let her hand drop.

It was up to Miss Sylvia now.

Her cell phone played the *Lawman* theme.

"Hello, Uncle Rex," she said. "I've found Zanna's necklace in the hospital parking lot at Summit. Can you come right now?"

CHAPTER TWENTY-TWO

The employee had no illusions. He'd worked for the boss since his twelfth birthday, turning tricks, sometimes in filthy alleyways. It had been painful and demeaning. He'd cried himself to sleep many nights. It took several months, but finally his former home took on a dream quality, an exalted dream, something nobody ever really had. Little by little, he accepted this life as his, set out to make it bearable.

Attitude. Always attitude.

The boss picked up on the change immediately, moved the employee out of the cold back room with the locked door, gave him a bed with covers and a lot more food, which in turn gave the employee more energy. He turned that energy to proving himself to the one man in his life who could make it better.

Inch by inch, with few backslides, he moved from captive to trusted agent. When the boss made him a guard over the women, his ego had leapt, but by then he'd learned how to hide those sudden moments of ego so the boss didn't see them.

He hadn't realized how hard it would be, however, to watch other people, even women, suffer as he'd suffered, hadn't known how difficult it was to control his almost overwhelming urge to save them.

Thoughts of what the boss would do kept him alive and working.

But even with his iron will, he'd not been able to hide these thoughts from the boss. He'd called the employee in finally, sat him opposite his immense and beautiful desk, put his fingers together, clearly showing the missing two, and began to talk about the lives the women had led before.

Degrading, disgusting lives, full of pain, starvation and abuse, working twelve to fourteen hours a day for nothing, their hands swollen and painful. Beatings if they complained, death if they attempted to revolt. He'd painted picture of such anguish, in fact, the employee left feeling good about the lesser degradation, abuse and starvation they now endured. It wasn't a perfect life, but it was better, and that was enough. After all, the boss provided condoms for every customer. Every employee knew to insist the customer take one.

Whether the customer used it or not was another matter.

The women were fed three meals a day, small meals, but certainly more than they got in their native lands.

Sometimes, when it was dark and he was alone, which was most of the time, the employee wondered how he would feel if his mother were one of these women. Or the sister he'd never had. His child. They were dark thoughts that squirmed in his belly like a pair of rats in a pile of grain.

It took lots of alcohol to make them go away.

He'd reached the pinnacle ten years ago, became the boss's trusted lieutenant, left the daily work and became a part of the management team. It was in this capacity he approached the current location with his teeth grinding, because somebody on his team had been stupid enough to snatch Rozanna Fucking Clark. Their mantra was keep a low profile. Clark was a profile high enough to destroy their entire operation.

He trotted up the marble stairs into the massive building with his heart in his throat. If they'd touched Clark, he'd cut their balls off. If they'd hurt her, he'd leave them in the alley for the dogs.

His boot heels rang on the marble as he rushed down the hallway toward the room where all the activity was. Ten men, sad-looking dudes with big bellies and dull eyes, waited their turn. He glanced at Sean as he passed him, checking that he was clean and fully intent on taking the money, handing out the condoms, sending his customers on their way.

A woman screamed somewhere near the back corner. Instantly, Miguel lifted from the far wall, ran in that direction, his long legs eating up the distance.

Abuse was tolerated. Torture was not.

The women knew what they'd get if they screamed just to get relief.

The room he sought was to his left. He swerved around the sheet-separated cubes, kept his gaze on the wall until he saw the slightly wider crack. There were six of these closets back here, once used to store the tables, cloths and paraphernalia of a finer time. Now, they were used to separate the new women from the old until the new could be seasoned.

He prayed nobody had attempted to season Clark. If she was still drugged, he'd drop her on a street corner somewhere. The only man she could identify was on his way to Peru at this moment, lucky to still have ten working fingers. He wouldn't be coming back to the States for a long time. She could identify *him* all day every day for all the employee cared.

He slid his key into the lock, fiddled a second until it found the tumblers, shoved the door wide. The light from outside spilled across the floor.

His heart sank.

A blanket, tossed as if she'd thrown it with all her strength, an IV stand with the needle stabbed into the line. Nothing else. Protocol. Fucking protocol. Begin the seasoning while they were drugged.

Goddamn!

He whirled back into the room, gestured to Miguel, who was again in his rightful place against the wall.

"Where is she?" the employee demanded as Miguel neared.

"Who?"

"Clark. The woman in that room?"

Miguel's face blanched. He leaned around the employee so he could see. His eyes widened. "Eyee," he said softly. "Where can she go?"

Confusion stopped the employee's intended next words before they got to his tongue. "You don't have her?"

Miguel shook his head. "I put her in this room, locked the door." He nodded toward the curtains. "No time to come back."

Relief spread through the employee like warm butter through freshly baked bread, then disappeared as quickly as it came. If Miguel hadn't sent her to be seasoned, where the hell *was* she?

"Did you check these rooms to make sure there was no way out?"

"Sí," Miguel said. "They are all the same. Little rooms with solid walls." Sweat popped onto his forehead.

"Get me a flashlight." The closets were not lighted. The back walls were in a deep shadow. He'd bet nobody had gone back there to check every single wall. They'd checked one, maybe two of the closets, decided the others were the same.

People got their fingers broken for just such incompetence. The employee intended to make sure they weren't his fingers.

The light played over the marble, sparking the gold in it. The sidewalls were made of overlapping marble panels, but in the middle of the back one, there was a large area that broke the pattern.

The employee's heart climbed into his throat.

He led Miguel to the back wall, handed him the flashlight. The damned thing looked solid enough. He tucked his fingers under its bottom edge. Immediately, it lifted.

"Shit!" the employee said.

He and Miguel together managed to tear it off. The patch was large because the hole beneath it was big enough for any adult to slide through. Like everything else in this old raveling monument to the excesses of another time, its edges were covered in dust an inch thick. Except for the bottom edge. There, the dust showed swirls, clean spots and fingerprints.

He shone the light around what he at first thought was the inside of a chimney. Bricks on all sides, a hollow column that stopped at the ceiling above. A chimney except there was no sign of fire. The bricks were dusty, not black. He danced the light around the pulley. Dropped from the ceiling, it clearly formed a part of what the odd shaft was all about. He leaned over, held the light at the end of his fingers, let it dangle into the hole, but he could not see the end of the shaft.

She left this room through this hole. Once more, he investigated the pulley, looking for something to say it had recently been used, but it lay sideways to the opening, so he could only see one side, which was covered in the same inch-deep dust as everything else.

If she'd jumped...*oh my God*! What did it cost a man when he shut an operation down a day early?

With Miguel right behind him, he raced through the room and down the back stairs to the network far below the building. He'd not spent much time down there but he had a good idea of the location of the closet in relationship to the downstairs. If Clark was dead, he'd dispose of her body so it could never be found; then he'd clear this place out.

Around the stairs toward the back of the place.

No door.

He retraced his steps, gazing at the high ceiling as he walked. If the closet was there, he put his hand on the spot, the shaft was— He took four steps toward the back.

Here.

He turned to Miguel. "Where's the fucking door?"

Miguel took the flashlight, played it over every inch of the wall.

There was no fucking door.

"Ah, shit!" the employee spat. "We'll have to get the women out of here," he said; then he stopped. If there *was* no fucking door, Clark was already where nobody could find her. He wouldn't have to tell the boss about her. They were leaving tomorrow anyway.

She was dead. Nobody could survive that jump. Dead and buried.

He took the flashlight, went over the wall one more time. No fucking door.

Just in case, he'd leave Miguel here. Because he'd learned long ago not to trust things to logic. If Clark had somehow managed to survive the fall and also had some wacko way of getting out of that shaft, she wouldn't get past Miguel.

* * * *

Neva waved as Uncle Rex's old battered pickup dropped over the hill. He parked two stalls down, came to her with his boot heels ringing on the pavement, wearing jeans and a shirt. She so seldom saw him in anything but khakis and pullovers, she pulled herself out of thoughts about her so-far awful day long enough to recognize how good he looked, in a mature Irishman's kind of way.

She handed him the plastic bag. He gave her a quick kiss on the cheek, then took a look.

"You're sure it's hers?"

"Absolutely. She put it on at her mother's funeral. Uncle Don about had a fit. It was huge for such a little girl, but she completely fell apart when he tried to take it away. She *bathes* with it on."

He rolled the ball back and forth on his palm, still inside the plastic, his gaze focused on it. "I found your rental car this morning."

Neva recoiled as if he'd slapped her. The air grew thick. "Where?" It was a whisper.

"In the river. She wasn't in it," he said quickly. "Her suitcase, did it have orange polka dots?"

"Yes."

"It was in the trunk. A backpack?"

"She always traveled with one." Neva sagged against the Mustang's front fender, her knees weak and her head pounding.

"I've been thinking about all the reasons somebody might snatch Zan," Uncle Rex said. "She's a celeb, so there's always a chance. I'm surprised she didn't travel with a guard. There's nothing in her background, nothing I can find, anyway, that would fit." He lifted his gaze to hers. "You and Zan look a lot alike."

"Moya thinks we do," Neva said.

"Red hair, same body style. She's taller, as I remember."

"Bigger ears," Neva said, but a niggle of unease wormed in her mind. She'd thought about this in the middle of sleepless nights, worried that the men who'd chased her from the cemetery might have mistaken Zan for her. They looked alike, after all, and Zan had Neva's rental.

But the information these people would need—the license number to the rental and where it was parked. How would they get that? *She* didn't know the freakin' license number. She shared this with Uncle Rex, who nodded his agreement and then said, "But they knew Ginger belonged with you."

A cold finger traced itself down her spine. They knew her movements, her friends and relatives, knew when she would be where. She had no chance against them. A dozen cops could be outside her house all day and night every day and they'd still find a way to get her.

"She was driving your car," Uncle Rex said, driving spikes.

It makes sense. It all makes sense.

She stared into the brush that grew beyond the end of the parking lot. "I don't want it to be because of me," she said, speaking more to herself than to Uncle Rex. "But it is, isn't it? I shouldn't have gone into the cemetery, should have called the police."

Uncle Rex sighed. "I don't think you made a mistake, honey. You'd run kids out of there for years. Couldn't have known this was different. You guys nearly rescued that poor woman whose baby was killed. It's just bad luck Zan looks like you. Don't beat yourself. Keep your eyes open, pay attention to what's going on around you. I've got men watching, some of them you'll never see, but that doesn't mean you can do stupid stuff."

"I shoulda warned Zan."

"About what?" His gaze jerked to hers. "She was picking up a rental car at the airport in the middle of the day. What's scary about that?"

Neva gazed at the asphalt. Her chest filled with tears. He could say what he wanted. She should have been smarter, should have protected Zan the way Zan would have protected her. Taken the damned afternoon off, picked her cousin up, made sure she was safe.

Uncle Rex used his forefinger to raise her chin. "Stop it. We'll find her. I promise. I'll take this downtown." He glanced at the necklace. "See if they can find prints on it or DNA. We'll need to keep it for evidence if they do. If not, I'll bring it back to you." He hesitated, looked away, then back. "One more thing. When I found your rental, I didn't exactly follow procedures. Don't tell anybody I've found it. Okay? Not even Moya."

"Sure," she said, biting back her questions.

"Was the tank full?"

The question seemed to come out of nowhere, and for a second, Neva didn't understand. Then she said, "Yes. Why?"

"It's still full. Which means she didn't drive far. That's good because it narrows the search area. But with this"—he rolled the necklace over his palm—"I'm guessing she parked here." He lifted his gaze toward the hospital. "Maybe she was injured, unconscious."

"I asked inside. They said they didn't have any unidentified patients."

"Okay. Now, about the cat. She was still in the carrier?"

"With the airline tags. She'd not been out of that thing since Zan put her in it. I can almost guarantee you."

"So somebody found the carrier? Why would they bring it to you?"

"That's the question. It had to be somebody who knew us all. The rental company wouldn't give them our address." She gazed at the parking lot for a second. "Anybody who knew us would have brought the cat inside; anybody who didn't wouldn't know the cat belonged at our place."

Uncle Rex stared at the asphalt in his turn before he said, "I'll have somebody make a couple of drive-bys every night. You guys stay home or go out together. Moya still pack heat?"

"Every day."

"Take her with you. Promise?"

"Promise." She sometimes pushed against all the people who watched out for her, chafed against their loving restrictions, but right now, it felt pretty damned good to have this man in her corner. She leaned forward and kissed his cheek. "I do not know what I'd do without you."

"Don't know what I'd do without you, either. Do what I tell you." He glanced over his shoulder. "There's your dad and mom."

Her father was leading Miss Sylvia slowly down the walk. Her mother's head was bent. Sudden guilt constricted Neva's heart. "They're probably mad at me," she said. "I told that quack off about ten minutes ago."

"The doctor?"

"Yeah. She's got Mom so drugged she sleeps all the time."

"Bobby's not looking good, either," Rex said, his voice soft and musing. "Must be hard taking care of your mom and running a business at the same time."

"Awfully hard," Neva agreed, watching how heavily her mother leaned on her father's arm. Her muscles were weak from disuse. Moya had warned that her patients who refused to help themselves weakened until they ultimately could not leave their beds. Miss Sylvia wasn't far from that condition now. Neva clamped her lips. She hated to think she'd hurt Miss Sylvia, but if that's what it took to wake the woman up, it was more than worth it.

If Miss Sylvia actually woke up.

CHAPTER TWENTY-THREE

Later that afternoon, Neva printed a picture of Zan from FaceGen. She added text offering a five-hundred-dollar reward for any information leading to Zan's whereabouts. The money was coming from her own savings account. It would clean her out, but she couldn't think of a better use for it.

Neva had called her Uncle Don, told him about Zan, asked if he'd heard from her. He said he would file a missing person's report as soon as he got off the call. Uncle Rex texted Uncle Don a pic of the necklace. He confirmed it as the one Zan always wore.

It was now official. Rozanna Deidre Clark was missing. Neva had expected to feel relieved once officialdom believed what she knew in her heart. In fact, she was more worried now than before the police agreed with her.

Officially missing.

Officially kidnapped.

Officially in the hands of some crazy goon who might like to play games with wire cutters and long nails.

The "misper," as Uncle Rex called the missing person's report, was hardly off the printer before the media came over the horizon like a herd of rats. They'd interviewed Uncle Rex four times in the past hour. Neva's cell phone rang constantly.

She sent them all to voice mail.

She made twenty-five copies of the flyer. She and Moya would paste those around town tonight. Her Facebook page, "Find Rozanna Clark," already had two hundred friends, some of whom posted helpful information, some of whom posted sightings that were all but impossible, such as seeing Zanna in Texas at a time when she would have been on the plane. Uncle Rex said they'd check all these leads out, no matter how stupid they sounded.

"Trouble brings the fruitcakes out of the cellars," he'd said with a shake of his head.

She was stacking the flyers when Ice came in. He didn't at first see her, so she had a minute to notice how tired he looked, how strained. It must get to him sometimes that in his mid-life, he was still toting bodies up and down the interstate.

"Whassup?" she asked.

He jumped and then grinned. "Nothin', like always. What are you up to?"

"Printing flyers."

He shoved his two gurneys against the wall and said, "For Zan?"

"Yes."

"Think that's smart?"

"Zan's missing," she said. How could he not know that?

"I know she's missing, honey, but I'm not sure it's wise to put your name and face out there. It's not been that long since you were missing. Know what I mean?"

A shiver told her he had a point. "I'm just trying to find Zanna."

"Of course you are." He put his arm around her shoulders, snuggled her close. "Because that's who you are, but it's not safe. Zan's disappearance doesn't need any more publicity. It's on the national news as we speak. Everybody knows she's missing."

"But they don't know I'll pay them five hundred dollars for information."

Ice picked up a flyer, held it at arm's length, squinting.

"Want me to hold it against the wall so you can read it?" she asked. Too vain to wear reading glasses, Ice was all but blind up close.

"Smart-ass," he said. "Five hundred, huh? Nice reward."

"I thought so."

He put the flyer down, turned her loose. "I still think it's a bad idea."

"My daughter with a bad idea?" Neva's dad said from behind her. "I can't imagine."

"Glad you're here, sir," Ice said. "Tell this idiot she doesn't need to get into Zan's thing." He jerked his head toward the flyers.

Neva tossed her dad a glance intended to have him take her side. He picked up a flyer. When he'd read it, he shook his head. "I'm sorry, sweetie, but Ice is right. Everybody knows Zanna's missing."

"But the reward—"

"That information can come through the police." His voice was hard, the way it was when he was scared for her. "You don't need to advertise it yourself."

"We'll put the flyers on telephone poles," she began, but her father was already shaking his head. "No, you won't. I saw your Facebook page. That's fine. But stop there."

Standing side by side, he and Ice stared at her, a solid bond of maleness protecting their woman.

For not the first time, she found herself loving and resenting them equally.

* * * *

Later at home, Neva slipped into her end-of-day outfit. Moya had a date with Ken tonight, so the house was Neva's. Normally, she read or watched television, talked to Davis before she went to bed, maybe washed her hair.

Tonight, she was on edge. Her mind roamed the many places Zan could be, chewed at imagined horrors.

She rubbed her jaw. The bruise was nearly gone, but she'd never forget it, hoped she'd never again feel as helpless as when she woke in the back of that van.

"Zan," she whispered, "we'll find you. I promise. Don't give up."

She grabbed a bottle of wine from the fridge, poured the deep ruby liquid into one of the delicate crystal glasses her mother had bestowed on her when her grandmother died. Wine tasted better from crystal.

Interestingly, milk did not.

She took it into the living room. She wanted to get drunk—knee-walkin', commode-huggin', specter-seeing smashed. Forget about Zan and her dad's business, just fall into a deep ruby glass and float mindlessly until morning.

Would anybody care if she did?

No.

Did she deserve it?

Yes.

But she couldn't think drunk, might miss the one clue that would take them to Zan.

One glass would be fine.

The door opened.

She jerked. Wine slopped onto the table.

Moya stepped in, gave Neva a smile.

"Hello," Neva said. "Why are you here?"

"Becauuuuse I live here?"

"This conversation sounds familiar. I thought you had a date."

"I did have a date."

"Yet you're here."

"Right. Ken broke his finger."

"He— Did you say he broke his finger?"

"Little finger, left hand."

"How?"

"Ken likes to fuck around with hammers and nails and dangerous machines on his day off. Wonder he hasn't cut a finger off. He laid this huge board on his worktable. When it fell, he tried to catch it. Little finger broke right in half."

"You sound angry."

"I *am* angry. I just don't know why. People have accidents every day. He's careful most of the time, was careful today. Things happen."

"But you're still angry?"

"Yes."

"And you don't know why?"

Moya stared over Neva's head for a minute. "I'm not angry at him. I want to go punch out the board."

Neva smiled, used her paper towel to wipe the wine off the table, and leaned back. "Methinks the lady is in love," she said. "Change, get yourself a glass, then come tell Aunt Neva all about it."

* * * *

Rozanna had made it down the dumbwaiter with only scrapes and a possibly broken toe gained when the platform spun out of control and slammed her foot-first into the bricks.

In total blackness at the bottom, she'd removed the heel from her boot, extracted her knife and cut the ropes. The platform fell with a thunk. Overhead, the pulley creaked into action, disgorging the ropes and sending them crashing down around her. At least, that's what she thought happened based on sounds. She could see nothing.

She'd done it, come down that long shaft on a rickety piece of wood held by ropes of indeterminate age and hit the floor alive and unharmed. She took a deep, celebratory breath and took stock.

Once before, she'd stood in unrelieved blackness in a cave deep in the Tennessee hills. The guide warned them not to move, then doused the lights and invited them to put their hands right in front of their eyes. She remembered the off-balance, floating feeling that had come when she realized she could see nothing, had no markers, no way to tell where she was in relationship to the things around her. One step, the guard had warned, could perhaps plunge her to her death.

Despite her eagerness now to find her way out, she squatted where she was and helicoptered her arms. They touched nothing.

Panic clawed for her throat. She filled her lungs until they could hold no more, held it for a long moment and slowly released it, repeated the process until she was somewhat in control.

"Probably a tiny room," she whispered to herself. "You'll find the door in no time, be outta here." Thing was, there was really no way to tell, and she wasn't in a position to take chances.

Dropping onto her knees, she leaned forward onto both hands, curled her lip when her hands sank into a half-inch of soft stuff— dust? Maybe. Or dried animal dung. She shook the image away. She had no choice here.

Way over her head, it sounded like somebody was trying to tear the wall down. Zan huddled where she was and craned her neck.

A beam of light shot across the shaft, flashlight from the looks of it. It caressed the pulley, then dropped down. Instinct urged her to shrink back, but she held still. The light didn't reach nearly low enough to help her see whatever lay ahead.

A high-pitched twitter alerted her seconds before a soft, warm, furry thing crossed her hands. Barely, she managed to get her hands over her mouth before a scream could escape.

Mouse. It was a mouse.

More disturbing than the mouse, however, was that they'd discovered her method of escape. She couldn't move without risking limb or life. They would be down here on her before she could do much more than find the wall.

Damn!

The thought was barely finished when she heard hard soles running her way. Tears clogged her throat. She swallowed them down, rocked back on her heels and pulled the knife out of her back pocket. They wouldn't take her alive.

A deep chill raced down her spine, but even as it did, she knew it was the truth. There were three ways out of this. Escape. Be recaptured. Or die.

"She's down here," a male voice said, muffled and indistinct so she couldn't tell if it came from in front of her or behind. Or maybe to her side. "It's the only place she can be."

A few seconds' silence.

"*Dios,*" a second voice said. "There is no door."

"Of course there's a door. It's a dumbwaiter. They loaded stuff down here, dragged it upstairs."

"But there is no door," the voice insisted. "I have touched the entire wall. There is nothing."

Nothing? It's a dumbwaiter. It must *have a door!*

Silence again, muttering, and then, "Goddamn it! We don't have time for this." A deep sigh. "You stay here. She comes out of that room, you stop her, but don't hurt her. Understand? Do not hurt her. Got it?"

"*Sí.*"

A single set of footfalls walked away.

There *was* a door. She would find it, manage to get past the guy outside and escape. She dropped to her hands again with her body shaking and her mind whirling. "Look," she whispered to herself, "there's a way out of here. If you make me crazy, I'll run around in circles. So shut the fuck up and let me think!"

If she moved in a fairly straight line in any direction, she would eventually come to a wall.

Right?

She wouldn't just move in circles, hitting the same places over and over and never finding a wall and maybe dying of thirst or—

Stop it!

* * * *

Zan had no idea how long she'd been in the dark. Thirst burned her throat and she was weak with hunger. As she had since she got to this place, she crawled forward with her knife stuffed in her back pocket. Her fingers were heavy with gritty grime. She knew from the weakness she couldn't hold out much longer. Dying in a sudden leap had seemed much more attractive than what she'd seen through the crack in the room upstairs.

Dying of hunger and thirst was not as attractive.

Something soft and smooth touched her hand. She jerked back, the image of a dead rat in her mind.

There is no smell. A dead rat would stink.

She felt around in the muck, found the thing, pulled it to her. It was smooth, not hairy. Not an animal. Sitting back, she explored with her hands like a blind person.

A bottle.

She shook it, heard liquid slosh.

A bottle of water!

Or rat poison.

She felt upward, found a twist-off cap, removed it, put her tongue against the opening, titled the bottle.

Tasteless liquid touched her tongue.

Rat poison would have a taste.

Right?

A larger swallow sent liquid down her throat.

It was water.

Wonderful water.

She drank and drank and drank.

When she was sated, she twisted the top on and poked the bottle into her bra. She was okay for the moment, but if there was one bottle of water, could there be two? She swept her hand out, found three more. These she stuffed down her T-shirt and hoped they would move with her.

When she swept her hand again, it hit something hard. She jerked back as what sounded like a stack of large sticks thudded to the floor.

Zan inched around it. Sticks wouldn't help her get out.

She moved along the floor one hand and one knee at a time, kept her ears trained on the back of the room, where tiny feet scurried and skittered and made her mind want to draw pictures of enormous rodents with teeth the size of piano keys.

The hair on the back of her neck raised. Her skin crawled. She crept along until, finally, her outstretched hand again hit something hard. Stones. Big round stones.

A wall.

Her throat grew tight; her eyes filled with tears. She'd found another wall. Unlike the other two, this one would have a door. It *had* to.

One thing at a time.

A sudden sneeze gathered in the back of her throat. She grabbed her nose between her thumb and forefinger, squeezed hard until the urge to sneeze faded.

Exhaustion overtook her, finally. She kept her hip against the wall, adjusted the water so it would stay inside her T-shirt and curled up with her head on her hands.

She woke stiff and sore. She needed to pee, and she was starving.

She took three steps from the wall, squatted and let loose.

Three steps back.

Her hand hit the wall. She explored it fully, top to bottom, found nothing that would resemble a door.

Keeping her hip against the wall, she moved slightly to her right, stood, inspected again. Nothing.

We will find the door, Zan. Keep the faith.

The voice was Neva's, but the thought belonged to Zan's dad.

CHAPTER TWENTY-FOUR

Neva polished the ornate, dust-catching legs of the small table in the last viewing room as if it were a diamond, while angry voices clashed down the hall in her father's tiny office.

At some point, she realized she was humming "Blest Be the Tie That Binds" under her breath, a subconscious prayer, perhaps.

Jody Talbert had done Oakley's accounts since Neva's grandfather's day, beginning right out of school and continuing to this day. But the tenor and volume of her father's voice and Jody's threatened to end that partnership.

The argument began with Jody's, "Damn it, Robert! I can't spin gold out of straw."

They'd yelled numbers at one another that dissected Oakley's present and destroyed her future. Neva could almost see them in there with their spreadsheets, both men stuffed in front of the computer in a space barely large enough for one.

As she'd figured, she and Ice were bringing in most of the income. The Nelsons' funerals, held Tuesday, were the first in two weeks. There were no more on the horizon.

Jody didn't have to tell her that their best income came from casket sales. Next was the rental on the viewing suites. What would her father do if he lost this place? Fifty-nine was a sucky age to start looking for another job.

He was trained for this, had done nothing else.

Ever.

She could branch out, she guessed, take in work from other funeral homes. They'd offered plenty of times, but until now, her workload wouldn't allow it. She'd talk to her dad about it tomorrow. Drennon might jump at it. Her lip curled, but his money would spend as well as anyone else's. Besides, it would be fun to see his face when she told him what her fees would be.

She gazed around the dimly lit room with its comfortable furniture, deep carpet and heavy drapes. She'd spent her entire life within these walls. This place was as much a part of her as her parents' house or her church.

One of her forever places.

She scrubbed the table leg the way she'd like to scrub Drennon's face. The rag whipped and twisted. What would *she* do if her dad lost Oakley's?

Working for another funeral home felt like betrayal.

Part of her anger was directed at her dad. He'd treated her like a child, kept the bad news from her, never given her a chance to help make things work. Protection was often simply a way to hold someone in a certain place, a safe, familiar place, an easy-to-handle place. She'd gone bonkers when Gray died. No doubt about it. She was sixteen. He'd blown his brains into her face.

Not many sixteen-year-olds could come back from that. It had taken a long time, but she was better now than she'd been even *before* Gray's suicide.

She was proud of that.

* * * *

Hours later, in her bedroom, Neva kicked off the covers. The clock said it was nearly two a.m.

So far she'd not slept.

She was worried about Zan, pissed at her father, twisting to find an idea for her next career. Mostly, she was worried about Zan.

With a sigh, she made her way to the kitchen. She stared at the empty refrigerator shelves for a good two minutes. Truth was, they could have been full and she still wouldn't have wanted anything in there. But she wanted something.

She stepped into Moya's room. "You asleep?"

"Nope."

"Worried about Zan?"

"Yep."

"Me, too."

"Let's have a milkshake," Moya said.

There it was. The one and only thing that sounded good. It didn't just sound good, it sounded *perfect*. Except...

"Can't. We're out of ice cream."

"Good thing they still make grocery stores."

Uncle Rex had specifically told her to take Moya with her. Moya and her gun. "That's why I keep you around," Neva said, moving into the easy sparring that they often adopted when things were bad. "You have the best ideas."

The nearest grocery store was at the corner of Cahal and Gallatin Road, directly across from Houston Drennon's refurbished funeral home. The funeral home was dark, as it should be at two fifteen a.m. Even the parking lot was dark. Obviously, when Drennon closed up for the night, he meant people to stay away.

Inside the store, they chose dark chocolate mint. Moya wanted rocky road, but Neva vetoed that. "Stupid nuts get caught in the straw," she pointed out.

The usually bustling store was nearly silent, the checkouts closed except for one where a cashier leaned against her machine, her eyes closed. The wheels on Neva's cart hummed along the floor.

They chose a half-gallon of milk to go with the ice cream, arguing over whether it should be whole milk or two percent. Neva lost that one and set the whole milk in the basket with a sigh.

"Don't pout," Moya said.

"I *never* pout," Neva declared, poking her lower lip out as far as it would go. "*Never.*"

Outside, Neva put their items in a foil-lined pouch designed to keep them cold.

"It's, like, six seconds to the house," Moya pointed out.

"I want my ice cream frozen hard," Neva said as she slid under the wheel.

The traffic light at Cahal was flashing yellow like every other traffic light along Gallatin Road. Neva glanced right, then left. An 18-wheeler, red cab, silver trailer came over the hill, chugging like it could barely make it. Its left-turn signal flashed. The driver swung wide for the turn.

Good thing nobody else was on the road.

Neva read the words along its side: "Brandon's Casket Company." Didn't take a genius to figure out he where he was going.

Neva turned left.

"Where you going?" Moya asked.

"I want to take a side trip."

"Okay," Moya said. "But I can hear your ice cream melting."

Neva drove past Cahal, turned onto the parallel route, Delmas Avenue, went around the block and approached the funeral home from its right, which gave her time to see where the truck was without being seen.

Nobody delivered caskets at three in the morning. Neva had never heard of Brandon's Casket Company.

Moya, who had said nothing until now, shifted in her seat. "I don't like this, granny."

Caught up in her sleuthing, Neva jumped at Moya's voice. "I won't go close," she promised. "Just want to see why they're delivering caskets in the middle of the night. Check something for me. Google that casket company, Brandon's."

"Okay," Moya said. "Don't get close. Like stop now."

Neva moved the car onto the adjacent grassy strip. From here, she could see the cab clearly because they'd backed the truck in against the building. A bright light streamed from behind it.

"You remember a door on that side of Bob's place?" Neva asked Moya.

"Bob?" Moya asked and then took a quick breath. "Drake. This is Drake's old place. I wouldn't have recognized it."

"Drennon's updated it a lot," Neva said. "It looks like he's added a garage on that side. Odd, since he has a huge one over here." She nodded at the Cahal Road side of the building. Nothing wrong with adding a garage. Nothing wrong with positioning it so deliveries were hard to see, either. Most people didn't like seeing dead bodies, even if they were tucked inside a body bag. The sight reminded them that no matter where they were or how much they had, death waited for them. To avoid this reminder, they shied away from the inner workings of the death business. School children, for instance, were never paraded through funeral homes to see the most inevitable of life's events.

"No such place," Moya said.

"Really. No Brandon's Casket Company?"

"Nary a one. Anywhere in the good ole U.S. of A."

"Think I'll take a closer look," Neva said.

"Granny—"

"I'll be careful."

"Right," Moya said, digging in her purse for the gun. "Last damned time you were careful, we nearly got killed." She stuffed the gun in her waistband. "Turn off the interior light before you open the door."

The night was warmer by far than Sunday had been, a temporary reprieve from winter's onset. Silence. Deep, unbroken silence. No traffic noise. No dogs barking.

Nothing.

It felt wrong.

Like delivering caskets in the middle of the night.

She tiptoed with Moya right behind her to the mouth of the alley. Bob's ancient hedge screened them from the new garage.

The truck's back doors rested against its sides, completely out of the way. Three men rolled a casket rack down the ramp they'd installed. The truck blocked her view of all but a crescent of the new garage, cement block walls and a concrete floor.

Nothing else.

Her gaze slid over the casket rack, then locked back as she realized how strangely it was loaded.

New caskets rode in four-tiered racks, each casket no more than three inches from the one above it. The fourth or top tier was generally within inches of the trailer's ceiling. Casket companies shipped as many as they could in one shipment, accommodated as many customers as possible in the same delivery run.

The thousand-pound gorilla in the casket company was located in Indiana. They ran their trucks in every direction nearly every day, packed them so the caskets nearest the door could be delivered first. By the time an Indiana truck got to Nashville, it generally was completely empty on the side nearest the door and completely full on the side nearest the cab. At that point, the racks would be rotated, making the next deliveries easier. This rack was filled with a snaggle-toothed combination of caskets on the outside and in, with nothing on the center rack and nothing on the top.

The rack rolled smoothly from the ramp to the floor. In a second, it would be out of Neva's sight. If she was to see more, she'd have to get closer.

Moya shifted, touched Neva's arm, jerked her thumb toward the car.

Girl could absolutely read Neva's thoughts.

A man's shout jerked Neva's gaze back to the garage. The pink casket on the third rack, the only casket Neva could still see, was open. A dark-haired woman who looked like she hadn't eaten in weeks grabbed the upright beside it, swung out, dropped lightly to the floor.

The second delivery guy burst into view, grabbed for her back as she ran for the door.

Neva rose.

Moya jerked her down.

"*¡Ayúdame! ¡Ayúdame!*" Her voice was high, thin. The cry raced down Neva's spine like boiling water. She couldn't have seen Neva, not looking from that blasting light into almost total darkness, but her terrified gaze seemed to capture Neva's in a stranglehold that made Neva's chest hurt.

The delivery guy managed to get his fingers on her thin top. Like Larissa, she twisted, jerked away, fought her way to the door, still shrieking that word.

"What does it mean?" Neva asked. The word sounded Spanish, a language Moya and her family spoke fluently.

"Help. It means *help me*," Moya said through gritted teeth.

The guy lunged, got a handful of the woman's hair, jerked her back hard, wrapped his arm around her waist, lifted her from the floor.

She slammed her bare heels into his shins.

He ignored her, carried her back into the garage, a gun tucked in the back of his jeans.

Seconds later, they both disappeared.

Neva rose.

Moya grabbed her arm. "No. We're calling 911. From the car."

CHAPTER TWENTY-FIVE

Neva dug her fingernails into her palms as the truck pulled out less than five minutes after their 911 call.

The light above the license plate was dark. She flipped on her lights. The rig stopped.

"Get the number," she said to Moya, whose fingers were already flying over her cell phone, capturing the precious digits and letters. Neva shifted into reverse. They could outrun the rig without breathing hard, but these guys were armed.

She wanted plenty of distance between them if any shooting started.

"Listen!" Moya said.

A siren. Coming their way.

The rig jerked into motion, swept through the turn onto Gallatin Road, headed toward the siren.

"Did you get it?"

Moya nodded. "Out-of-town license," she said. "Indiana."

Neva barely let the cop get stopped against Drennon's outside wall before she tapped on his window. "They just drove that way." She pointed toward Nashville. "You can catch them if you hurry."

Short and squat, he let his gaze travel from her head to her feet with a stop along the way at her breasts. She held her gaze on his face and waited until his came back. "Hurry," she said. "They're getting away."

He motioned for her to step back from the car, crawled out. "See your ID." he said.

"Didn't 911 tell you about the kidnapped woman? We don't have time for this!" she said as she fished her license from her pocket and handed it over.

He wrote the information down in a slow, careful hand while she fairly danced with impatience. "You have to call it in." When he didn't respond, "We've got the license number. Call it in!"

"Calm down, lady," he said slowly. "We'll catch 'em."

"Whaddya mean you'll catch 'em? You aren't even trying!"

Moya squeezed Neva's elbow.

He handed Neva's license back, went through the same thing with Moya while Neva's internal clock ticked so loudly she could barely hear Moya's responses.

"Okay," he said, finally. "What's this all about?"

Neva managed to thwart a huge eye roll. She told him what they'd seen. Moya read off the license number, and Neva again begged him to call it in.

"You ladies sit in your car while I call this in." He turned for the cruiser.

Neva slid into her car and immediately dialed Uncle Rex's number. This cop was an idiot.

"Did you say the officer's name was Sims?"

"Yes."

"Lock your car doors. Should take me about ten minutes to get to you."

"But what if he orders me—"

"He has not charged you with a crime. Be polite. Just don't open the door. Tell Moya to keep her gun in her purse."

Neva clicked off to see Moya staring toward Gallatin Road with her head cocked to one side. "What in the hell is that noise?" she asked.

It was a siren, but where a normal siren dropped smoothly in decibel level, then rose again, this one chattered in hiccups before it rose. Neva twisted around just as a patrol car slid to a stop at Cahal, signaling for a turn. He cut the lights and the siren as he pulled into the parking lot.

"Uncle Rex says do not leave the car until he gets here and"— she nodded at the weapon in Moya's hand—"to leave your gun in your purse."

This officer had dark hair. His uniform stretched over the muscles in his shoulders. He tossed a comment over his shoulder at Officer Sims, strode directly to Neva's car and grabbed the door handle as if he meant to tear off the door.

The handle balked.

"Open this goddamned door!" he shouted.

Neva opened the window a crack.

"Open the mother-fucking door!"

"My uncle, Detective Rex Mason, is on his way. I will open the door when he gets here."

"Mason?" For the first time since he arrived, the cop actually looked at her. "He's your uncle?"

"Yes."

The officer, whose nametag said, "Floyd," turned and nodded at Officer Sims. Together, they moved to a spot behind the building. They turned their backs to Neva and Moya, bent their heads together.

"Wonder what that's all about," Moya said.

"I don't like the way they're acting," Neva said. "If Uncle Rex doesn't get here soon, I'm calling Dad."

The purr of a finely tuned engine brought her glance over her shoulder just as a long, scarlet Jaguar flowed into the parking lot, stopping with its nose against the building. The man who curled out was taller than Neva's dad, a big man. He glided toward the officers with his head back, a frown on his face, clearly irritated. He exuded a sense of power, obviously a man accustomed to getting what he wanted. His gaze met Neva's in the rear-view mirror in a cold, soulless stare.

"Houston Drennon," she said. She'd never seen him before, not in person, but the newspaper ran pictures of him when he opened this place.

"My, my," Moya said. "This is becoming quite a party. Good thing we have ice cream."

He met the officers behind the building.

"Wish I knew what they were talking about," Moya said.

"I wish they'd go after that truck." Neva's fingers played along the door handle. She pulled them back, clasped her hands in her lap, did what she'd been told to do.

Finally, Drennon turned toward her car. The cops lined up behind him like ducklings.

"Leave the gun in your purse," Neva muttered. "But keep your purse close."

Moya tapped her fingers gently on the leather beside her. "Got it."

This was the showdown, then.

Neva's shoulders tightened.

Headlights hit the back of her windshield.

Uncle Rex's sedan pulled in beside Drennon's Jag.

Drennon stopped. The ducklings came to heel.

Uncle Rex nodded at her as he went by the car, said something to the two officers, then flashed his badge at Drennon. Neva left the car, met Moya on the other side.

"My niece tells me she saw something inside your building, Mr. Drennon," Uncle Rex said.

"They're gone," Neva said. "If you'll get somebody after them—"

"We sent a car," Floyd said. "The truck was stopped"—he glanced at his wristwatch—"seven minutes ago. They searched the trailer, the cab and all caskets. They found nothing."

"Then she's still in the garage!" Neva said. She stopped as an awful thought hit her. If they'd stuffed the woman back in the casket she'd come from, she didn't have much air. "Let's hope she's still alive."

"I'll open it," Drennon said. He removed a remote control from his car, pointed it at the back of the building. Then he took the lead with Uncle Rex right behind him. Officer Floyd fell in next, then Officer Sims. Neva followed Sims. Moya followed Neva.

She spotted the pink casket the second she entered the garage. They'd shoved it against the far wall. "That's it," she said, stepping around Officer Sims. "That's the casket."

She braced herself. God knew what they'd done to the woman.

Drennon lifted the lid.

The casket was empty. But what sent shock bolting through Neva was that its white satin lining was pure and unsullied.

She had some experience with what living bodies did to satin. Two boys in her fourth grade class sneaked into Oakley's, hid themselves in a couple of new caskets, waited until Neva came into the room to pop out.

They'd expected her to be terrified. Instead she was furious. Both caskets had to be returned to the company for new linings. The dirt on their shoes had marked the satin badly. The oil in their hair left stains that no amount of detergent would ever remove.

Nobody had been in this casket.

Ever.

She turned to the group. "It must have been another—"

"That is a one-of-a-kind casket," Drennon said. "I ordered it for a customer whose teenage daughter lost her battle with cancer. You are right about one thing, however. They did deliver it tonight, along with the one beside it."

Uncle Rex raised an eyebrow at her.

"There's another room," Neva began, but Drennon was shaking his head before she completed the sentence.

"Not yet. We will be adding other rooms and connecting the garage to the main basement, but we haven't yet. This is all there is." He lifted his arms toward the ceiling and let them fall.

"I saw her," Neva said.

"So did I," Moya confirmed.

Uncle Rex looked confused.

Sims and Floyd looked disgusted.

Drennon had no expression whatsoever.

"They probably dropped her off somewhere before the truck was stopped," Uncle Rex said.

It made sense, was the only thing that did, but the back of Neva's neck prickled. She wasn't convinced.

"I hope you're comfortable now, detective," Drennon said to Uncle Rex.

"I apologize, Mr. Drennon, but I hope you understand. We have some human traffickers around right now."

"I fully understand, detective. Fully. I heard what was found at Oakley's. I can't understand how anyone could be so clueless."

Uncle Rex caught Neva's eye just in time to keep her from telling Houston Drennon to go fuck himself.

* * * *

Ten minutes later, Neva set the foil bag on the counter. She'd chewed over the night's events all the way home. Moya was right to keep her from putting them in danger. Absolutely right. Neva had no doubts about Moya's courage or the fact that what was happening to that poor Spanish-speaking woman tore Moya's heart out. And yet, Moya had the good sense Neva had lacked.

So why did she feel like a coward?

They were no more outgunned than they'd been in the cemetery. *You barely got out of that one alive, and Larissa is dead.*

"Still up for a milkshake?" Moya asked and stopped Neva's dark thoughts.

"Sure," Neva said. "I love milkshakes for breakfast." The ice cream was still frozen. Not hard frozen, but good enough. She scooped it into the blender and added milk. She couldn't let her concern about this other woman sidetrack her from Zan.

"You remember playing in that old funeral home?" Moya asked when the blender stopped.

"Yep," Neva said. She poured a glassful, handed it to Moya, then poured one for herself.

"You think we're strange because we grew up around dead people?"

"Probably," Neva said. "It's as good an excuse as any." She licked a dribble off the glass. "Mmmm, that's really good."

"Been better with rocky road."

"Stupid nuts get stuck in the straw," Neva said.

They drank in silence until Moya said, "Remember that key Drake kept in the false brick?"

Neva reached for the memory, found it and said, "I'd forgotten it."

"I could always find it," Moya said. "Third brick from the bottom on the edge of the building."

"Which is no longer the edge," Neva pointed out.

"True. That's actually what brought it to mind. Wonder if we could find it?"

"Probably. In the daylight, the new bricks will be a different color from the old. I'll bet he'll paint the place when he's through with it, though. After that, I don't know whether I could find it."

"More?" Moya held up her glass.

"Little piggy," Neva said. She made the second glasses only half full.

"Did you see Drennon's hands?" Moya asked.

"No."

"Man has no pinky fingers."

"Pinky…little fingers?"

"Duh." Moya held up her two smallest fingers. "Pinky fingers. His are gone."

"Like he never had them?"

"Like somebody cut them off."

"Euwww."

"It looks pretty odd," Moya said.

"Probably chewed them off because some poor, hard-working funeral director wouldn't let Drennon steal his place."

"You're just prejudiced."

Neva swallowed a mouthful of chocolate mint milkshake and said, "Ya think?"

CHAPTER TWENTY-SIX

Cee shivered under her shawl. Compared to winters in Chicago, where she had spent most of her adult life, Nashville's were quite mild, but the unrelieved gray skies of November, December and January got on her nerves the way snow never did.

She and Rex had fought like a couple of old married people when she told him she was coming back to the streets after only a few days off. It was risky, but she had the experience and, most importantly, she had the acceptance to be the eyes and ears they needed right now to find Zan.

Rex didn't think she'd learn enough on the streets to justify the risk. Rex had never been on the streets, didn't understand the deep relationships she'd forged. The homeless trusted her completely. That was hard to give up. So, here she was, fresh contacts in her eyes and clean cotton in her cheeks, at the start of another rotation.

She'd taken the usual bus, stored her things at the mission. Scott was about as happy to see her back as Rex was to see her go. She swung down Broad Street, past Tootsie's Bar and Grill toward the river. She turned at Third because Second was already stuffed with *turistas* with new blue jeans. They also had new cowboy boots, so half the street was filled with hobbling neo cowboys who didn't know leather boots took a lot of breaking in before they were good for a long walk.

Unless you enjoyed blisters.

The sky was gray with filth, the sun a weak beacon somewhere above it. Claudia normally didn't notice the weather, not past "is it raining" or "is it cold," but even she felt the wrongness in the earth.

The weatherman said the high pressure that had stopped the rain for so long showed no sign of moving.

As she walked, Claudia glanced in the doorways and down the alleys, looking for Lisa or Large George or somebody, but the streets were empty of homeless, as if a dancing flautist had piped them all into the river.

She crossed Woodland Street, moved past the huge courthouse with its enormous marble columns and fountains out front, then turned onto the Victory Memorial Bridge.

At the World War II memorial, she ran her finger down the short list of Nashville servicemen who'd given their lives for freedom, found her mother's uncle's name and rested there for just a moment, remembering how his son, her Uncle Ben, had tossed her into the air and caught her as she fell back. She'd shrieked with delight. He'd laughed and said she should have been a boy.

He was right, she discovered later as she fought her way up the ladder of the then-male-dominated law enforcement world. She understood it again when she'd tried to be a wife to three different men, all of whom wanted her to be somebody she wasn't.

Her relationships with men had been so difficult, she briefly wondered if she were gay, but she'd never lusted after a woman the way she had and still did after men.

She'd found her place in Chicago, gone as high as she could go without being a politician, then retired to Nashville, not meaning to work at all, but when the call came, she answered it. Right now it felt good to be back on the streets, but by the end of the rotation, she'd be eying a comfortable life again.

Where in the hell is everybody?

She swung down the stairs from the bridge to North First, then down the narrow road beside the Department of Transportation's motor pool, cars parked behind a tall chain-link fence topped with barbed wire. The attendant, a near-toothless man named Wallace, spent his workdays from seven thirty in the morning until three thirty in the afternoon, ferrying people in a white van from the building downtown to the motor pool, where they would check out a state-owned car, a perk for TDOT executives to drive on business trips. When they returned the state-owned cars, Wallace would take them back to the headquarters building.

She suddenly realized she was not shuffling, being Claudia, not Cee. She leaned against TDOT's fence, grateful the homeless population was missing.

What was she thinking?

Instantly, she knew the answer. Being Cee was a lot of things, but primarily it was old and slow. That hadn't seemed bad when Claudia was younger, but now it came too close to the person she was quickly becoming. She took a slow step, dragged Cee's left foot slightly. It felt awkward. She didn't want to do it. She forced herself, one slow step at a time, until her resistance melted. By the time she shuffled across the refinery's property, it felt right.

Cee was back.

Nearer the river, the air gained a bit of moisture, which, combined with the cold, sent a deep ache through Claudia's bum knee. The bullet wound in her shoulder soon joined the misery.

She broke character long enough to say, "I am too damned old for this crap." Already resenting the hardship. Maybe she really *was* through with this life.

Maybe.

The refinery property ended at the river. Claudia rounded the bend to the earthen steps. They'd been carved into the hillside so long ago nobody knew who'd done it. They rose in a tilted, staggering pattern to the top of the hill, where a dozen patched tents stood side by side with cardboard huts and a few wooden structures made from material filched from construction sites.

The centerpiece was an ancient pop-up trailer whose top would never again pop down but which boasted an honest-to-God bed inside. The zip-up windows had been gone forever, replaced by squares of green oilcloth that made the trailer resemble a monochrome circus tent.

She rubbed her aching knee.

They should put a disclaimer on the application to the police academy: "Be aware that service in this profession will leave you with aches and pains that will never heal. Oh, we'll never pay you a living wage, either."

She genuinely limped up the old steps, no need to pretend. Halfway, she saw Large George emerge from the far end of the briar thicket. He didn't see her at first. She had a chance to see the grimness in his face, the thin line of his mouth, his clenched fists. Rusty stains covered his jacket and ran down his blue jeans to his knees.

Blood.

She stopped.

When he saw her, his face split into a huge smile that would have been reassuring had she not known George so well. Trouble was, this smile got nowhere near his eyes. Something was up George's butt big time. When he was near enough, he said, "You okay, Miss Cee? You been gone."

"Yes, George, I'm fine. Just a little time with my sister. *You* look worse for wear." She touched the bloodiest spot on his sleeve.

Fury raced through his gaze. Claudia braced herself. Seconds later, the smile slowly returned. "Got me a rabbit this morning, Miss Cee. I guess I ain't as good at skinnin' as I thought."

A lie, but convenient for them both. Until she knew more, she wouldn't push George. Not when she was alone and unarmed. "Rabbit sounds mighty good, George."

"I'll do us a stew, Miss Cee. We'll eat it tomorrow." George stepped around her, jogged on down the steps, his shoulders stiff.

Claudia watched him. She was no bloodstain expert. George, like everyone else, ate what he could find. But she'd skinned many a rabbit when her dad and brother brought them home in the fall. The animal would have been lying on the ground, not held on George's shoulder as the blood pattern seemed to say.

She'd defended George against Rex's suspicions years ago when they'd found the private detectives murdered down here. Good thing Rex hadn't caught sight of George today.

She rose to the next step, groaned when pain sliced through her knee and swept her gaze along the various hovels, all of which seemed to be abandoned. George had emerged from the far end of the briar hedge, which meant the town's population was back there.

Something was wrong.

The briar hedge that separated the ramshackle buildings from the plateau behind appeared impenetrable. It actually was, except at its far end where the vines had grown around an enormous wooden wire spool. Over the years, the spool deteriorated into nothing, but the hole, just large enough for one person to walk through, remained.

In the fall and winter, the homeless kept the passageway covered with part of an old billboard. In summer, the vegetation did the covering for them. When gangs got after them, the homeless disappeared through the passage.

Claudia made her way down the long hedge, set the heavy sign to the side, stepped into the tunnel and slid the sign back in place. Behind the tunnel was a good ten acres of open land. There'd been some dumping along the back part years ago. The earth was still heaved where the city covered the refuse. There were no geographical features of any note. Just a long stretch of flat, open land covered now with patches of anemic yellow grass that had somehow sustained a spark of life.

Claudia stepped into the clearing behind twenty or more people who stood with their backs to her, moved quietly into the back row and whispered to old, wizened Sam, "What?"

"Lisa's got her a woman in there." Sam nodded toward the front of the crowd.

Claudia rose on her tiptoes. They'd hung a large, red oilcloth over a rope between two small trees. To make sure the oilcloth wouldn't fly away, they'd secured it with a second rope in its middle and a third at the far end. These were fastened to stakes.

"A woman?"

Sam shook his head. "Terrible shape, Cee. Somebody done beat that chile 'til she should be dead."

Claudia remembered George's bloodstained clothes. "Where'd Lisa find her?"

Sam spat a line of tobacco juice on the ground. "Large George done found her." He glanced behind him. "Only we ain't s'posed to tell nobody, Cee. You won't tell, will ya?" When she didn't answer, he put a hand on her arm. "I mean, they'll blame 'im for it, Cee. You know how it is."

"Yeah, I do, Sam."

A murmur ran through the front of the crowd. Lisa emerged from the makeshift tent on her hands and knees. Her hair was tousled as if she'd torn at it. Her eyes glowed.

Terrific. We're in our manic mode.

Lisa climbed to her feet, squared off at the crowd. "She needs medicine."

"You'd best take her to the mission, Lisa," Sam called out. "You ain't no doctor."

"She's too sick to take anywhere," Lisa said. Her gaze swept over Claudia and then jerked back. "Come up here, Cee." She gestured with her hand. "You need to see her."

Claudia twisted through the crowd, reminding herself to move at old Cee's pace.

"You gots to help her," Lisa said with a sweep of her hand at the tent.

Claudia put a gentle hand on Lisa's shoulder, gave it a squeeze and dropped to her knees. The ground was hard as the proverbial rock. She gritted her teeth at the pain in her knee and crawled quickly through the low opening.

They'd found an old lounge chair somewhere, piled enough blankets over the girl so no part of her was visible. Claudia pulled the covers gently back until she could see the face.

A savage beating. Worse than she'd seen on Larissa Nelson.

Again, George's bloodstained clothes rose in her mind. He'd appeared the day she found Larissa. Suddenly there like a genie from an enormous bottle.

Had he just dumped Larissa? Was the man in the alley trying to tell her who killed Larissa. She didn't make a career in law enforcement by ignoring possibilities. Bad as she hated to admit it, George was a possible.

The girl whimpered, a mew from a nearly dead kitten. God knew what kind of pain she was in. She might offer the key to finding the perp.

If she lived.

Claudia hurried back to the crowd. They hated officials of any kind, even meter readers. No matter what she said, they'd never let her lead paramedics back here.

The girl was very fragile.

Had to be handled gently.

But first, Claudia had to handle the crowd.

CHAPTER TWENTY-SEVEN

Outside the tent, Claudia pulled her jacket around her and took a deep breath. Twenty expectant faces waited for her words. She chose them carefully. "She won't live through the night if we don't do something."

"She needs medicine," Lisa said, her mouth set in a stubborn line.

"I know we think Lisa can work miracles, but none of us can save this girl. She's got to have medical help." She rushed on before any of them could speak. "We can't let them come here, of course, but if this were our sister, we'd want somebody to help her, right?"

A few nods.

"Wallace. You know, the guy at the TDOT motor pool?"

More nods.

"He's gonna go for his last run soon. We'll leave her for him to find."

"He'll run over her," Lisa said.

"We'll put her somewhere he can't run over her, but also can't miss her."

"On his porch," Lisa said.

"Yes. On his porch."

In the end, it took four of the largest men, one at each end and one on either side. The old lounge sagged in the middle, but held while they moved like clumsy elephants across the clearing.

Claudia tried to measure the distance with her gaze, decide whether or not they could get to Wallace's enclosure before he returned from his last run. The guys were practically stepping on one another as they made their way across the clearing. Any faster, and they *would* trip.

The similarities in their wounds had brought her to connect this girl with Larissa. But it could be she was beaten by some drunk dude who should be castrated with a rusty tin can.

When her gang reached the refinery, she stopped them. "We'll hear him leave in a minute," she said.

Wallace had an assistant, a nice woman who was always around during her working hours. She opened the gates at seven thirty every morning and got things rolling. Her shift ended somewhere around three o'clock. After that, only Wallace remained behind the tall fence.

Wallace's old van had made enough noise to wake the dead, but she'd noticed a new one parked beside his porch today. She'd have to listen closely to hear that new engine rev.

In fact, she didn't hear the engine rev. She heard his tires crunch on the loose gravel as he pulled out. "He's on his way," she said to her ragtag band.

Turned out Wallace's porch was too small for the chair. They set the lounge right in front of the steps that came down the side of his trailer. Claudia was touched at the care with which the obviously exhausted men handled the girl. When they had set her safely down, Claudia lifted the covers and folded them below the girl's chin. Gasps rose from those behind her, but Claudia ignored them. The face was awful, but Wallace would be in a hurry, ready to end his day. If he saw nothing more than a lounge chair full of blankets, he might leave it for tomorrow.

Lisa took time to fuss over her patient, so they had just turned the corner near the refinery when Wallace returned. Minutes later, Claudia heard the sirens. She exchanged smiles with everyone. Wallace had found their poor lady. Soon, she would be on her way to the hospital.

The Indian summer was gone, replaced by another cold front. The temperature had dropped a good ten degrees since the morning. The air's bite was deep and vicious. Claudia glanced at her band and realized all of them were shaking with cold.

She led the way back to Homeless Town. Sam disappeared, returned with a box of instant hot chocolate packets. Claudia would normally have shaken her finger at him. She tried to make them understand stealing would get them banned from the riverbank, but they needed so much and had so little, they sometimes took what they wanted.

She warned them, but she understood.

She was too cold to shake her finger at Sam, too grateful for the water now boiling in their big pot over the open fire, another no-no in Nashville's air quality region. She could already taste the chocolate, feel the scalding liquid on her throat.

Ten minutes later, when the ambulance drove away with its siren wailing, she had her aching hands wrapped around a cracked and chipped cup she'd stolen from the Krystal one dark, snowy night. *Do as I say, not as I do.* Her feet were stretched out toward the fire. She was as warm as she was likely to get tonight, but her comfort wouldn't last long.

The man who beat that girl, if it was the same man, had killed before and would surely kill again to keep his victim from naming him. Claudia had no intention of letting him kill this one and take what was perhaps the only chance they'd get to find Zan.

CHAPTER TWENTY-EIGHT

Neva's headlights caught Davis leaned against a concrete column at the airport's pickup area.

His blond head was bent over his cell phone.

He'd hooked his thumb into his jeans pocket. One leg was bent back against the column.

A gorgeous hunk in a casual pose. He looked like an advertisement for blue jeans.

She'd thought the love she and Gray shared was a once-in-a-lifetime love, that she would live alone and unloved forever, a gray and bitter soul roaming the earth searching for why.

It was partially true. She and Gray were young, their emotions new and fresh. They were lost beneath the drumbeat of their hormones so every moment was either painfully wonderful or so pain filled she could barely breathe. Gray's every glance, touch, every word shimmered. If he was unhappy, which didn't happen often, she was devastated. If he was happy, she was delirious.

She and Davis shared mature love. They'd lived through the wars, seen the bad of life, come out on the other side. Hormones could be harnessed to do what she wanted them to do. If it missed the high peaks and deep valleys of teenage love, it more than made up for that with its depth and growing trust.

She'd been an idiot to distrust him. Davis was carved from the stone of responsibility and doing the right thing. She could save her worries for other things and other people.

Davis would always tell her the truth.

Not because she was special.

Because he was.

He glanced up as she stopped beside him. Light filled his eyes and then his face. She grinned at him, knowing her own face mirrored his delight, jerked a thumb over her shoulder and pulled the trunk lever so he could store his bags.

Seconds later, he slid in beside her, smelling of cold air and that something minty that was forever around him.

"Hello, beautiful." He slid an arm around her shoulders, dragged her to the middle of the console for a deep kiss. "Dear God, I have missed you," he said when he let her go.

"Right back atcha, dude. Flight okay?"

"Yeah," he said. "I read a lot. Don't usually sleep on the way home so I can get back into this time zone. How about you? Any more news about Zan?"

They'd talked every day since he left, so he knew most of it, but she brought him up to date. She did not tell him about her rental car. That was her secret, hers and Uncle Rex's. Not even Moya knew.

"So tell me about your trip," she said.

"I now know how to do this, which is a big step. But I'll have to tear up the old tunnels to do it."

"Is that a big deal?"

Davis sighed. "Yes and no. Structurally no. Parts of them will be incorporated into the new tunnels. The parts that aren't will be sealed off or left alone. It's the historical preservationists who may stop me. During the Civil War, abolitionists moved runaway slaves through those things. Got historical significance out the wazoo, not to mention secret rooms with incredibly unique doors."

She raised her eyebrows.

"They're round," he said, making a circle with his hands. "Roll across the interior wall, pop in and out of a hole fashioned so that when it's closed, there is absolutely no way to see the door from outside. There is but one other example, or a similar style. It's not nearly as sophisticated as these. The Derinkuyu underground city in Turkey. Amazing stuff. Amazing enough to maybe kill my project."

"Let's hope not!"

"Let's," he agreed.

"Secret rooms, huh?" Neva said.

"Very secret."

"How frequently do people actually build secret rooms?"

He glanced at her. "Not too often. Why?"

"Well," she said, "you're not going to like this, but…" She told him about her trip to Drennon's, held up her hand to stop his lecture. "We called the police. When we got inside, there was absolutely no sign of the woman. There was also no sign of the casket. Logical conclusion was the casket guys took her with them, right?"

"Does seem so," Davis said.

"They found those guys. The trailer was empty. Caskets were empty. Cab was empty. No woman, nowhere, no how." She turned onto Donelson Pike. "Let me ask you something."

"Okay."

"If the woman was already in the truck and was being taken back to the truck, which is the only thing that makes the slightest sense, why the hell bring her into the garage at all?"

Davis shrugged.

"Exactly," Neva said. She dropped onto I-40 West. "They would have left her and the casket on the truck. Easy, peasy."

"But they didn't find her or the casket on the truck."

"Exactly."

"Doesn't that mean it wasn't there?"

"You'd think so, but since it wasn't in the garage, and it wasn't on the truck, where the hell?"

"They off-loaded it somewhere."

Neva bit her lip. "That's possible, I guess. But again, why take her off the truck?"

"Doesn't make a lot of sense," he said.

"Unless it and she are still in Drennon's garage."

"Oh. I see."

She waited for him to laugh at her. He stared out the window until she made the sweeping turn onto Briley Parkway.

"Did you see anything in the garage that looked odd?"

"You mean, other than Drennon?" She used her hand to erase that statement. "Sorry. I hate that son of a bitch. No, dammit, I didn't. Looks like your ordinary concrete block building with a really big overhead door. Had three embalming tables. That's about all."

She waited for him to say something. When he didn't, "So," she said. "Whaddya think?"

"I think," he said, "you should not even consider looking for a pocket room. You aren't, right?"

Neva shifted instead of answering.

"Promise me."

"Think with me, Davis. If I'm right, what I saw will be the tip of the iceberg. Pretty easy to cart living people around in caskets if they're made so enough air gets inside. Took me a while to remember it, and I got only a quick glance, but I'd swear there was filigree along the side of the one I saw, filigree beneath which holes would be easily hidden. Drennon's got a nice new garage that's practically invisible. Casket dudes bring boxes in with the women inside. What could be more normal than a funeral home with caskets? It's *perfect*."

"Have you told your uncle?"

"Yes."

"What does he say?"

"He can't go back in without a warrant."

"And this is not enough to get one?"

She lifted her palm. "It's not only not enough, it's nothing. I'm guessing. Maybe it's informed guessing, but I've got nothing to back it up. There's a key to the basement where the old wall ended. Third brick from the parking lot. But"—again she held up a hand to stop him—"I would be worse than stupid to waltz into the nest of the viper."

Davis nodded.

She glanced quickly at him and back to the road. "What if Zan's in there, Davis?"

They rode in silence for a while and then Davis said, "Secret rooms sound more like my game than yours. Let me see what I can do."

CHAPTER TWENTY-NINE

"Thank you for seeing me, Mr. Drennon," Davis said. "I promise not to take a lot of your time."

"I admit to being intrigued, Mr. Pratt," Drennon said.

Davis struggled to keep his gaze on Drennon's flat, gray eyes. It was tough. Drennon's stare went through Davis and out the other side, a cold intrusion probing for his deepest secrets. Davis could have ignored that, kept his gaze tight on the other man's, had Drennon's office not been a study in fascinating contradictions.

Drennon's desk would retail for fifty thousand dollars or more. Yet his credenza obviously came from a big-box store.

"Let me get to it, then," Davis said, wrenching his gaze from the jeweled globe in the corner. The thing cost $39.95 online, and they'd throw a personalized cup in with it. It sat on a piecrust table that was worth more than two hundred.

"I'm an architect." He slid his business card across the smooth rosewood. "Your place here is a marvelous blend of federal and neoclassical architecture. The two styles are obviously not mutually exclusive because you have a blend right here, but I think I'm safe in saying this may be one of the few such buildings in Tennessee. You added the front porch and the columns, am I right?"

"Yes," Drennon said. He spread his hands. Davis noticed the little finger on each was nothing more than a stump. "I preferred the original look, actually. Nice clean lines, but I was advised that Nashvillians prefer the more ornate style. I wanted to re-brand the place without destroying it."

"Good idea," Davis said, impressed at the man's business acumen. "I wish more people would realize how important a building's facade is to the success of their business."

Drennon said nothing.

"I know you're terribly busy," Davis rushed on. "But if I could have just a quick tour of your interior, primarily the basement. That's where the original footprint will be. Won't take more than a half hour." Davis gently bit the inside of his cheek, focused on Drennon's gaze and said nothing.

If Drennon had much to hide, he was not likely to let someone rattle around. In which case, Davis would express his thanks and take his leave. If Drennon did allow him to investigate the basement, Davis needed only a few minutes to make an educated guess about a pocket room.

The minutes ticked by almost audibly while Davis's nose itched, his legs threatened to grow knots and his eyes dried.

Finally, Drennon stood. "Follow me."

Davis, who towered over many men, felt quite short as he walked down the long hallway beside Drennon, who silently marched straight through the kitchen into a small cross-hall. He selected a key from the ten on his ring and opened the door. "We don't use the older area for preparation yet. I've built an addition on the side. We will use the addition until we can modernize this place. It's in complete disrepair."

The basement stretched out below the stairs in a dingy, outdated collection of embalming tables and leftover equipment.

"I assume the outer walls interest you," Drennon said.

"Yes." Davis was becoming accustomed to Drennon's taciturn nature, appreciated it now, since he was planning his moves as he went. The lack of polite chatter made it easy to think.

At the bottom of the stairs, he deliberately turned for the back wall. The construction was not concrete block as would be the case today. It was brick, doubtless handmade and certainly laid old-school, each brick carefully cut and shaped to fit just its place and none other. Each course looked to be positively plumb along the wall. The light was dim under the stairs.

Davis pulled his flashlight from his pocket, sent it roving. Half his mind grooved on the artistic workmanship; the other half was looking for anomalies. At the end of the wall, he found what he sought.

The brick to this point had been perfect. Here, they ended in a snaggle-toothed mismatch.

Davis turned deliberately away, ran his hands down the wall to its other end, even though he'd easily seen that the workmanship there was as perfect as in the middle. If there was a pocket room, it was where the bricks got sloppy. He went over the other walls as well, moving swiftly, actually losing himself in the realities of the design. His lie was proving true.

It *was* a most unusual building.

When he was satisfied he'd looked innocent and competent, he said, "Well, that's it, Mr. Drennon. This is one hell of a building. The craftsmanship alone would make it important. Have you considered seeing if it's eligible for the National Register?"

"I have," Drennon said. He'd taken up a stance in the middle of the room, from which he could see Davis's every move. Was his gaze sharper, less friendly than before, or was that Davis's imagination? "But I don't want those people giving me a problem if I decide to make changes here," Drennon finished. "Have you found what you need?"

"I have. Thank you very much." Davis moved toward the stairs.

Drennon didn't move. "I noticed you spent time in that corner, Mr. Pratt," Drennon said. He nodded at the place where the pocket room's wall intersected with the back wall.

"That is an oddity, sir. The remaining wall is done with total perfection, but there's a lot of variation in that spot."

"What would that mean, in your expert opinion?"

Davis scrambled for an answer, kept his face bland. "Could mean a variety of things, actually, but I think the location gives us the answer." He went to the spot, put his hand on the irregular brick. "It's difficult to see into this corner. I think the craftsmen used their leftovers here rather than somewhere more visible." He dusted his hands together. "It's just a theory, sir, but it is an educated one."

Drennon captured Davis's gaze. Davis stood his ground, mentally added and subtracted large figures to keep any expression from his face.

"Very well, then," Dennon said, finally. He mounted the stairs.

At the front door, Davis held out his hand. "Thank you, sir. I want to do more research on this building. I'll let you know what I find."

Drennon engulfed Davis's hand with his huge one, gave it a squeeze and turned it loose with, "See that you do."

He opened the door and stood by while Davis walked through. On the porch, Davis turned to thank him again, but the door was already closed.

CHAPTER THIRTY

Neva turned from the elderly man on whose cheeks she was brushing a bronze mixed with gray that would give him a hint of life without giving him so much life his family would worry whether he was actually dead, and answered her cell phone, which was jingling with "Evil Woman."

"I guess," she said as she answered it, "this is your daily call to tell me you won't be coming home. Was it something I said? Did? Don't you *love* me anymore?"

Moya's chuckle was quick and light. Neva loved what was happening between her best friend and Ken Stasher. Like Neva and Davis, they spent almost all their free time together, seemed to be growing closer every day. Moya glowed with a light Neva recognized. It was the same light that filled Davis's face when he looked at her. The light that said, "This is *my* person."

"You're one to talk," Moya said, adding pretend shock to her voice. "You're never home."

"Not true, dearest friend, which you would know if you ever actually graced our front door. Davis is tied up trying to save this humongous project, burning the midnight oil as it were. But, puleeze, don't worry about me there in our sad little house alone with a book. I will be"—she changed her voice to the finest melodrama of the early talkies—"fine, my deah. Simply fine."

"Well," Moya said, "I would rather spend my evening with you, but if you insist, I shall instead spend it with the aforementioned hunk."

"Give the hunk my best," Neva said. "Don't forget the condoms."

"You are so full of it," Moya said, but she was laughing when she clicked off.

Neva turned back to the prep room, feeling uneasy.

Her mother had developed "one of her spells," as her dad referred to them. He'd left at noon. She had no one with whom to ride home. She gazed at her cell phone.

Better safe than sorry.

"I'm in Murfreesboro," Uncle Rex said. "Getting new tires."

"In Murfreesboro?"

"Found a deal. I've been here for two hours. So far my car hasn't moved once. I'm guessing it'll be another two before I can leave here, but I'll send a car. They'll follow you home."

"Thanks," she said.

The cruiser showed up in less than ten minutes, followed her home, flashed his lights as he drove away.

Great service.

Halfway down the hall to her bedroom, she realized she was out of toilet paper. Not sorta out. Not gonna be out tomorrow. There was none in the house.

If she'd thought, she would have borrowed some from the funeral home.

The night was deep, but there was what Moya called a "cheat-ya-right," a curb market, just down Gallatin Road. She could walk to it if she wanted to.

Which she didn't.

Before she could scare herself to death, she grabbed her purse and headed for the garage.

The Mustang's leather seats were still warm. She slammed the door, hit the lock so both doors were secured, then put the key in the ignition and turned it.

Since the car returned from the repair shop, its engine had been especially good, idling in perfect timing, racing when she hit it, moving with smooth and quiet operation the rest of the time. She'd not paid for a tune-up, but she wondered if she received one, nonetheless. In keeping with the idea that even good things came with a price, the new engine had apparently awakened a stockcar-driver gene in her she'd not known existed. Twice in the last week, she'd found herself speeding down Gallatin Road at more than fifty miles an hour, a sure-fire way to draw a cop if one was around.

As usual at five thirty, the traffic going north on Gallatin Road was bumper to bumper. A like stream would be traveling north on I-65, east on I-40 and south, even though TDOT swore it was east as well, on I-24. From five thirty until seven, the best idea for Nashvillians was to have another beer and wait.

Beer.

This would be a good night for it. Since she was going to the store anyway, she'd grab a six-pack.

And a good book. Something sweet and not scary.

Because her life had all the scary she could handle.

Lost in thought, she was oblivious to her speed until the blues flashed in her rear-view mirror. She glanced at the speedometer. Fifty miles an hour.

She was so screwed.

She pulled into a tiny parking lot. The cop came in behind her, but didn't quite have enough room to get out of the street. He left his cruiser, jotted down something on the pad in his hand, her license number, she assumed. As he approached her window, she saw his nameplate: Mike Floyd. The cop who'd tried to tear the door off her car. She raised her gaze to his, expecting something smart-assed, but he looked at her as if he'd never seen her before.

"Oh, hello," she said, driven by something she couldn't have explained to make him acknowledge he knew her. "You don't remember me, I'm sure, but I was at the funeral home a couple of nights ago. The girl who wasn't there?"

He nodded and smiled. "I do remember. Sorry I was so rough. I get a little hot under the collar about mistreated women."

She smiled in response, not sure what to say.

"I wonder," he continued, "if you'd mind pulling around this building for me. All those people out there"—he nodded toward the road, where even the southbound traffic was fairly high—"have to pull over a lane if my lights are flashing on the roadside. Backs traffic up. You mind?"

His response was polite, professional. He'd explained his rudeness, and now that Neva thought about it, Uncle Rex had warned her about his partner, the fat one, Sims. He'd said nothing negative about Floyd. "Not at all," she said. She'd been in her share of cop jams. Good idea to give an officer plenty of room to do his job, but a single flashing blue could back traffic up for miles.

Neva pulled into the alley, parked on its left side.

Floyd pulled up behind her again, left his blues flashing, came back to her window.

She handed him her license and the registration for the car. "I'm sorry. I wasn't paying attention to my speed."

"Happens to the best of us," he said. His gaze was on something below the window, his ticket pad, she figured. In a minute he'd tear one off, hand it to her. Good news was it would just be speeding, not reckless driving. Bad news was, she'd never had one before and was pretty proud of that record.

Gone. She'd soon become a common driver.

She stared through the windshield at the bushes, watched them sway in the light breeze and waited for him to get through with his paperwork. Cops had tons of it, she knew from Uncle Rex's and Claudia's griping, but it did seem to her he should be able to write a simple ticket without delaying her beer much longer.

Something stung her upper arm. "Owww," she said.

He pulled the needle out and gazed into her eyes as the world tilted and darkened.

She jerked the door handle, shoved against it, but he'd blocked it with his body, trapping her inside. "Let me go!" she managed before her head spun and the lights winked out.

CHAPTER THIRTY-ONE

Claudia had left the hot chocolate and roaring fire less than twenty minutes ago, but her fingers already ached with cold.

She rounded the bridge piers and was nearly to the stairs when a dark shape detached itself from the wall. She reached for the weapon she wasn't carrying, then threw out a hand. "Stop!" she shouted, putting every ounce of authority she could muster into it.

"It's me," Rex whispered.

"Goddamn, you scared the shit out of me." She patted her chest to calm her racing heart. He took her hand, drew her back under the bridge with him.

The dark was deeper there; the cold, colder.

Rex wouldn't be here if it weren't important, but she needed to get to the hospital.

"Sorry, Claudie," he said. "But I gotta do something. I want you to know before I do it." He sounded like a man who intended to throw himself off a cliff. Claudia put a hand on his arm. She knew this man, knew his cadences, the way he thought. Best be silent until he got to it.

Rex shuffled his feet. Gravel gritted. "I caught Floyd and Sims sending Neva's rental over the bluff."

"Was Zan—?"

"No, thank God. But her suitcase and backpack were. I sent the car and everything else to the FBI lab for testing, got a few friends who came through. They've found DNA that matches Sims for sure. Not so clear about Floyd. Now that I've got proof, I'm going to the captain."

Claudia shook her head, fighting panic at what this meant for Zan, then admitting she'd known all along. Zan being held somewhere. Else, Zan would have let Neva know she was all right. Claudia shook her head again, this time to clear it, and said, "The captain and Floyd are very close."

"That's why I'm telling you. Something happens to me, call this number." He pressed a small rectangle of cardboard into her hand. "Tell him everything you know."

"Who is it?"

"The friend with the Feebs. You can trust him."

Dread that had nothing to do with Zanna fell on Claudia. "I don't like this, Rex. Why don't you let the Feebs handle it?"

"Because somebody's got Zan." His feet crunched the gravel again. "I can't sleep thinking about what they're doing to her, Claudie. I can't stand it. Not a fine woman like that. I mean, it's not okay for any woman to be treated that way, but—"

"—but you know Zan, care about her. I understand."

"Yes." Rex's voice carried relief. "If I can get the captain to act, we can find her."

Claudia grabbed his shoulders. "You be careful, Rex Mason."

She felt his hands on her waist.

"I will, Claudie. You be careful, too. I don't like you out here." He pulled her to him, wrapped his arms around her. She laid her head on his shoulder, smelled the Old Spice he always wore, inhaled it with a sense she might never smell it again.

For a long moment, they clung together, and then he pushed her back. "Thanks," he said.

"Sure."

"Tell me you'll quit when this is all over."

"I'll quit when this is all over," she agreed. "I've made up my mind."

* * * *

Claudia caught the downtown trolley at the corner of Charlotte and Sixth, ignored the driver's glare and took a seat. The trolley's heating system was in high gear. She tried to pull enough warmth into her bones to keep from freezing on the long walk down D.B. Todd Boulevard to Meharry Hospital.

Bob Foster's Exxon at the corner was her first stop. It probably cost Foster a fortune to keep soap in his bathroom for the homeless. She blessed him for his charity as she locked the door behind her and snatched the wig off her head.

Above everything, she hated that wig. It rode her head like a heavy, furry animal. Her own hair wasn't too bad now, because she'd been back such a short a time, but it still needed a good wash. It always needed a good wash when she was on the streets.

Once she'd stripped off all three layers of clothing, she laid the wig in the middle of the outer and inner garments and rolled them into a neat bundle. The middle layer, which was exposed to neither the city dirt nor her body, was the cleanest and the one she would wear to the hospital.

She scooped water from the sink, poured it over her head until her hair was thoroughly soaked, then rubbed soap into it until it lathered, rinsed and blew it dry by contorting herself under the hand dryer.

When her body was lathered, rinsed and paper-toweled dry, she slipped on the long, orange and green skirt with the saucy ruffle she'd found in a bag of free clothing at the Goodwill, topped it with the gold sweater and finger-fluffed her hair.

When she'd finished, the mirror showed her an eccentrically dressed older woman with dark brown eyes.

She tucked her clothing roll under her left arm, pulled the leather jacket on, opened the door and took a quick look around. The street was empty.

At the hospital, Claudia handed the receptionist the expired driver's license with Cee's picture on it. Barely glancing at it, the woman went back to her spreadsheet with a jerk of her head toward the green door to the right.

Softly, Claudia opened the door and stuck her head through. The green hallway was long, narrow and empty, the ceiling low and decorated only with sprinklers and a couple of ancient speakers that clung to the corners, so dusty Claudia couldn't imagine how they could manage any sound.

The doors on either side of the hallway were staggered so a patient in one room could not possibly see a patient in the one across the hall. All the doors stood open. Claudia peered into each room as she passed until she saw her girl. The room was large enough for the bed and a chair and a set of white shelves that were loaded with towels and pitchers and plastic bags. A couple of vomit trays finished out the collection. Claudia slid inside, flopped into the chair beside the hospital bed.

The girl was covered to her chin with thin hospital blankets. Claudia sneaked a peek beneath them. They'd somehow removed her clothes and slid her into a hospital gown. It had tiny ballerinas on it, reminded Claudia of the wallpaper in Neva's girlhood bedroom.

Neva'd had her share of hard knocks, but had not once been touched in anger. This girl had probably not spent a pain-free day since she had her first period. Maybe before.

Claudia's stomach twisted with dark anger. Sons of bitches! Somebody should feed them to the alligators one stinking piece at a time. She balled her hands into fists and held on until she could shove the anger out of her way. The doctor would be in soon. Claudia had her story, but she wanted to bulletproof it.

"Oh!" a voice from the hallway said. "I didn't know anyone was in here."

The nurse was short and heavy, not a young woman by any means, but she had a kind face and sweet eyes as dark as Moya Vargas's.

"The receptionist said I could come on back and I—" Claudia said.

"No problem," the nurse said. "You're a relative?"

"Her aunt."

"Good. We've been hoping her family would come." She lifted the covers, pulled out the girl's good arm and stood in silence gazing at her watch. When she finished, she said, "You can see she's had a hard time."

"I can see she's been nearly beaten to death," Claudia said, allowing the horror she genuinely felt to show. "Do you know what happened?"

"No," the nurse said. "She was actually found in the TDOT motor pool. They're looking for the people who dumped her there, hoping they'll have some answers."

Wouldn't count on it.

"What's her name?" the nurse asked.

"Yvonne. Yvonne Miller. She's had such a hard time," Claudia said, grateful the name popped into her head so easily. "Been in Bulgaria of all the places, trying to write a novel. I didn't know she was in the States until she called this afternoon, begged me to pick her up, said she was under the bridge near the Titans' stadium. When I got there, she was gone, but some state employees down there said they saw a woman carried off in an ambulance. You're the third hospital I checked."

"The doctor will be in as soon as he can," the nurse said. "Would you like a cup of coffee?"

"I would love coffee. Cream and sugar, please."

CHAPTER THIRTY-TWO

Davis let Neva's phone ring until it went to voice mail. He'd told her earlier he had to work late, but he'd finished early. If she didn't have plans, he wanted to share a nice dinner somewhere, tell her what he'd learned at Drennon's.

He called the funeral home's main line and then winced when Neva's dad answered. "I am so sorry, Mr. Oakley," Davis said.

"Davis, we've had this conversation about a dozen times. Name's Robert. I'd actually prefer Bobby, but Mr. Oakley is my dad. He's seventy-five years old. So no more Mr. Oakley, right, son?"

"Right, sir." Davis winced again, feeling like a twelve-year-old with a stutter, as he often did when talking to Neva's dad. "Sorry to interrupt you. I called your lovely daughter, who didn't answer. I forgot you always answer the business phone. Thought she might have left hers downstairs and would answer this one."

"She never answers this one," Bobby said, slowly. "She does, however, always answer her cell phone." The worry in Bobby's voice sent a cold spear through Davis's stomach.

"She was probably in the bathroom," Davis said. "I'll just call her back."

"You do that, Davis. When you two finish talking, you tell her to call her father."

"I'll do exactly that. Thank you, si—Bobby."

His next call to Neva went to voice mail as well. Moya answered her cell phone sounding like she'd run a mile. "Davis!" she said when he identified himself. "Are you lost?"

"I'm hoping your beautiful roommate is with you, that her cell phone has broken and you will hand her yours."

A man's voice, near enough for Davis to hear clearly, panted, "Who is it?"

There was a pregnant pause and then, "I'm not at home, Davis."

"Yes, I understand," he said with a laugh that sounded like a fourteen-year-old caught buying condoms. "I'll keep trying until I get her."

"When you do get her," Moya said, "you tell her to call me." She paused a minute. "Well, maybe she should wait a half hour."

"I understand," Davis said, so eager to hang up he had his finger on the button before he said good-bye.

Once more, his call went to voice mail.

He parked in the driveway behind Neva's house, killed the engine and sat looking at the back door for a few seconds. He didn't have a key, didn't need a key. Neva slept with him at his house, but now he wished he'd asked for one.

Just in case.

There was no key that unlocked every door, but locks came in types, even the new ones. The master key he used to gain entry to Pratt-designed buildings for their last inspections opened most cylinder locks. Ones like those on this old house were especially easy to manipulate.

Blessing the high hedges that surrounded the house, he first knocked on the back door, knocked hard enough so anybody inside could not fail to hear. When no one came, he slid his master key into the lock and manipulated it through the puzzle of metal that made up the lock. Took a second to get through.

The door opened smoothly. The house was warm and smelled of perfume and wine, a smell he'd come to associate with Neva over the past year. It also had the cavernous, reverberating feel of emptiness.

"Neva?"

A lovely red and white Maine coon came around the corner. It stopped when it saw him. Its eyes, the same reddish gold as its fur, widened.

He loved cats, but there was no time.

The room was neat, clean. No signs of struggle, nothing tossed, torn. If she'd been taken from here, she'd not had time to fight.

Running, then making himself walk, then running, he checked her bedroom, the bathroom and Moya's room. When he didn't find her in the kitchen, he punched in her uncle's phone number, panic coiled in his chest, waiting to strike.

"I don't want to sound paranoid, sir, but she's nowhere. Nowhere. I've talked to her dad and Moya and...well..." How fucking lame could he get? Davis drew in a deep breath. "Thing is, I think they've got her. I don't have any proof, but—"

"I sent a car to follow her home earlier, Davis. See if her car is in the garage."

Davis swept through the kitchen and into the garage. "No car."

"Signs of a struggle?"

"Nothing."

Mason was quiet for a moment. "Wait there until I call you back."

One of the reasons Davis liked architecture was its measured pace, where a thought could be examined from all angles and a course of action developed in stages so deadly mistakes were not likely to happen. He'd been told he thought well. But he wasn't adept at thinking quickly.

Now, he cursed his nature, tried to force reason and thought into his head, thought that made sense, that would lead him to the one, and only one, spot where Neva was. Because from what he'd learned of the human trafficking business, she was likely to be there only a few hours. When they moved her, his chances of finding her dropped to below zero.

Law enforcement was just beginning to take trafficking seriously enough to develop methods of tracking them.

If Neva was still in Nashville, if she was still whole—

Savagely he wiped the image of her abuse from his mind. That way lay madness.

He had no time to go insane, no time to lose his way, no time to make mistakes. For the most important decision of his life, he had to move like lightning. Yet if he was wrong, he would lose her forever.

They would move her to another state or another country, to places he didn't know about, places so remote or so ordinary, finding the proverbial needle in a haystack would be child's play compared to finding her.

Tears bubbled up from his chest.

He coughed them away, checked his cell phone as if it might have forgotten how to ring. He'd seen the evidence of the pocket room, heard her logic that was the place. Why was he pacing her kitchen floor, waiting for a phone call, waiting for permission to do the only thing that might save her?

If she wasn't in the pocket room, he'd likely spend a night or two in jail.

Small price to pay.

Weaving into and out of traffic, speeding at more than sixty miles an hour, he snatched the cell before it could ring twice.

"Davis?"

"Yes."

"You find anything?"

"No, sir. But I think I know where she may be."

"You're on your way there now, I'm guessing."

"Yes."

"Drennon's. Look, I can't get a warrant, not until she's been gone 24 hours."

"Too late."

"Yes. I want you to park across the street from the funeral home and wait for me." Rex Mason described his personal car. "It'll just be the two of us. You armed?"

"Yes."

"Good. One more thing." There was a short pause. "For reasons I can't explain, no matter what happens, I don't want you to call 911. Okay?"

"Don't know I can promise—"

"There are things you don't know. Calling 911 is a real bad idea. Could cost her life."

CHAPTER THIRTY-THREE

Rex Mason clicked off the phone. Pratt was a good guy, smart enough to ask for help. Rex knew how he felt. Rex loved Neva. It would kill him if she were harmed. But bad as that would be, if something happened to Claudia… Yet there she was on the streets of Nashville, where anything could happen. She had no protection except Stan, whose loyalty was unquestioned, but who could not be in ten places at once. She'd said she would leave the streets after this rotation. He hoped she'd meant it.

He checked his weapon, made sure he had plenty of ammo.

His phone rang.

"Hey, Mason."

"Officer Sims. To what do I owe this honor?"

"I got info on that Clark girl. I don't wanna give it over the phone. The NSA might be listening. How about I stop by your house."

"If you can be in and out of here in five minutes, Dale. I'm on my way out the door right now."

"I can do it in two," Sims said.

Rex stuffed his gun into the back of his belt. He wasn't worried. Floyd, now that would be a different thing, but Sims was a lightweight.

True to his word, Sims knocked on the door in less than a minute.

"You musta been in the damned driveway when you called," Rex said as he held the door open.

"Right," Sims said.

Screen door, old as the house, slammed like a gunshot unless Rex closed it himself. He closed it, shut the inside door and then turned. "So, Dale, what's this all—"

Dale Sims was straddle-legged in the middle of the room with his service revolver pointed at Mason's chest.

"Keep your hands in front of you," he said. "Lay your weapon on the floor. Kick it to me. That gun in your boot—I want that one, too."

Cursing himself for being an idiot, Rex did as he was told. He'd have a chance later, maybe, but right now, Sims was in control. "What's this all about, Dale?"

"None of your business, Mason. You and me, we're going for a ride."

"From which only one of us will return?"

"Turn around," Sims said. "Put your hands behind your head, lock your fingers. You know the drill."

Rex held his hands out together. "Do it in the front, Dale. You got the only gun. No reason you gotta make me miserable."

"Regulations—" Sims began.

"Regulations my ass. You're about to murder me. There ain't no goddamned regs that cover one officer murdering another. Here, put the fuckers on."

Sims stared at Rex for a long minute, his piggy eyes contemplative. "Tell you what, Mason." He tossed a pair of cuffs across. "You put one on your wrist and the other on that doorknob."

"You're handcuffing me to my own doorknob?"

"You want to be front-cuffed, you do as I tell you."

Rex fastened the cuff around his left hand, then hooked it onto the doorknob, which was much too large to allow the cuff to slip over.

Sims laid his gun on the table. Rex's heart sank. He couldn't snatch Sims's weapon while he was worrying with the cuffs. Rex's opinion of Sims's intelligence went up a reluctant notch.

Sims used a second pair of cuffs to shackle both of Rex's hands, then removed the first.

He retrieved his weapon and said, "Now, Mason, open the door and go on out."

A thousand things flashed through Rex's mind. Turn and butt Sims in the face, kick back into his shins. Trouble was, Rex knew how Sims was trained, knew he was ready for just those moves and knew how to deflect them, knew that when it got too bad, the right thing was to shoot the perp, put him down.

Which was what Sims had in mind for Rex anyway. He was just keeping Rex alive so he wouldn't have to carry Rex's body to the dumping place he'd selected. Somewhere remote so Rex's body wouldn't be found until it was nothing more than a skeleton, if it was ever found.

Sims's car was parked with its nose right against the garage door. He hooked his hand in Rex's right elbow with the automatic touch of a man who'd done it a thousand times before.

Rex's backyard was perfectly private, something he and Marilyn, his now-deceased first wife, had selected so they could enjoy nude sunbathing and swimming. His neighbors' houses were as deeply insulated as his. If they heard him scream, they'd think it was a cat.

Sims put his hand on top of Rex's head as Rex slid into the front seat.

His mind raced. He'd talked to the captain yesterday afternoon, told him what he'd seen Sims and Floyd do, told him about the car, confessed that he'd violated about thirty rules and broken a few laws.

When Captain Jordan asked where the car was, however, Rex lied, told him it was still with the FBI.

Jordan stared into his eyes for the longest time, during which Rex had hope the captain was one of the good guys. But when the captain's gaze slid to the far corner of the room, Rex's father's ghostly voice whispered, "Won't look at you. He's lying, son."

In the end, Jordan asked him to say nothing about this until they could get more information, thanked Rex for coming and shook his hand. Rex left feeling like he'd tattled to the principal.

A principal who didn't like *him* very much, and who liked the fact that he knew what he knew even less.

CHAPTER THIRTY-FOUR

They let Claudia into Yvonne's regular hospital room at nearly six p.m. The girl was attached to at least four machines. Tubes and wires ran into her broken body. The CT scan found broken ribs and bruised kidneys, but her spleen survived the beating. Surgery on her face was scheduled for tomorrow. Tonight, thanks to Claudia's presence, Yvonne would stay in this room, but the nurses said they'd be in every fifteen minutes.

Suited Claudia fine. She would be happy if they pulled up a chair and stayed.

She laid her head back against the vinyl chair and bounced the rod that should be holding the lamp together gently off her knee.

A long steel rod had many uses, as did the lamp's heavy base with its tall wooden handle. Better than a baseball bat.

Exhaustion teased her with thoughts of a nap. Nurse would be back in ten minutes. Nothing was going to happen in that space of time. Just a quick snooze.

She forced her weary limbs out of the chair, paced the room. Didn't take long for that to get old. She cut off in mid-stride. She really needed to pee, but that involved leaving the girl alone. Maybe looking out the window would keep her mind off her aching bladder.

The parking lot swept back two city blocks. It should be an oasis of light, but half the lights were burned out. Deep shadows stretched along entire lanes.

A real gift to a predator.

She'd called Rex earlier, left voice mail. When he didn't call back, she took a risk and called East Precinct, explained about the girl's injuries and asked them to send a guard for the night. In light of what Rex had told her, that might not have been her smartest move, but keeping Yvonne alive was the most important thing right now.

Headlights bloomed at the entrance ramp. A Metro patrol car cruised swiftly down the nearest row past several open spaces. Exhaustion kept her gaze on him until he pulled into a space three rows back, a space so dark the car disappeared when he turned off the lights. She drifted into an alpha fugue, stirring just in time to see the officer emerge into the lights near the entrance.

She straightened. About damned time. She couldn't push her bladder any further.

She'd been in the bathroom for what felt like no time when hard-soled shoes rang across the floor.

"I'm in here," she called. "Be right out."

He walked on in the direction of the bed.

"Helloooo," she called. "I'll be right out. Can you hear me?"

A cacophony of bells, buzzers and alarms answered her.

Hard soles raced for the door.

She tore at the suddenly obdurate doorknob, burst into the room just as the hall door flew open.

Nurses tumbled over one another. An orderly with a crash cart led Dr. Clark, whose bright red hair stood in pillow-driven tufts.

"What happened?" he asked Claudia as he slid to a stop beside Yvonne's bed.

"I don't know. I was in the bathroom," she said, hugging herself.

Stupid, stupid, stupid! Rex warned you about Floyd and Sims. You should not have let East know what was going on.

She ran to the window.

If she could get a look at the officer…wouldn't be a slam-dunk eyeball witness identification, but it would give her a possible.

Right now, she had nothing.

The cruiser sped out of the parking lot in light too dim for her to see anything but the outline.

Feeling like a complete failure, she turned back to the drama behind her.

Dr. Clark had both hands on Yvonne's chest.

The monitor found a blip.

Claudia held her breath.

I shouldn't have left her.

The team was synchronized. Their arms crossed one another; their knees often touched.

Claudia wavered between anticipation and horror.

Minutes sped by like seconds.

Finally, as if someone had turned them off, the team dropped their hands, stood immobile, their gazes on their patient.

Dr. Clark pulled off his gloves. "Time of death: 8:33 p.m."

He lifted his weary gaze to Claudia. "Would you like time alone with her?"

"Yes."

Claudia closed the girl's eyes, brushed her hair back with a gentle hand, perhaps the only gentle touch she'd ever known. Too bad it came after she was dead.

She gazed closely at the body. No bruises around the neck or mouth, nothing to indicate the intruder had touched her.

Claudia would tell Dr. Clark what she'd heard, see if Rex could get an autopsy done.

She'd failed Yvonne.

At least twice a day she told herself she was too old for this shit. She meant she was past being able to handle the discomfort and inconvenience, but the truth was, she was past being effective.

Which was when a good cop retired.

CHAPTER THIRTY-FIVE

Davis called Mason, listened to his call go to voice mail, left a message. Mason hadn't wanted Davis to call 911, but without Mason, Davis was alone, a single guy with a gun in his belt against God knew how many armed men, desperate to keep a secret that doubtless made them all rich.

He opened his phone, hit the 9 and then a 1, then stopped. Mason was Neva's uncle, if not by blood then by relationship. He'd said calling 911 might get her killed. Logically, then, Mason had some reason to believe things weren't right with the police.

Davis glanced at his watch. How much time did he have? An hour? Ten minutes?

The things he didn't know made him crazy.

Go on; get her. Don't wait another minute.

He grabbed the door handle, stopped when he heard brakes squeal from Gallatin Road, a big rig stopping hard. Seconds later, the rig stopped at Drennon's drive with another sharp squeal, then turned into the parking lot. A red cab, just like the one Neva had described, jugged past. The trailer turned behind it, "Brandon's Casket Company" emblazoned on its side. What was that she'd said?

Brandon's Casket Company didn't exist.

He'd waited too long. Until now, the pocket room would have been filled with silent, drugged women while the men watched television or told stories. If he'd not waited for Mason, he'd have her by now, be on his way.

If Neva was right, they would pick up the women here and move them to another market. His research had told him they would have several such markets, all considered safe houses.

Davis leapt from his vehicle, hit the ground running, ducked into the darkness behind the building and forced himself to think. The truck was at the back, which meant there was a door to the pocket room back there. It was entirely possible there wasn't one in the old part of the basement, but if there was, he still had half a chance.

If he could find it.

His hand shook so hard he barely got his master key into the lock. He twisted it.

Nothing happened.

Once more.

Ah, shit!

His heart dropped to his shoes. He gave the only window one longing look and then turned for the other side of the building. A key, she'd said. Hidden in a brick. Third brick from the parking lot.

Davis ran down the wall. They'd added the new section. The old brick would be behind it. He slammed his hand into his pocket, fumbled for his keys, flipped on the keyhole light he carried there.

Weak, diffused light hit the brick wall, just barely enough to see where the old bricks ended and the new began. Three bricks from the parking lot. He grabbed it, jerked hard.

Nothing.

"Please, God," he whispered to the night while behind the building, the garage door rose and the truck's brakes whined as the driver inched it back toward the opening. "Please."

If they'd paved the parking lot recently, the third brick might now be the second. Davis grabbed it, tugged hard, unprepared for it to slide out quickly, lost his balance and sat down hard on the asphalt.

The brick cantilevered, its top already open.

Inside was a gold key.

Now, if Drennon hadn't changed the locks.

"You hear somebody over there?" a voice asked from the back.

Davis froze, the key in his palm.

"Naw. You're always hearing shit, man."

"I tell you, I heard somebody."

Davis clutched the key hard, raced to the opposite edge of the building and slid around, pulled his weapon. If the dude came this way, he wouldn't be going back.

A flashlight beam cut across the parking lot, played up and down and then cut off.

"Told you," a voice said. "You got bugs in your ears. Come on. We got a lot to move."

Davis listened to their footsteps retreat across the parking lot, waited only until he was sure they'd turned the corner to slide around again.

They would move the women now.

Cursing the delay, he slid the key into the lock and stepped inside, ran to the corner under the stairs and put his ear against the wall.

Shuffling feet and creaking metal. They were already at it, and he didn't know whether there was a door here, let alone where to find it.

The truck idled on the other side of the building, waiting for its sad cargo.

Thoughts shot though Davis's brain like bullets, shattered his concentration. He couldn't trust his shaking hands to find the door. He had no time, no knowledge and, right now, no brain.

Desperately, he leaned his head against the wall, let the bricks cool his face.

This is a job. Just another job. You're trained for this, remember? Calm down. Think, dammit!

With every corpuscle throbbing with the need to hurry, he moved his hands methodically, carefully across the bricks, pushed, poked and pulled on every single one, then went for the spaces between the brick.

Nothing.

Think, Davis. That expensive education should work for you here.

Okay. Probably a lever. Probably tucked beneath a brick. Probably hard as hell to find.

Forget that. Easy to find. Just have to know where to look.

Which he did not.

Time ticked in his head while images he couldn't stand to see flashed through his mind.

Where were they now? Was Neva already in the truck? He'd do what he had to, but his best chances were through this door.

If there was a door.

He nearly missed the lever. Would have, except for the tiny barb that caught his little finger as his hand swept by.

Relief almost did him in, but he stiffened his sagging knees, held his breath, shoved down on the lever.

The wall popped open a crack.

Now, if Neva was still inside.

A door stood open at the other end, let in enough light so he could see the caskets. Their tops were open, the women's heads visible on their silk pillows.

Three rows.

Two against the walls and another down the center.

This "pocket" room was quite large.

His gaze bounced from face to face until finally it caught on the glint of auburn. She was near the opposite door, had to be one of the next to go.

Too late, too late, too late. His heart beat in his ears. Too late, too late, too late.

Shut the living fuck up! Davis screamed internally. The cadence stopped, but his heart continued to pound.

The door at the other end was against the front wall; this door was against the back. The light slanted across the room but was blocked by the center caskets from reaching this door. Davis had cover to slide behind the caskets along Neva's wall.

His plan was as simple as it was dangerous. Pick her up and run like hell, shoot if he had to, kill if he couldn't help it.

Ducking beneath the light, he sidled into the room, flattened himself against the wall, slid past three caskets and then dropped to his knees when the first of the two men came in the far door.

Except for the noise they made, the room was so silent Davis's harsh breathing sounded to him like airplane exhaust. One of them was already suspicious that someone else was around. If Davis couldn't get himself under control, they'd hear him for sure.

He leaned against the wall, put his head in his hands and talked himself down. His breathing still sounded harsh in his ears, but the casket was between him and them.

It might work.

He leaned to one side, caught sight of the second man as he came into the room, and stiffened. It was the man he'd seen in Bobby's cemetery, the short, dark guy who might be Stephen.

Stephen stopped at the door, seemed to literally sniff the air, then shrugged and said, "Let's clear out the center first."

"What the fuck for?"

"It'll make it easier to get the others out."

So like Stephen to make a plan. So methodical. So careful.

His buddy only grunted, but in a minute, Davis heard one of the center caskets roll toward the door.

He had five minutes.

Tops.

He jerked the IV out of her arm, threw it behind the casket.

She was deadweight, limp, laid across his shoulder like an enormous rubber doll.

He raced for the door, slid through and gently kicked it shut.

They'd concentrate on the center caskets for a while, might not notice she was gone. He should have plenty of time to get her into his truck and get away.

CHAPTER THIRTY-SIX

Rex's heart tried to pound its way out of his chest. His throat tightened, made it hard to breathe. As inevitable as it was, he'd always thought of death as a long-term thing, something that would eventually lay him down, end it all, send him to whatever waited. Everybody died. No big deal.

Imminent death had a far different feel. Rex shoved his thoughts aside, focused on his breathing, lowering his heart rate, finding a calm place before fear drove him into a stroke and saved Sims a bullet.

"What's this all about, Dale?" he asked.

"You'll find out soon enough."

"You're a good cop. You wouldn't be doing this if Floyd weren't making you. I understand. He can be a tough guy."

Sims ran a hand over his jaw. "Mike's not in this."

"You don't have to lie to me. I'm gonna be dead in a while."

Sims said nothing.

"The captain's a good guy. If Mike's pushed you into something, he'll help you."

Sims barked a nasty laugh. "You're pitiful, Mason. Detective rank and you don't know shit about what goes on."

"You saying Captain Jordan's in on this?"

Sims's mouth tightened. He gripped the wheel. "Shut up."

"I'm trying to help you. Everybody at East Precinct knows Floyd's using you. He talks about you all the time, man. Things no partner should say."

"Like what?"

"Like the time you threw up all over a perp. Had to bathe him before you could bring him in. Or the time you shat your pants. Floyd said he made you walk home that night so you wouldn't mess up his car. Stuff like that."

They were driving down North First Street. At this hour, in this part of Nashville, a man could die because he stopped at a stop sign. Kick a cop out on these streets and the gangs would make sure his death was ugly and painful.

"Floyd told you that shit?"

Rex jerked his thoughts back to Sims. "Where else would I hear it? I'm telling you, he's gonna lay all this at your feet when it blows. You know it'll blow."

Sims was silent for such a long time, Rex was gearing up to press his advantage when Sims said, "You don't know shit, Mason. Not shit. Now shut up or I'll pop you right now no matter what kind of mess it makes."

Rex settled back against the seat. No need to feel sorry for himself. Not a single man or woman alive knew the hour of his death. But he had thought he had plenty of time. For another marriage perhaps, a long vacation in Hawaii maybe. A trip to Ireland. He and Marilyn had no children. Bobby Oakley was the closest thing he had to a relative.

Who would miss him?

A vision of Claudia stretched out beside him at the pool made him suddenly hard. Would she miss him?

He shook the image away. The conversation with Sims had calmed him enough so he realized there was a persisting niggle in his stomach, the niggle that usually meant he'd missed something.

He left Sims to his single-minded driving and focused on the personnel file he'd poured over last night. He'd been Sims's supervisor for a few months and the system thought he still was.

Most of Sims's reviews were good, facts provided by Sims and corroborated by Floyd in separate interviews. Six years on the force, came straight out of Volunteer State Community College with the required grade average of a C+. He'd done reasonably well with the physical, a little slow, but fatties were always slow. Gravity, Rex thought.

He teamed up with Floyd at the academy. They'd been more or less inseparable since.

Sims's breathing became audible, which felt like a sudden thing, but when Rex put a mental finger on his place in Sims's file, he realized he'd been hearing it for a while.

They must be nearing the place of Rex's demise.

Why would that make Sims uneasy?

They were still going down North First, approaching the interstate bridge. Rex waited to see if Sims would access the super slab, but he drove past the Jefferson Street entrance without slowing.

Sims's record was fine. He'd distinguished himself often.

Rex didn't have access to Floyd's file, but he was positive if he did he would see that in those moments in which Sims distinguished himself, he was beside Floyd, shared in the golden one's glory.

Rex's thoughts stopped as Sims's breathing accelerated to real panting.

Approaching the Victory Memorial Bridge overpass now. Sims's foot went to the brake.

He flipped on the turn signal.

This road led past the TDOT motor pool, past the Ashland Oil Refinery and then, with a nice walk, to Homeless Town. Once past the refinery, there would be nobody to see them and a billion places, including the river, to dispose of a body.

Rex's stomach clutched.

He focused on controlling *his* breathing, although Sims probably couldn't hear it over his own. With an effort similar to pulling a rusted bolt from a piece of metal, Rex forced his mind back to its mental review of Sims's file.

By the time the cruiser bounced over the curb past the refinery and began driving along the grass beside it, Rex had remembered all of it he was going to remember.

Without finding that elusive fact that still niggled.

Sims pulled the cruiser into the deepest shadows beside the refinery and glanced at Rex. "You okay?"

"Just peachy," Rex said, holding his shackled hands up.

"We're going for a walk. I'm gonna walk behind you. You make one stupid move, I'll shoot you here. Don't wanna do it that way, but if you make me, I will."

"Take a deep breath, Dale," Rex said. "Way you're hauling in air, you're gonna hyperventilate. I'll have to find somebody to carry *you* back to the car." Rex's tone was jaunty, but his attention was back on the file, speed-reading now.

He wasn't completely familiar with Homeless Town, but if Sims had parked the car, it couldn't be far.

"Shut up, Mason," Sims said as he shoved his belly out of the car.

Rex fumbled with the door handle, put off by the awkwardness of the cuffs, finally got it open and stepped into the cold air. "Sure you want to do this, Dale? It's not too late to back out."

Sims gestured with the gun that Rex should walk ahead of him. "Help if I knew where to," Rex said.

"I'll tell you when to stop," Sims said, his voice shaking a bit, but whether from nerves or the cold, Rex couldn't say. "You don't worry about a thing."

Now that they were out in the open, Rex's chances of helping himself were better. In the classes he taught for rookie officers, Rex emphasized that a handcuffed perp is not by any means helpless. Nashville officers were overcome every day because they gave up a single opportunity, which was all Rex asked for here. One single opportunity.

Clearly, he couldn't count on Sims to volunteer it.

He stole a glance behind him. Dale Sims was a good three feet behind, too far to jump, too close to give Rex a clear chance to run.

Good job, Sims!

Dammit.

Rex turned. "I gotta pee. How about I step under that tree over there." When Sims hesitated, Rex said, "Aw, come on, Dale. I don't wanna die peeing down my leg. Won't take more'n a minute. You got somewhere to be or something?"

"I'll be right behind you, Mason."

Just where Rex wanted him.

He hadn't lied about needing to go. He stopped at the first tree he found, struggled through unzipping his pants. While his warm stream sizzled in the cold air, he watched Sims from his periphery.

The man never moved. Again, Rex was forced to admire Officer Sims's adherence to his training.

Rex assumed a casual tone to hide the fact that his heart was again trying to knock a hole in his ribs. "So, Dale. You're gonna kill me in a few minutes. How about telling me why?"

"You know why, Mason."

"The hell I do. I thought we were on the same team."

"We were. Then Detective Yates poked her nose in where it didn't belong." He glanced at Rex. "You didn't get our first message."

"First me—" An image of the big rig sliding across the road came to Rex. "Ah. You sent the truck."

"We got lotsa friends. Thought you got the message until you went to see the captain, told him about that car. You shoulda said something. We'da cut you in."

"In on what, Dale?"

"I hate it, Mason. I really do. You're a nice guy, always been fair to me, but the man says you gotta go."

"What man?"

"Now, see, there's a question that ain't gonna do you no good. What difference does it make who? You ain't gonna tell nobody. You ain't gonna make the bust."

"Then tell me, Dale. What harm can it do?"

"Get my ass killed if Mike finds out. That's what harm it could do."

"How would he find out? I'll be dead. Come on, Dale. I just wanna know before I go to my grave. Who's running this thing?"

"Walk 'til I tell you to stop."

The grass crunched so loudly under Rex's boots, it might have been ice cubes. The gurgling of the river, still not visible around the final bend in the road, filled his head. Distinctly, he heard a fish break water and splash back.

The specter of death had apparently heightened his senses.

Sure hoped it didn't heighten the feel of a bullet tearing through his chest.

From somewhere up river, a barge horn hooted, the sound as bleak and lonely as Rex felt.

There was not much time left.

They rounded the bend.

"Up the hill," Sims said.

"That where you do your killing, Dale? Up the hill?"

"I ain't no killer, Mason."

And there it was.

In Sims's entire file, there was not one killing, not even a shooting. Rex knew Floyd had his share of justified shootings and a couple of dead bodies, but not Sims.

"That's right. You're the good guy." Rex raised his voice, hoping there was somebody to hear. "But after tonight, you're a rogue cop."

"Shut up, Mason!"

Rex smiled at the stress in Sims's voice. "You can't have it both ways, Dale. Can't claim to be a good guy, then off a fellow cop. That ain't how this works. When they close that jail door behind you, you'd better have a jar of lubricant up your ass. You know how them prison boys love ex-cops."

"Shut up! I told you. Shut up!"

"Big guys in jail, Dale. Big all over. You'll have fun." Rex stopped at the base of a set of earthen stairs carved into the hillside. At their top, large shapes huddled under the darkness.

Homeless Town.

They had arrived at his place of death.

CHAPTER THIRTY-SEVEN

Neva bolted upright from a deep, dreamless and yet disturbing sleep to find herself in a powder-blue casket on the top rung of one of three racks in the back of an 18-wheeler rolling at top speed. Sunlight blasted in through the cracks between the doors. Morning, then.

She gazed at the other caskets, all closed. Hers was the only one open. She raised her cuffed hands. A sharp pain bloomed in the bend of her left arm. An IV line, its bag hanging from the casket top.

How the hell?

She'd gone for toilet paper—that cop. What was his name? Floyd. Officer Floyd. He'd drugged her. That explained the fuzz in her head, the warning from her stomach that moving fast would be a bad idea.

The mush that covered her brain, an after-effect of the drug, made it hard to decipher what she was seeing, but the mush was lifting fast. As it did, she began to understand. They'd got her—the traffickers.

Images of her future shriveled first her stomach and then her heart. Rape, torture, degradation—*this* was her future. A whimper escaped her rigid lips, but she bit back the torrent that wanted to follow it.

"So, you're awake."

She jerked at the sound of his voice.

His head just cleared the casket's side. His eyes were red, as if he'd been weeping, and so full of sorrow, she wanted to comfort him. Before she could say a word, he held out a frosty plastic bottle of water. "Can you take this with your hands like that?"

Always worried about her comfort. He'd come for her like a knight, only without shining armor. Just like always, Ice was there when she needed him.

He'd already removed the cap. She sucked down half of the water before she pulled the bottle from her mouth. Her throat felt like an army of owls had roosted in it. "How did you find me, Ice? That cop—he drugged me. I guess he put me in here. Did they get you, too? How'd you get free?"

His silence brought her around to see his eyes brimming. She reached for his face.

He caught her hand, held it tightly. "I'm so sorry, Neva," he said. "I did everything I could to stop you, talked them into leaving you alone for a while. But you just couldn't stop."

"Talk them…talked *who* into leaving me alone? What are you…" He held her gaze, waited while she stammered, her brain frozen. "What are you saying? You tried to stop…"

She held out the water bottle to him. Strong as Ice was, he couldn't lift her out of a casket that was above his head. She'd have to climb down. For that, she would need both hands.

Ice's pale blue eyes darkened. He shook his head, gently shoved the water back at her.

The truth slowly made its way to her brain.

Ice wasn't here to save her.

He put a soft hand on her arm. "Bad things are coming, Neva. You'll get through them if you keep your head on straight. Do what they say. *Always* do what they say. It's not fun at first, but eventually you'll get used to it. Then you'll be fine."

Her mind twisted away. She could not have trusted Ice, loved him, believed him, could not have put her life in his hands so many times if he was—

"Just fine," he repeated. "Just fine."

"I don't want to be *fine*, Ice. I want *out* of here." When he didn't say anything, she added, "Please."

"I wish…" He shook his head. "They'd kill me." He lifted his left hand so she could see the splint around his little finger. "Brought Zan's cat back to you, rescued you from Juan after you tore holes in his body. Talked the boss into believing you knew nothing for a while, but you could not stay out of it. He broke my finger because of you, Neva. Where the boss is concerned, failure is not an option. I'm not gonna die for you."

Again, she saw herself raped, sodomized. Watched her body shrink, her hair fall out.

"Ice," she whispered, steeling herself against the answer she knew was coming, "did you take Zan?"

"That was one stupid mistake." His face twisted. "Sometimes these guys act like they got born yesterday. They had a description of your rental car, thanks to me. So they follow you to the airport, watch you park and leave the car, thinking you were flying out. When 'you' returned, they snatched 'you' and got Zan instead. Dumb-asses."

"But you know where she is."

"I know where she *was*," he said. "She... You don't need to worry yourself over Zan, little girl. Not now."

She lost the ability to help Zan when she left home alone and then let a crooked cop talk her into hiding herself and him where nobody could see what he was doing.

Ice's hand was curled around the edge of the casket. She grabbed it, peered deeply into those strange blue eyes, searching for the Ice she knew and loved. He had to be in there. Nobody could fake the love and concern he'd had for her—not for long. "If you won't help me escape, Ice, kill me. Or give me your gun. Just let me have it for a second. Please, Ice, *help* me!"

He wiped a tear from her cheek and then one from his own. "Stop, Neva," he pleaded. "They will literally kill me. If I could, I would. I've done what I can. I lowered your dose because your dad always said you are sensitive to drugs." Strain and doubt filled his gaze, and with a shiver, she realized he was telling the truth. He *would* help her if he could.

"How do I raise the dose?" Neva asked, eyeing the IV sack. She *was* sensitive to drugs. So sensitive she'd slept for twenty-four hours after a simple wisdom tooth extraction.

He seemed to consider it for a second before he shook his head. "They'd know I did it. It could have been an accident if I'd done it at first, but now"—he shook his head again—"I should not have come back here." He stumbled away, head hanging, shoulders slumped, a picture of anguish.

"Ice, please!" she screamed.

Without turning, he pulled out his cell phone. She heard him say, "Stop the truck. Do it now."

The rig pulled to the right and angled down.

"Don't leave, Ice! Wait!" She threw a leg over the side of the casket, jerked it back as the box threatened to capsize. Her drug-slowed mind struggled to find something that would touch the soft part of his heart, make him help her.

The truck stopped. Ice shoved one of the doors open. Sunshine, traffic noise and the smell of hot asphalt flowed in—the sounds of life, ordinary, everyday life.

"Ice!"

The door closed. The lock clicked home.

Neva kept screaming even after the truck resumed its speed and Ice was much too far away to hear her. She screamed until her body was so wrung out she could barely raise her cuffed hands and her screams nothing more than forced whispers.

Then she fell back against the satin pillow, laid her hands together on her belly as she'd arranged thousands of dead bodies, consigning herself to the death pose even as she was consigning herself to a living death far worse than any real one.

Soggy lethargy pressed on her chest, forced her eyes to close. She took an enormous breath and let it slowly out.

She shouldn't fuss so.

She'd succumbed to depression after Gray's death. It wasn't her mother's depression exactly, but it was a deep, dark blanket under which she had hidden from her pain.

She'd cured herself of it, but now it offered her an escape, the easiest escape in the world. Lie back and relax, let the drug do its job. Sleep. Drop down through the layers of softly welcoming ooze. Give up.

She slipped beneath gray, lifeless waters. Slowly, her lungs became gills and her skin burnished gold and coral with a lightning blaze of silver. She breathed water like air and allowed herself to drop down, down, down to the bottom of the pool.

The first raw scream brought her straight up.

It sounded like he was being cut in half.

Halfway down the casket rack beside her, a bronze casket jumped and skittered. Its top bounced up and down with his screams, but it couldn't open because someone had tied a long belt around it.

By the third terrifying screech, she recognized the voice.

Davis was living his nightmare.

The hair on her neck lifted.

She jerked her right hand back against the cuff. It hung on her thumb joint.

With Davis's raw screams cutting through her head, she slid her thumb into its second position, then tugged her hand back again. The cuff caught on the almost-invisible hump that remained.

She lifted her hands, kicked the bottom half of the casket open, put her foot between her hands, groaned as the cuff dug in; then with a sudden pop, it was free. The IV slid easily from her vein.

"Please, Davis," she said. "I'm coming." Her words were drowned under his shrieks.

She would need her toes. She jerked off her tennis shoes, threw them to the floor, grabbed the upright piece of angle iron at the corner of her rack, swung out, fitted her toes around it, then walked hand over hand down it with the stupid cuff clanging against the metal like a dinner bell. When she was close enough, she dropped to the floor.

The box bounced like a beach ball in high waves as Davis pounded his fists against the casket's lid and threw himself against the side.

She grabbed her shoe, slammed it on his casket lid.

He quieted, stilled.

She worried the belt's knot until it was loose enough to slide the end through. She was nearly there when Davis kicked the lid. It slammed against the belt and retightened the knot.

"Damn it. Stop!" She slammed her shoe again. The casket lid dropped back.

The second the belt was untied, he flung the top back. His hair stood on end. His fingers dripped blood. He tore the IV from his arm, looked through her, leapt from the casket so quickly he seemed to levitate out.

She jumped back.

Landing on his toes, he rolled like an acrobat.

"Davis, wait."

He raced blindly for the trailer's back doors, hit hard, bounced off, backed up and went for them again.

Neva grabbed his right arm, tried to turn him.

He flung her away like an irritating sack of potatoes.

She stumbled against the middle rack, got her balance, tried to think. He was nearly a foot taller than she, outweighed her by sixty pounds.

The rig must be doing at least seventy miles an hour. If the doors opened, he'd hit the pavement. If the impact didn't kill him, traffic behind them would.

She ran past him, turned. He roared toward her, his eyes frantic, his face blank.

She planted her feet, strengthened her back, waited until he was almost on her to sock him in the solar plexus with all her strength.

Davis dropped to the trailer floor, both hands clutching his throat.

He gaped like the fish she'd imagined herself. Air battered against his lips but could not move past his spasmed solar plexus.

Holding her aching hand, she scooted to him. "Say something." It didn't matter what. Any sound forced upward through the frozen muscles would relax them. He managed to squeak out something that might have been, "Okay." His face changed. He gulped air, rolled to his side.

She spooned herself into him. He trembled against her, his breathing harsh.

"You okay?" she asked finally.

Nothing.

"Davis?"

She crawled around him. He gazed at her without recognition for a second, then managed a wan smile. Finally he said, "That was attractive."

"You were hysterical."

He struggled up, crossed his legs Indian-fashion and rubbed his chest. "How many times did I hit the doors?"

"Twice. Sorry about your chest. I couldn't stop you—"

He waved it away. "You saved my life." His gaze wandered to the casket racks. He stood and took in the whole scene. "They've got us."

Such a simple statement to encompass the end of life as they knew it.

"Yes," she agreed. "They've got us." Dark water rose in her mind. Savagely, she shoved it down. If there was a way out of this, they would find it.

"Ice was here earlier," she said.

"Ice? *Your* Ice?"

"Yes. He's part of this. I begged him to help me, but he—" She swallowed tears and stopped. After a moment, she said, "A cop drugged me. How'd they get you?"

"I found you at Drennon's. You were spot on about the pocket room."

She listened as he described how he'd risked his life to find her.

"I had you," he said. His hands curled into tight fists. "Had you nearly in my truck." He rubbed his shoulder. "Something stung my shoulder. That's all I remember."

"Ice said he gave me a smaller dose than he gave the others. That's why I'm awake."

"Musta given me the same as the women," Davis said. "He forgot I'm a lot bigger." He was silent a second. "Was there anyone with Ice?"

"No. Why?"

He told her about seeing Stephen.

"Are you sure?"

"I'm pretty sure he's the guy I followed to the cemetery." He rubbed his arm and winced. "I wish I could reach him." He glanced quickly at her face. "I'll kill him if I have to," he said as if she'd accused him of something. "But if I could just talk to him, let him know who I am, who *he* is. I've looked for so long, and now that he's near…"

"Wish I could make things different," she said.

"Me, too," he said with a sigh. "But you can't." He gazed at the caskets again. "There were lots of women in that room."

"Ice said Zan isn't here."

"And you believe him?"

Neva's gaze moved among the caskets. If every single casket held a sleeping woman, there must be… She counted them, subtracted herself and Davis from the count, and came up with sixteen.

Sixteen motivated people, even starved, drugged people, could work miracles.

She grabbed Davis's arm. "You're right," she said. "See if you can find Zan. And get those needles out of their arms."

"You have an idea?"

"We're going to launch an army."

CHAPTER THIRTY-EIGHT

"Climb them steps," Sims said.

Make him mad enough to do something stupid.

The steps were rock hard, baked by the summer sun, then dried by the drought. No chance they'd collapse under Sims's weight.

Rex glanced behind him. As he'd done before, Sims was positioned perfectly, two steps behind Rex. His gaze was on the steps, but he quickly raised it to Rex's face. "Look where you're going."

Rex wanted to shove the guy's gun up his ass, but anger would cloud his thinking. Not a good thing right now.

Enough light flowed across the river from Nashville's riverfront for Rex to see that the shapes he'd seen before were shacks and huts dotting the hillside. He knew little about the homeless, but he wasn't counting on them to come to his rescue. From what Claudia said, they stayed pretty much to themselves.

Rex had often imagined his death. It involved multiple shooters, several of whom didn't survive, and a final battle in which Rex's lethal shot and that of his opponent were fired at the same moment. As each man lay dying, his opponent managed to say, "You're one hell of a cop, Rex Mason."

A far cry from dying with his hands shackled, staring into the muzzle of a service revolver.

Rex reached the top, stepped off onto the still-rising hillside.

"Keep movin', Mason."

"To where?"

"On up. Up until I tell you to stop."

Of course.

Sims would want a private spot for his first kill, where no one could see him lose his dinner or pee his pants. Rex's first kill brought a sudden rush of urine he barely managed to stop. He'd seen it hit guys like speed, seen them stalk around like gamecocks, damn near crowing as they strutted.

Sims looked like the toss-your-cookies type.

"Think I'll stop here," Rex said. He faced Sims, moved his feet apart for stability.

"Up there." Sims flicked the gun barrel toward the darkness.

"Nope. I'm not climbing another hundred feet to die. Do it here."

Sims shifted, gazed up the incline.

Rex pulled his hands in against his belly, rose to his toes. Sims's gaze snapped to Rex's. "Thinking of trying something?"

"Trying to warm my hands," Rex lied. "It's cold out here."

Sims was shorter than Rex. Right now, he was lower on the hillside, too, which brought his head to the height of Rex's chest, a fact that seemed to bother the fat man. Keeping his weapon right on Rex, Sims circled above him. "Turn around, Mason."

Too late, Rex realized the man's strategy. Sims was now not only taller than Rex, he was uphill, which meant Rex had less chance of charging at him. Rex should have jumped the son of a bitch when he had a better chance. For the first time since he'd managed to calm himself, Rex thought he might actually die tonight. Instantly, his heart rate skyrocketed. His throat closed against his breath.

Take it down, boy. Take it way down.

Trouble with panic was it made a man do really stupid stuff like rush at Sims when the man was as solidly placed as a football goal. "Okay," Rex said when his breathing settled. "You gotta do what you gotta do, but how about letting me in on why. You're gonna kill me. Not like I could tell somebody else."

"I been thinkin' about that. Reckon a dead man can't hurt us none. Me and Floyd, now, we're not dirty, not the way you're thinking. We're on the take, but only from this one guy. I don't know his name. He talks to us through another guy named Jerry somebody. But they got a business going that makes millions. Millions, Mason. Me and Floyd, we're knocking down a thousand a week apiece just watching doors for them and maybe doin' a couple other chores. We get all that dough and women. All the women a man could want. They do everything. E-v-e-r-y-t-h-i-n-g. Mike, he really likes that part."

"And killing cops? How much does he pay you for that?"

"We ain't never killed a cop before. Mike offed a couple of private types, but they don't count. This one's for free."

In the glow from across the river, Rex could see Sims's eyes. He focused on them, knowing it was there Sims would signal the final moment between them. "They bring those women in here, right,

Dale? Have parties and then take them out. Women from other countries."

"Well, now," Sims said, sarcasm and disappointment dripping from every word, "ain't you the smart one."

Stupid move!

A mental midget like Sims would want to stretch out the telling. In fact, had Rex let him talk, Rex might have earned sympathy from the fat man. Instead, he'd cut through the bullshit and ruined it all.

"I ain't smart, Dale. Not like you and Floyd. Hell"—Rex shrugged his shoulders—"I ain't pulling down no thousand a week just for watching a door. Ain't getting no strange. I ain't a bit smart."

Sims's angry face split slowly into a nasty grin. "That's right. You ain't. Okay, Mason, now you know. Make your peace."

Sim's weapon wavered in an arc from dead center of Rex's chest to the left and back again.

There was no time for anything other than a suicide move.

Rex balanced on his toes, inched his left foot back for stability.

He'd die, but he'd die trying.

Somebody moved in the deep shadows behind Sims. Sims was focused on his weapon. He breathed in hitches, so close to sobs it was difficult to tell the difference.

The figure was too far from the lights to be distinct.

It was human.

It was coming fast.

Any noise it made was covered by the river's gurgle and slap.

If Rex didn't do something, the guy would barge into this and Sims would kill him.

Rex cleared his throat.

Sims jerked up, stared at Rex, then dropped his gaze to the gun again.

The shadow came on with that dogged swiftness, directly at Sims.

Closer to the lights now.

A woman in a long skirt. She moved with the grace of a panther. The light didn't get to her face. Crazy bitch. She was going to run right into Sims, get her head blown off.

Sims sucked in a huge lungful of breath, blew it out, wiped away the river of sweat that streamed down his face and said, "Sorry,

Mason. I don't want to do this." He pointed the gun between Rex's eyes.

Rex forced himself to ignore the gun even though his eyes couldn't focus on anything else. He cleared his throat, raised his voice. "Before you shoot me with that gun, Dale, I have one final question."

The woman stopped.

Sims lowered the quaking gun. "What is it?"

"Where do the women come from?"

"Russia or Ukraine, most of them. They bring them through Mexico. Get this, Mason, they move them around in caskets. Like dead people."

In his periphery, Rex saw the woman's retreating back. He was both glad and sorry he'd stopped her.

She'd live.

That was good.

But Rex would not.

Would the homeless tell Claudia of his death? Or were they afraid to talk about murders that happened in this place even among themselves? Would Rex rot under a tree somewhere, his britches full of his postmortem shit while Sims and Floyd made thousands and perhaps millions?

He'd prevented himself from railing at unfairness while cancer ate the life out of his wife. Now, he couldn't stop.

The woman/shadow turned, squared her shoulders, tossed her head in a gesture so familiar it stopped Rex's breath.

She broke into a run, moving like a ghost across the grass between herself and Sims, swift, soundless, running at an armed man with nothing but her courage.

Terrified at what might happen to her, his heart still soared at her courage, her spirit, her magnificence. He pulled his shackled hands into his stomach, watched her speed down the hill, stood firm even though everything in him wanted to move out of the way. If he so much as blinked in her direction, Sims would shoot her.

That, above all, could not happen.

She was right behind Sims.

She'd tucked her skirt into her waistband to reduce the rustle. Like a bird taking off from a hillside, she suddenly rose, her head higher than Sims's, who, perhaps sensing her nearness, whirled, firing as he went.

She made no sound as she slammed into him. Rex leapt aside, hit the ground hard on his left shoulder and rolled so he could see. Sims buckled under her attack. They rolled down the hillside, their limbs twined, two dark lumps turning over one another.

A shot sounded.

Sims cried out.

A second shot.

Then they were still and silent at the bottom of the earthen stairs, their limbs tangled, their bodies pressed against one another.

Rex shoved himself up.

Pain knifed through his shoulder.

He ignored it, raced down the hill, praying with every step that she was alive. Unhurt was too much to ask. Just let her be alive.

"Claudia?" he cried as he ran. "Are you okay?"

"Get him the fuck off me!" Her voice was muffled but strong.

Rex's knees weakened at the sound of her voice, so he more fell than dropped when he reached her.

Sims lay across her chest, one arm thrown across her face.

"Is he alive?" Rex asked. Sims looked dead, but he was jerking in spasms as if he had Tourette's.

"He's too damned fat for me to get him off." Ah. Sims was jerking because Claudia was shoving at him. He outweighed her by a good ninety pounds.

Rex dragged Sims's arm off her face. Her eyes appeared, wide. Even in the half-light, he could see the strain in them. Still using the arm as a handhold, he leaned back, dug his feet into the earth, pulled with all he had.

Sims inched back slowly. As soon as her hands were free, Claudia shoved from her side.

Finally, she slid from beneath. She climbed slowly to her feet, rubbing her knee.

"Are you hit?"

"Hell no. Missed me, probably hit a damned tree up there somewhere. Stupid son of a bitch. What the hell, Rex?"

He couldn't take his gaze off her mouth, imagined those full, ripe lips beneath his own.

He'd escaped death by less than a minute and all he could think about was how her breasts would feel under his hands.

"What is wrong with you?" she asked. She sounded angry, but he could tell by the look in her eyes, she was beginning to use that fine mind, as sexy as her body, to assess what they should do next. "I thought he was going to kill you," she said. "I wasn't sure I could stop him."

"He *was* going to kill me," Rex said. "You were wonderful. An Amazon. Wonder Woman. You are my hero."

"Stop it," she said, but a smile played along her mouth. "Let's get those cuffs off."

He helped her roll Sims over. She dug the key out of Sims's pocket, then wiped her hands on the grass. Sims had peed himself as he died.

An unexpected tidal wave poured through Rex. Sims, not Rex, died tonight. Sims peed his pants. Sims would rot in a hole.

His euphoria evaporated in a sudden longing that made him bite his tongue to keep from crying.

When she removed the cuffs, he massaged his wrists. She'd had no weapon. She never carried one in the field, so the bullet that killed Sims came from Rex's service revolver. "Listen, Claudia. About the way this happened." She stared at him as he continued. "That's my weapon in his hand."

"He shot himself with it," she said.

Rex stopped. "He shot himself?"

"I guess so. I never had a hand on it. You can check the prints. I thought at first he'd hit me, but then he went limp. You got a cell phone?"

"No. He does, but we can't call for help. Not yet." He expected her to argue with him, but she cocked her head to the side in a sexy move that sent his libido into overdrive and said, "Because Floyd and Sims are connected to this trafficking thing."

"Right," he said. "Sims knew just what I told the captain. We can't go through channels, but I know some good cops and we'll— Oh, shit!"

"What?"

He told her about Davis's call, his worry about Neva. "I was supposed to be there hours ago. Goddamn!"

Claudia pointed at Sims. "You in his car?"

"Yes."

She dug her hands into Sims's pockets once more and brought out his car keys. "Let's go," she said.

CHAPTER THIRTY-NINE

Robert Oakley pulled the covers over his head, trying to hide from the vibration against his chest bone.

Sylvia moaned beside him. He woke enough to realize it was his phone.

He'd been asleep no time, too worried about Neva to sleep until exhaustion finally won out. Now he was fuzzy-headed.

"Shhhh." He patted Sylvia's shoulder. "It's okay. Go back to sleep." The clock beside his bed, viewed through eyes so bleary the numbers doubled, seemed to say it was four a.m.

Robert stepped into the hallway. "Hello."

"Bobby," Claudia said, "listen to me. We're tracking a human trafficking ring. We think they're bringing the women in and out of Nashville in caskets. How would that work?"

"Claudia, Neva's missing."

"I know, honey. We're on it, but I need you to focus now. How would they carry them around?"

"They'll need some way to get oxygen in the boxes. Look for filigree along the sides of the box. Something ornate around which they have carved slits. They'd deliver them just like they do the empty boxes. Where are you?"

"On our way to Drennon's place."

Robert's jaw literally dropped open. "You think *he's* doing this?"

"We think he's in it up to his ass."

Robert thought for a second. "That's why he wanted my place. He needed the burying space."

"Yes," Claudia said. "He's probably pulling out of Nashville as we speak."

Robert swallowed hard. He didn't want the answer to this next question and yet he could not stop himself from asking. "Claudie, is it possible they've got Neva?"

"Anything's possible, Bobby, but we have no proof they have her. You stay there. I'll report in every hour so you'll know what's going on. But if Neva comes there, I want you to call me immediately, okay?"

"Okay," Robert said. "Find her, Claudie. Find her and bring my baby home." His last words were choked through tears.

"I will, honey. I promise." Robert turned back to check on Sylvia, to make sure she had enough cover, wasn't thirsty, hadn't found a spare razorblade with which to slash her wrists. Neva out there being— And he was stuck here with this woman who couldn't live life because it was *so* hard.

Robert was shocked at his anger, but the shock didn't stop it, didn't even diminish it.

Neva had suffered for years, growing up without a mother. For the first time, he realized the loneliness and guilt in Neva, knew she felt responsible for Sylvia's condition because it began when she was so small.

That damned doctor had played on her guilt, used it to excuse her own bad medicine.

Their bedroom was dark, Sylvia nothing more than a lump beneath the covers. Robert stepped into the room, intent on closing the door before he headed downstairs.

"Robert?" Her voice was high, thin, her usual whine. "I'm thirsty."

More than twenty years of being her caretaker slammed into Robert like an iron fist. "Then get your ass out of bed and get something to drink. I've got a life to live. And so does Neva!"

Her astonished face rose from the covers like a snake out of its hole. Guilt stabbed him, but he stalked out anyway, slammed the door behind him and ran down the stairs.

The bottle of Irish was right where he'd left it.

He poured three fingers in a glass and threw himself into the chair, still seething even as remorse began to pour through him.

CHAPTER FORTY

Neva stacked the IV tubing in the far corner, figured it might come in handy later. In that same corner, she found extra crossbars for the casket racks. Each had a sliding fastener, which would connect it to the uprights. The false bars would be firm and seem impossible to remove if the border guards bothered to check them.

Pretty smart process.

Now they had to wait.

If Ice came back before the women woke, their plan would be difficult, if not impossible to implement. If they pulled it off, they'd all be free.

After the shock of what she found in the first two or three caskets, she'd forced herself to ignore the condition of the women, their thinness, dull hair, the obvious signs of abuse and the harem-like outfits they wore that exposed their every part.

But when she opened the ninth casket, she sagged against its side, her legs so weak she would have fallen otherwise. Ten, maybe eleven, the girl still carried enough baby fat to look near normal. Given the emaciation of the others, it was clear they shared their meager food with her.

Children.

How could anybody— Neva stopped. She was quite experienced in pain, anguish and horror. She was completely naive about hunger, illness and torture.

Did this cesspool have no bottom?

She worked steadily, but with each raised casket lid, the hope that she'd find Zan dropped.

She found two more girls, somewhere between the ages of fourteen and sixteen.

Finally, all the caskets were open but one.

Davis put his arm around her, held her while she opened it.

The woman inside was not Zan.

A sob caught itself in the back of Neva's throat. Davis turned her to him, held her while she fought the tears.

"I shouldn't have hoped."

He hugged her, then shoved her back and gazed into her eyes. "We're getting out of here, and we're taking them with us." He nodded at the racks of sleeping women. "We'll find Zan, too. Don't doubt us, Neva. We can do it. You *have* to hope!"

She grabbed his belief, held it tight.

"How long will they sleep?" he asked.

That was the question.

Her army was small, weak, starved, beaten, abused and drugged.

But it had more reasons to fight for freedom than the U.S. Navy. Their days, weeks or years of abuse were filled with things Neva didn't understand or want to understand.

She and Davis would give them freedom.

If it killed them both.

CHAPTER FORTY-ONE

A woman whimpered near the back of the trailer.

Neva, who'd paced like a caged animal for the past hour, stopped, unsure she hadn't conjured the sound out of the nervous energy that made her legs tremble.

Once the excitement of having a plan subsided, doubts flooded in. She'd done research on this monstrous business. Most trafficked women were foreigners, kidnapped or coerced in their native lands, brought into the States, where they knew no one and could not speak the language.

Coalescing different people into a cohesive whole sounded daunting enough, but when you added in the language barrier and their appalling physical condition, it began to seem impossible.

But impossible was not an option.

She needed a slam-dunk way to motivate them. Traffickers often employed a Judas to control the women. She was fed more, given more freedom, extra privileges. In return, she tattled on insurrectionists, dampened hopes, counseled compliance.

Neva hoped one of these women could serve in a similar capacity—explain the game plan, encourage rebellion, raise hope.

A tall order.

Motion caught her eye. The casket at the end of the first rack rocked forward. An emaciated leg kicked over its edge; the foot found the floor. The woman was tall. Her hair had once been chestnut. Neva could imagine its once-golden highlights.

Her eyes were deep, dark pools of pain and fear, dull from lack of nourishment, but behind all that, Neva thought she could see a tiny flame of intelligence.

The woman raised her gaze first to Neva's face, then moved it to Davis's and stepped back. "Who are you?"

Stunned that she spoke English, Neva rushed to introduce herself and Davis, then added, "We're here to help you." *Really? Could you have found a more lame way to say it?* "What is your name?" she asked, somehow stuck in this rigid, monosyllabic exchange.

The woman's gaze shifted from Neva's face to Davis's and back again, searching, Neva thought, for something to tell her where they fitted, what part of her torture they carried, what awful thing they would do to her and the others. The sharpness of her gaze, the intelligence behind her eyes all conspired to worry Neva that she might be the Judas despite her emaciation.

Would she work with them?

Or against?

"Luisa," the woman finally said. "You will not get out of here." She nodded at Neva. "You have the hair of fire. They will—" She turned her back to them, moved to the next casket, brushed hair off the forehead of the child Neva had wept over. "She will not escape." She turned to face them both. "There is no escape."

Her flat tone, the pain in her eyes stabbed Neva's heart. Hopelessness would kill them all. Hopelessness drained all energy, thwarted all efforts. Hopelessness was depression by another name. It was the one thing Neva could not allow here. "There is escape," she said. "But only if we work together, only if we all believe."

"They will beat you until you think you are dead, then beat you more. You cannot escape them. They have guns. They're everywhere. They will make you feel pain that tears holes in your mind."

Groans from around the trailer said other women were waking. Neva needed Luisa on their side.

"Look, Luisa. Look around you." She swept her hand at the open caskets. "There are eighteen of us, including the children. That's a lot of people. The cab up there"—she pointed toward the front of the trailer—"cannot hold eighteen people. We've got them outnumbered."

"They have guns," Luisa said with a shake of her head. "They will win."

She sounded so much like Neva's mother, Neva had to bite her lip to keep from screaming at her. But these women had lived through things that would have killed Miss Sylvia. Far from hopeless and pitiful creatures, they were heroines who survived even when survival was the worst choice. Neva blushed as she thought of how she'd begged Ice to kill her.

If she'd been willing to die to prevent this future she'd not yet experienced, how could she ask these women who'd lived it for so long to take a chance on making it worse? What if they failed? What if— *Oh, shut up!*

She took a deep, steadying breath. Her job was to radiate hope like the rays of the sun, to infuse every other person here with the firm belief that they *could* escape. To do that, she had to believe it herself without reservation.

She held up her wrists.

Luisa's eyes narrowed.

"They put the cuffs on both wrists." She let Luisa chew that over for a minute. "And yet I managed to remove my wrist from this one. All it takes is belief, Luisa. Belief that you can."

"You have no weapons."

"We have many weapons." She pointed toward the back corner, where she'd found long angle-iron rods and realized how the traffickers got across the border. The rods were affixed to the casket racks, turning them into regulation racks, stacked so nobody could get inside the boxes. Once across the border, these false rods were removed to allow the women to climb out when they woke. "Long, hard rods are weapons; teeth and fingernails are weapons. Your own hard head can be a weapon. We are not helpless. Please believe that."

Luisa gazed at Neva for another minute before she turned away without a word, moved among the caskets, speaking softly.

Was that a yes? Was she whispering encouragement or was she warning them against the crazy people?

The women rose and shuffled one by one to the trailer's side, got a bottle of water from the stacks in the far corner and then huddled together. If they had any interest in Davis and Neva, they hid it well.

"If we can't get past this—" Davis said softly.

"We have to," Neva said. She moved up beside Luisa, who was now speaking softly to the child, a lovely blonde with huge, cornflower blue eyes. "Who is this?" Neva asked.

"Bianca," Luisa said. "She will be eleven tomorrow. It is her birthday."

"Happy birthday, Bianca," Neva said.

Bianca flinched and tossed up a hand to guard herself. Neva threw up her hands in response. "Tell her I won't hurt her," she requested of Luisa.

Luisa spoke in a guttural language that might have been German. Bianca seemed to listen, but until Neva stepped back from the casket, the girl refused to leave it. Neva watched Luisa interact with Bianca, recognized the love she carried for the child.

Neva turned and gazed at the women now sitting along the trailer's side with their water bottles. They all loved this child, she suspected. Loved and protected her and the others. Women, no matter how traumatized, would gather together for the protection of a child if it killed them.

Which it often did.

The thought gave Neva an idea.

Luisa was also watching the others. Neva put her hand on the woman's shoulder. With a quick gasp, Louisa shrank away from the touch.

Neva dropped the hand to her side and said, "Think of Bianca, Luisa. She's a child. Don't you want her to have a real life, to have a chance? If you won't fight for yourself, fight for her and the others."

Luisa shook her head. "You will fail. They will beat us all, not feed us for days, give us only water. The children will be given no mercy."

"Only if we fail," Neva pushed. "We can do this, Luisa. Together, we can take these women away from this…" Neva stopped, out of words to describe their lives.

Luisa turned toward the child, who had snuggled against one of the other women, her water bottle in her hand.

"She still has a chance," Neva whispered. "Help me give it to her."

"Most Hated Guard," Luisa said, speaking as if to herself, "he likes her pain, asks for her always. It hurts even to listen."

Neva's stomach turned, but she swallowed it down. Was this the beginning of a possibility? "You'll help us, then? Talk to the others?"

"I will talk to them, but they will not listen," Luisa said. "The guards—they have…" Her voice trailed away, leaving Neva with images that made her squirm.

"We'll convince them," Neva said, shoving confidence she didn't necessarily believe into each word, each syllable.

"Tell me what you would have us do," Luisa said. She didn't look convinced, and perhaps she wasn't, but she was willing to try. If they could convince the others to try as well, they had a scant chance, which was one chance more than if they did nothing.

Davis explained their pathetically simple plan to Luisa.

When all the women were awake, Luisa gathered them around her near the truck's side. Neva and Davis stayed near the caskets, continued to refine and hone their ideas while the others talked, their hands fluttering. Neva watched their interaction with Luisa, still not convinced what her role among them was, but when she noted how the leadership of the conversation moved seamlessly from one woman to another, when she saw anger flare across some of the faces and withdrawal on others, she began to believe Luisa was on their side, was not the Judas woman she'd feared.

Little by little, their murmuring lowered until there was only silence.

Davis nodded toward the group. "I think they've finished discussing it."

Neva turned.

They sat side by side against the wall, seemingly totally unaware of their nakedness. Luisa's head was back, but as Neva approached, she saw that Luisa was staring at the ceiling. Neva sat down beside her.

"Some will help," Luisa said with a sigh. "We will fail, but"— she gazed down the line of women and children—"if there is a chance for the young ones…"

"I know it doesn't make sense to you," Neva said. "But this isn't how it's supposed to be. Women aren't supposed to be used like…like…"

"Like plastic dolls," Luisa said. "Like toilet paper. Like wooden things that cannot feel pain."

"Yes," Neva said.

They had their leader, albeit a reluctant, not totally convinced one. Everything hinged on these women. If Davis failed, it would be they who moved into place, they who formed Neva's army, they who carried the day.

Her already too-simplistic plan depended on a group of battered, tortured women who'd had the hope and energy beaten out of them years ago. The drug was still working in them all. The children, in particular, dropped off anytime they were left alone for more than a minute or two.

The truck slowed, moved right, then angled down. Davis leapt to his feet, his face pale. Sweat popped onto his cheeks.

Neva put a hand on his arm. He covered it with his, gave her a wan smile.

Then he and Luisa shooed the women toward their caskets. Neva helped the children. When they were all inside, she climbed up to her casket with the hanging handcuff again clanging against the metal, left the top open and curled her legs Indian-style. She taped the needle back to the bend of her elbow, folded her hands together, tucked the right cuff under her right wrist, which pulled the connecting part across the wrist.

Wasn't perfect, but if nobody looked too closely, it might work.

One of the cab doors slammed, then the other, and Ice's voice wafted back. "… pee like a big dog, dude."

"Yeah, me too."

They walked away.

If they'd just stopped to take a leak, they might not check back here. The plan would work if it was done before the truck reached its destination. Eighteen to two was just about the right odds, given the condition of the women. Eighteen to ten would be impossible.

Five, long, heart-stopping minutes later, she heard heels ring on the asphalt, the sound too far away to tell if he was coming this way or going back to the cab.

They grew louder.

She was forced to move her carefully placed hands to wipe the sweat off her forehead.

It all depended on her now. Seventeen people, three of them children. If she fucked up, every broken bone, every smashed mouth would be her fault and hers alone.

Dear God, help me.

"Better check the hens." Ice's voice.

A key rattled in the lock.

The door on the right opened, admitting sunlight and the smell of hot tires. Neva reached for yoga-style peace, failed to find it and turned to watch him vault into the truck. When he saw her, he smiled. "Well," he said. "Get any sleep?"

"A little," she said.

"You're calmer."

"Yes."

"Give up?"

"Do I have a choice?" It sounded as bitter as it felt.

"Not any more. Price you pay for not listening to me."

"For not... Dear God, Ice! Are you *hearing* yourself?"

He spread his hands. "Not my fault, honey. I did all I could."

"Do not call me *honey*," she said.

Behind Ice, the casket lid on the far rack rose slowly.

Keep Ice talking.

She gazed into those incredibly lovely eyes with their deep blue ring. Their crystal-clear, faint blue seemed tinged with black now, as if she were seeing a part of his soul, a soul she'd once considered selfless and loving. A soul that had been instead cunning enough to live a role designed to hide its real self.

But it was still a soul that knew her every thought, had watched her every move since she was six. The slightest flicker of her eye would alert him. Once again, she reached for her yoga training, emptied her mind of her surroundings, focused on his face and nothing else.

"Please, Ice," she whispered. "Let me go."

He lifted a piece of her hair, let it fall. "He likes redheads."

"Who?"

"The boss. He'll take a shine to you."

"Is he mean?" Neva asked.

"He's"—Ice seemed to search for the word—"efficient," he finally said. "You do what he says when he says or else." He held up his bandaged hand again. "See?"

Her sphere of vision encompassed the area behind Ice where Davis moved like a shadow, one silent inch at a time. The air in the trailer was taut with tension bled from the closed caskets, but Ice leaned against her casket rack, one arm on the edge of the casket, the other by his side, the picture of comfort, seemingly oblivious.

It all depended on the silence of the women, on their ability to lie still with a wad of silk practically touching their noses, to draw even, soft breath through the tiny slits along the filigree in the back of their caskets. It depended on their willingness to take whatever punishment the rest endured, because if they all remained silent and yet Davis failed, they would share in the brutality.

Neva slammed a mental door on that thought, afraid it would write itself across her face.

Davis's face disappeared behind Ice. Neva controlled her heart rate with a savage effort.

Seconds later, Davis snaked his arm around Ice's neck. Ice clawed at it with one hand while he reached for his gun with the other.

"Get his hand!" Neva cried. Davis grabbed Ice's right hand with his own, jerked it up behind Ice hard enough to make Ice yell.

But now Davis had no hands with which to get the gun.

Neva hooked her fingers in the angle iron on top of which her casket rested, leaned far out of the casket, ignoring its sudden tilt, and snatched Ice's gun from his pocket. When she was upright again, she pointed it at his face.

"Damn, Pratt," Ice said. His voice forced itself through the restriction on his throat. "You got a problem. Little girl here can't stand to touch a gun, let alone use it."

"Little girl will blow your fucking brains out if you don't shut up," she said. She flipped the weapon so its business end was toward her and held it out to Davis, who dropped Ice's arm and, in one smooth move, took the butt of the gun and then rammed the barrel into Ice's side.

Ice kicked back. Davis cried out, then tightened his hold on Ice's neck until the man's face reddened. "And so will I," he said. "Your best idea is to stand perfectly still. In fact, that should be your only idea."

Ice went slack, but his eyes darkened. He might be under control for the moment, but they couldn't give him an inch, not one second's opportunity.

Casket lids popped all over the truck, disgorged wide-eyed women with ghostly pale faces. If Ice so much as looked at any of them, they'd likely faint.

Davis stepped back, trained the pistol on Ice's head. "Turn around." Davis backed away, putting distance between them, reducing the possibility that Ice could jump him.

Neva waited until there was no chance Ice could reach her before she climbed down.

"You don't know who you're fucking with, Pratt. My guys will tear your eyes out."

"You have one guy, Ice. There are eighteen of us."

"Women!" Ice sneered. "They'll fold like cheap paper the first time we hit 'em."

Neva collected the IV tubes to tie Ice.

She came back, walking through the racks, her gaze on Ice and Davis. Two of the most important men in her life: one, the song in her heart; the other, a wound in her soul she thought would never heal. His entire life with her had been a continuing lie. She'd been a means to an end, nothing else.

While he carried her on his shoulders and wiped away her tears, he'd willingly destroyed the lives of untold numbers of women. Every ounce of her love for him was gone. The sight of him made her nauseated. But she knew him as well as he knew her, and the look on his narrow face was so much the hawk waiting for the rabbit to make a wrong move, she called out, "Watch him, Davis. He's just waiting for a chance."

"I'm just waiting for him to take a chance," Davis said in a voice she'd never heard before, a voice that should have made her shudder but was instead welcome.

The plan depended now on speed. They needed Ice trussed and gagged in a casket before his buddy came looking for him.

She'd barely finished the thought when hard heels rang on the asphalt.

"Hey, Jerry." He came around the truck, obviously clueless about what was happening inside, but his dark eyes widened as he apparently saw Davis and Ice.

The shock of recognition nearly made Neva drop the IV lines. Stephen Pratt or his double. So much like the picture she'd aged, he seemed a figment become flesh. She shook off her shock, took two steps back, doing what she could to hide herself from his view. His gaze was tight on Ice and Davis.

She didn't think he'd seen her.

Luisa tried to lead the women to the back of the trailer, but they seemed frozen where they stood. Bianca, in particular, who'd come to rest much too near the truck doors, seemed unable to move even a step.

Neva laid the plastic lines on the floor.

Davis kept his gaze on Ice's face. If he recognized his brother, he gave no sign.

"Shoot him, Ronnie. Shoot him now," Ice called out.

Stephen grabbed for his weapon.

Ice lunged to his left, which gave Stephen an open shot at Davis, but Davis's weapon was still pointed at Ice's head. If Stephen shot, Davis would kill Ice. A standoff.

Apparently realizing this, Stephen turned his gun on Bianca. "How 'bout I shoot the kid? Maybe a coupla the women?"

"How about I drill your buddy here?" Davis called out.

"Ain't my buddy," Stephen said. "Sombitch got me in trouble plenty of times. Shoot his ass."

Neva had promised the women that if they believed, if they worked together, they could do this. They'd given her what she asked, and now they would all die because they believed.

People said it wasn't hopelessness that destroyed; it was the shimmer of hope, and that's what she brought into this trailer with her—the allure of possibility, a promise of a better life. She'd backed it by using their love for the children.

Without giving herself time to think, Neva raced down the rack beside her, burst from the cover of the caskets, shrieking like a female bobcat in heat.

Stephen's eyes widened. He hesitated half a second before he swiveled his gun to her. She had no protection, nothing to fight with, no real plan. She'd launched herself to make a difference. If Stephen's bullet found her, then so be it, but she would die knowing she'd done all she could to keep her promise.

A gun roared. Neva flinched and ducked but didn't slow until the top of Stephen's head exploded into fragments. Bone, blood and brain matter sprayed out.

She skidded to a stop scant inches from his falling body, paralyzed by the sight, thrust back ten years to the moment Gray's head had exploded that same way.

With Gray's brain no longer controlling his body, it had crumpled toward her.

She'd instinctively thrown up her hands, but his weight bore her to the floor, pinned her there while his brains and blood rained into her face. Somewhere somebody screamed and screamed and screamed. Until Gray's mother screamed his name from the hallway, Neva didn't realize it was she screaming beneath Gray's dead carcass, clawing at the floor, her hands sliding through his blood and brains.

Sheila Ledbetter pulled Neva from beneath her son, then gathered him into her arms. Neva slipped and slid to the hallway, fell onto her face and listened as Sheila said, "Gray, Gray! I am so sorry, so very sorry."

"Get him!" Davis's yell jerked her back to the present.

Ice had seized the moment of Stephen's death to leap for the door. Neva whirled just in time to see him disappear around the truck's side.

Davis leapt after him, Ice's gun still in his hand.

Shuddering from her vision, Neva nonetheless slid off the truck. Stephen's gun was somewhere. She intended to find it. The thought of Ice hurting Davis made her sick, but if Ice managed to take Davis down and come back for her, she'd be ready.

Stephen lay on the asphalt in a pool of his blood, again so much like Gray she had to bite the inside of her lip to remain focused. Behind her, the women gazed down on his lifeless body, watched as she rolled him over.

The gun was beneath him, dropped from his lifeless fingers. Without a moment's concern, she picked it up, wiped off the blood and gore on the nearby grass and stuffed it into her front jeans pocket as she'd seen Ice do a thousand times. She stared at the body as she'd not been able to stare at Gray's, taking in the difference, the deadness of the thing, the leftovers from a life misused.

A lump in his pocket caught her attention. She slid her hand into his blood-soaked, now-cooling pocket, ignored the slime and came out with a cell phone. With it came a gold handcuff key.

The phone still showed a signal despite its blood bath.

She cleaned both off as she had the gun and stuffed them into her right pocket just as she heard footsteps running her way. Soft footsteps. Tennis shoes, not boots.

Davis.

"I lost him," he panted when he came around the truck. "Are you okay?"

"I'm fine," she said and turned her gaze to Stephen. "I am so sorry. If I hadn't—"

"If you hadn't moved, Bianca would be dead. You saved her."

He probably meant it. But his eyes were sad and pain-filled. Could he ever see her without thinking of this moment? She'd saved the women. Had it cost her a life with Davis?

As if to confirm her thoughts, he said, "I wish… But he was a grown man, made his own choices. I just wish I could have helped him." He lifted his brother in his arms, slid him onto the back of the trailer. Neva handed him the handcuff key. In silence, he released her left hand, stuffed the cuffs into his pocket, then helped Neva into the trailer.

"We'll put him in one of the caskets," she said. "The women won't want to look at him."

"Neither do I," Davis said. His voice was as grim as his face.

CHAPTER FORTY-TWO

Stephen's cell phone vibrated in Neva's pocket. She checked the face.

"It's Ice," she whispered to Davis.

Davis's shirt was covered in his brother's blood. His face was chalky, his eyes haunted. She wanted to hold him, try to make him feel better, but there was no time. He took the phone, tore out the battery, handed them both back to her. "Ice can track us using the towers if he knows how," Davis said. "We've got to get out of here. No telling how many of his buddies he's already called."

"Can you drive this thing?"

"Drove one when I was in college," Davis said. "It was smaller, local deliveries and such, but they have pretty much the same operating system. You stay back here and take care of them." Davis nodded toward Luisa, who was huddled with the others against the far wall. "I think they're okay. Luisa is, anyway, and she'll help the others. The gunfire didn't do them much good."

Neva followed him to the door.

He stopped, gazed at her as if she might disappear at any minute, then pulled her into his arms. She laid her head against his chest. His heart beat a rapid tap-tap-tap-tap. "We're going to be okay," he said. "I promise. I'm not going to stop until we get home, but if I do and somebody comes to the trailer, if they're not whistling 'Rocky,' it's not me."

She pulled back.

He seemed to think for another long minute and then he said, "If they force me to come back here, I'll whistle 'Folsom Prison Blues'."

"'Folsom Prison' is bad. 'Rocky' is good."

"Right." He pulled her into another quick hug and then he was gone.

Neva staggered to the truck's side, slid down beside Luisa. "It's going to be all right," she said, raising her voice so they could all hear. "We're going home. All of us."

Luisa said nothing, but there was a new look in her dark eyes. Neva chose to believe it was respect. Neva had promised, and she'd delivered.

An hour later, she woke to find Luisa squatted beside her, face drawn, dark eyes worried. "Do you hear it?" Luisa asked.

Neva heard only engine noise and the sound of the tires racing over asphalt.

Luisa led her to the back doors. "Listen."

The hum of the tires was hypnotic, probably one of the reasons she'd fallen asleep, but then she heard that odd siren, the one with the chatter at the end. That cop who'd drugged her, his cruiser had a siren just like that.

"It is Most Hated Guard." Luisa spat onto the floor. "He likes the pain, the screaming, likes to be begged." Her gaze wandered to Bianca. "He hurts her again"—Luisa's eyes burned and her face flushed—"I will kill him."

Neva glanced at the trailer's front. It, several feet of connecting steel and the back of the cab were between her and Davis. No chance he could hear her no matter how she screamed.

The women woke as the siren grew, their eyes wide. Bianca whimpered in her sleep. Two of the women scooted near her.

Luisa grabbed Neva's arm, her gaze pleading.

"I'm thinking," Neva said. She had Stephen's gun, but the cop had one, too. He was just one man against seventeen women and Davis, but it didn't take a genius to see that where this one man was concerned, these women had long ago been cowed to the point they likely didn't have the ability to fight him.

She'd be on her own, and a wild run into the face of death probably wouldn't end the way the last one had.

The siren grew steadily closer until the sound cut through her head and Bianca woke screaming. Luisa gathered the child in her arms, but Bianca tore loose and ran to the back corner, where she squatted with her hands over her eyes.

CHAPTER FORTY-THREE

Davis wiped sweat off his forehead and peeked again at the side mirror. This damned cop was persistent, he'd give him that.

Davis had taken the back roads, fearing Ice had alerted his buddies. They'd been nearly to Memphis when they pulled off their miracle. A Nashville police officer had no jurisdiction here. This guy was either a loon or a problem.

The rig wasn't made to wag its tail, but that's exactly what Davis had it doing. Every time the cop moved into the other lane, Davis swung the trailer right into his face, then pulled it back when the guy moved. The last few glimpses Davis had of the cop's face were not pretty.

Stephen's broken head rose in Davis's mind. He thrust it away.

The cop's angry face appeared in the side mirror again.

Davis fought the steering wheel around. He didn't have time to make these sweeps gentle. He worried about the casket racks. One of them broke loose and—

He cut that thought off, too. He had to stay focused on the cop. Neva would take care of the women.

A bullet shattered the side mirror. Davis shied back, missed a chance to swerve.

It was all the cop needed. He rabbitted down the side of the rig. To stop him, Davis would have to knock the cruiser into the other lane, risk wrecking innocent on-coming traffic.

The cop ducked in front of the truck, pointed to the shoulder with the barrel of his gun, began to slow. Davis's choices were to go around him, impossible now that the stream of on-coming traffic had returned, try to roll over the cop's car, taking a chance on tearing loose the casket racks in the back, or stop.

He hit the brakes, rolled behind the cop until he found a shoulder wide enough and pulled the rig to a halt. The cop got out, gestured for the traffic behind Davis to come around, then came down the passenger side. The cop opened the door with his gun in his hand and said, "Crawl over here and get out. Don't raise your hands. I know what's in that trailer. You fuck with me and your redhead will be first one I drill."

Davis allowed his weapon to drop beside the seat and did as he'd been told.

He hit the ground in front of the cop, headed down the side of the trailer whistling "Folsom Prison."

"Shut the fuck up, Pratt!"

Davis had never seen this man before. The only way he could know Davis's name was if Ice told him.

Wonder how many other people Ice had been chatting with?

"Sorry," Davis said. "'Folsom' is one of my faves." If Neva hadn't heard him whistle, she certainly heard that.

"Wait for me at the corner."

Davis stopped at the truck's edge.

The officer, Floyd, according to his nametag, stepped around Davis. "You are so fucked, boy. Man who runs this outfit eats guys like you for dinner."

Davis barely heard him. His attention was focused inside the truck. Neva had a gun and sixteen females in there with her, thirteen of whom were old enough to fight.

"Open the doors," Floyd said, gesturing with his gun.

Davis slid the key into the lock, made a show of twisting it and said, "They're stuck."

"Yeah? How about I send a couple of slugs through them. You think that might unstick them?"

Davis twisted the key for real. The lock easily slid back.

He glanced quickly at the officer. Floyd was close enough to drill Davis between the eyes.

He opened the door, which put it in Floyd's face for a split second.

Neva was at the trailer's edge, her gun in both hands. She nodded for him to continue with the door.

Floyd had apparently been ready for something like this. He slid around the door before Davis could move, pointed his pistol at Davis's head. "Drop it, little girl. Drop it right where you are. Kick it off the trailer. Do it carefully, now. Don't want to hit your boyfriend here with it."

Neva's face paled.

Davis's hope died.

She dropped the gun to the trailer's edge, then leaned down to shove it off and mouthed, "Duck, Davis. Now!"

Davis dropped, heard Floyd's shot go over his head. He bounced up, hit the gun with his elbow, knocked it to the ground.

Struggling with Floyd, Davis was barely aware of the women dropping off the back of the trailer until Floyd screamed, "Get off me!" He whirled in a wild circle, his hands clawing at Luisa, who was attached to his back with her teeth sunk into his shoulder. A second woman bit Floyd's arm. Blood oozed around her lips. Then they were all on him, teeth and nails flashing. He fought, knocked a couple to the ground, but they popped right back up and went in for more.

Years of abuse, pain and degradation seemed to stoke their fury, which grew in intensity as if Floyd's screams were gasoline poured on their fire.

He went down under their combined weight. His screams reached inhuman intensity.

Shocked by the savagery of the attack, Davis first threw his hands over his ears. Then, with a grunt of disgust at himself, he grabbed Floyd's gun and tossed it to Neva, who was still at the truck's edge.

Floyd's shrieks cut through him like a knife.

"We can't let them *kill* him," he said.

She gazed into his eyes for a moment and then nodded. "Much as the bastard deserves it, you're right."

He helped her down. Together they managed to pull the women off Floyd.

The officer looked as if he'd been in a bad vampire movie. Blood oozed through his T-shirt and pants. His arms were riddled with bites. His whimpers reminded Davis of a beaten dog.

Luisa gazed over Davis's head.

He turned to see the three girls at the edge of the trailer, their gazes on the quivering officer, who had curled around himself like a wounded animal. Their expressions were difficult to read, but Davis didn't see an ounce of sympathy in them. Luisa swung back into the truck, led them away.

Davis turned to Neva, who tossed a baleful glare at the trembling cop. "Better handcuff him."

Davis shackled the cop's hands, but he honestly didn't think it was necessary.

Mike Floyd's eyes were blank; his mouth hung open. The savagery of the attack had sent him scurrying deep inside himself.

CHAPTER FORTY-FOUR

Zanna woke. Her time here had morphed into two types: when she was awake and searching for the door and when she was asleep. Without sunlight to mark the time, she had no reference points. Had she slept an hour or six hours? Had she been in this room for a day or three?

Her only gauge was her hunger, now a ravenous beast that clawed at her mid-section like an angry bear. Her legs trembled when she walked; her entire body trembled even when she lay on the hard, filthy floor. They'd find her someday, a pile of bones in a corner, bones with long strands of red hair. There would be all sorts of investigations once they knew who she'd been. Books would be written about the mysterious death of Rozanna Clark. How did she get in that room with no door?

She shook her head hard. She was not going to die in this filthy room. Somewhere there was a way out. She remembered or she'd dreamed a good bit of noise upstairs, feet moving, things clanging. She listened carefully now, but there was nothing.

Today. She would find the door today.

She kept one hand on the wall as she moved along, her hand sweeping up and down the wall, searching for something, anything that might open a door. She stepped to her right. Her elbow smashed against something long and hard. Her funny bone kinked. She grabbed it and held it against her, waited until the pain passed, then reached out slowly.

Nothing.

Dammit, she'd socked the hell out of her elbow on *something*.

She tried again, swept her arm up and down, gritted her teeth against the possibility of hitting her elbow again. Her hand cracked against what felt like the same thing. She grabbed it, ran her aching hand down its shaft.

Long, round, thin. A broomstick! A *broomstick* stuck in the wall?

She shoved against it. Nothing. Pushed up, then down. Still nothing. Frustration and hunger made her grab it in both hands and pull back as hard as she could. Part of the wall popped into the room. Light flooded through the cracks around it.

Zan leapt back, grabbed her knife out of her back pocket and held it at the ready, sure somebody would force his way inside momentarily.

Nothing.

She put her ear near the opening, which wasn't yet large enough for a person to use, but she kinda had the idea now. The thing was a huge wheel cut out of the wall itself. When it was closed, it slid into the wall.

In here, if there was any light, which another glance around the room said there was not, the wheel would be ultra visible. Listening for noise outside, Zan studied the wheel. To allow it to slide along the wall, there could not be any mechanism for closing it from the outside. Any protrusion would be torn off as the wheel rolled across the wall.

If you could only open and close the wheel from in here, whoever brought the water in could not have left. She peered back into the room.

Scant inches from her foot lay a set of bones, long and short, a rib cage and a skull, surrounded by empty water bottles. The skull had a hole in the forehead, a small, round hole with cracks radiating from it. Several empty bottles that once held water lay around the skeleton.

A human skull.

She rolled the door a bit more, which filled the room with a dim light. Two other skeletons were laid precisely, the way an engineer might have done. The skeletons cut the room into thirds.

A suicide pact? No, there would be at least one gun.

Zan forced her gaze from the skeletons. Time to get out of here. The wheel left a large opening that began about two feet from the floor. Zan lifted her long legs over the tall threshold and flattened herself against the wall.

It was a tunnel with a high, high roof and a concrete floor. The walls were far apart. Except for the drip of water, she heard no noise at all.

She moved slowly down the wall with her senses wide open, knife at the ready. The tunnel was long, probably a quarter of a mile. At its end, she could see sunlight. A wave of relief washed through her. She ran a couple of steps, then made herself stop.

This place seemed empty.

That didn't mean it was.

She'd go to the police, describe the men she saw in that room and the women. She shuddered at what could have happened to her. Confidence, they'd said. Walk with confidence. Assailants want an easy mark. A confident woman isn't easy.

Nobody could walk with more confidence than Rozanna Clark. Yet here she was.

She'd hire a guard just like her father had begged her to do. Might hire one for Neva and Moya, too. Skimming so close to the flame her wings got singed had taught her a lot.

Keeping one eye on the end of the tunnel, she stopped every few feet to look behind her. There were cross-tunnels. Anybody could hide in one of those.

When she reached the end, she blasted through the opening into sunlight, flung her hands in the air and lifted her face to the sky. Even in its drought-dry murky yellow, the sky spread above her in a dome that could have been heaven. She whirled in a circle, stumbled, tried to catch herself.

Her feet slid.

She fought to stop, sat down.

The land crumbled beneath her.

The last thing she saw was huge rocks rushing at her.

CHAPTER FORTY-FIVE

Claudia rushed down the long, deeply carpeted hall at Oakley's Funeral Home, her head pounding. Her brother had said she and Rex should get to Oakley's as quickly as possible, that Neva and Davis were there, that they were all right.

"All right" doubtless meant they were whole of body, but what had the girl suffered that she wasn't sharing with her father? Claudia zipped through yellow lights and at least one red one in her hurry to see firsthand whether her niece was "all right."

A wave of babble had hit her when she opened the funeral home's front door. Babble wasn't usual in this place. Everything in it was designed to help visitors keep their voices low, their demeanor appropriate. This sounded like a sports rally.

"What the hell?" Rex was right behind her.

She half-ran to the kitchen, then slid to such a sudden stop, Rex ran into her.

"Oof," she said.

"Sorry. You shouldn't have—" Rex went silent, seeing, Claudia figured, what she was seeing. Women wrapped in bed-sheet togas sat at the kitchen table. Not all women, Claudia amended, because three of them were clearly girls, despite the aged pain in their eyes.

The long, wooden table groaned with leftover sandwich fixings, chips and cookies. Three empty gallons of milk sat in the center of it all.

At the far end, Neva's bright head was bent as if in prayer. Claudia swept around the table with a wave and what she hoped was a bright smile for the others. She knelt beside Neva's chair, caught her breath as the girl raised a pale and worn face. Her sapphire eyes seemed to have aged a year since Claudia last saw them.

On impulse, she put a hand on the girl's leg. With an exhausted sigh, Neva covered it with her own. "Hey, Auntie C."

"Are you really all right?"

Tears sprang to the girl's eyes. "I'm okay, Auntie C., but I have a lot to tell you." She stared into Claudia's eyes for a long moment, then smiled. "I wasn't raped, if that's what you're asking. It's just that…Zan. We didn't find Zan, and Davis…"

Claudia gazed down the table to where Davis Pratt sat with his head in his hands, looking like he'd lost his best friend. "What happened?"

"I don't want to talk about it here," Neva said. "Tell you later."

Claudia patted Neva's hand and rose.

Admiration for her niece drove tears to her eyes. Unless she missed her guess, these were rescued trafficked women. Neva and Davis had pulled off a miracle. Claudia could hardly wait to hear how, but right now, the women must be moved to safety.

Davis and Neva as well.

She was counting heads when her gaze landed on Mike Floyd, who was so torn up she barely recognized him. He was slumped against a large piece of plastic they'd laid over one of the overstuffed chairs. The plastic was streaked with blood.

He held a bloody paper towel against his ear.

Whoever had taken Floyd down had done it in a savage and effective way.

Claudia bent to Neva's ear, tossed her head in Floyd's general direction and whispered, "Do you want to talk about that here?"

"Not in front of them." Neva nodded at the women. "I'll tell you all about it. Right now, we've got to decide what to do with them."

Rex went to Floyd, spoke in a low voice. When he turned, Claudia gestured to the hallway. "We need to get Floyd to a hospital," he said when they were outside the kitchen.

"Yes, but not until we know for sure what happened. Neva's not going to tell me everything with Davis around. How about you take him to a room? I'll take her to another. We'll compare notes."

Claudia listened more with her eyes than with her ears as her niece told a story of insane risk and stupid courage. She was shocked to hear about Ice. Neva told the story in a calm voice until she began talking about Davis's brother. Then the tears flowed. "Davis saved my life, Auntie C. Killed his only brother. You know how long he's been searching for Stephen. Shot him in the head." Emotion threw her from the chair to pace the deep rose carpet. "He'll never forget it. He would deny it forever, but he'll never really forgive me, either." She turned to stare at Claudia with a face so filled with hopelessness, Claudia put her hands on her niece's shoulders. "We have no future, Auntie C. I know it."

"Forgive you for what? Saving that child's life and probably his as well?"

"He says that, but I don't think he really believes it. Would you? I mean if you had to kill Dad, wouldn't you blame the person who'd made it necessary? Even if that wasn't fair?"

"Don't want to think about shooting your dad right now, Neva. But no, I wouldn't blame you if I were Davis. I would hate it that my brother was dead, of course, feel guilty about my part in that, but I wouldn't blame you. He's in shock right now. You both are. Give it some time. I don't know Davis well, but I think he loves you very much. Will his brother's death affect him? Of course. But his brother could have saved his own life by not trying to take yours. That's where Davis will find peace, probably already has."

Neva stepped into Claudia's arms, rested her face against Claudia's shoulder. "I hope you're right," she murmured.

"You'll see," Claudia said. "Rex and I need to talk now. I'll catch up to you later."

Davis was leaving the viewing room when she stepped in.

"You okay, son?" she asked.

His smile was wan but it was genuine. "I'm alive, Neva's alive, and all those women are free," he said. "I'm fine."

She patted his shoulder as she passed.

Rex was sitting in the easy chair with his hands tented, his forefingers bouncing off his front teeth.

"What do you think?" she asked as she slid onto the couch.

Rex shrugged. "Can't ask the precinct for help. But we've got to get some firepower here before it's too late."

"How about the favor you called in from the Feebs?"

"My buddy's too low-level for this," Rex said. "We need big-time help."

She considered.

There was rot in the force. Likely limited to East Precinct, but still, rot in the system could affect a lot of people. The right people to investigate the police worked for the FBI.

"Have I ever mentioned Lottie Wilson to you?" she asked.

"No," Rex said, still bouncing. "I don't think so."

"My college roommate. She went on to the FBI. We've kept in touch."

"Ah," Rex said, dropping his hands to the chair arms. "You should reach out."

"That's what I thought."

CHAPTER FORTY-SIX

Neva caught up to Davis in the hall. His eyes were red-rimmed and bleary. The skin on his face was loose. He seemed to have become his father instead of the vital young man he'd been yesterday.

She knew the women had affected him. Davis's heart was huge and soft, but it was Stephen's death and the specter of having to tell his parents that was bleeding the life from his soul.

"Are you okay?" she asked.

He sighed and spread his hands. "I don't know whether I'll be glad when this is over or not. When it's over, I have to go home and tell my folks what I did."

"Tell them you saved my life."

His smile didn't reach his eyes. "I will, and they will understand. It's just that...I mean...you know how it is. I'd already jumped to a preview of my mother's face when she saw him, my father's, too. They've waited so long. And now—"

"It *will* be hard for them," she said, trying to suppress her own anguish. "This isn't what any of us wanted, but at least there won't be any more nights walking the floors wondering. These years must have been awful for them, Davis. And now they're over."

"You think they'll look at it that way?"

"In time," she said, hoping she was right, hoping she got a chance to see that day.

"You know," he said with a deep sigh, "I would give my left arm for a drink."

"Follow me."

She led him down the hallway to her father's office, dug the Irish whiskey out of the credenza. She had to wipe the extra tumblers out with a tissue to get rid of the dust, but she figured the whiskey would sterilize any germs. She poured two fingers for each of them and handed Davis a glass.

"I'm sorry about Zan," he said after his first sip.

The overhead light stabbed through the amber liquid, lit the crystal diamonds on the bottom, drove fire through the whiskey. It reminded her of the rhinestones Zan used to work into her hair on New Year's Eve. "I thought for sure she'd be with the others."

"Are you sure Ice doesn't know where she is?"

She shook her head.

"Do you think he would tell the truth?"

"Why not? I was caught like a butterfly in a spider's web. What harm would it have done?"

"Lots if you managed to get loose. I didn't get a chance to talk to him, but from what I've seen of how Ice felt about you, I imagine he was pretty sorry you were involved."

"Not sorry enough to let me go," she said.

"No," Davis agreed.

"I can't stop, Davis." She lifted her gaze to his. "I know it's crazy. What they would have done to me, what they will do to me if they catch me again makes me want to pee my pants." A hateful, uncontrollable energy shoved her out of the chair. "I see her in a deep hole somewhere, starving to death. I see her in a dumpster among rotting vegetables. I can't stand it. She wouldn't leave me. You don't know Zan. She'd claw her way through a mud bank to save me. I feel like I've muddled and messed up and failed and—" She turned away to hide the tears. Behind her, Davis's chair creaked. If he left the building and never came back, she couldn't blame him. He'd followed her into hell. They'd nearly lost everything. She could hear him saying he couldn't watch her put herself on the line again, couldn't stand by while she invited the worst of the worst to come and get her.

"What do you want to do?" he asked softly from behind her.

She whirled. His hazel eyes were open, their gaze direct, if weary. Was he for real, this man? Would he risk his life along with hers? Could she ask him to do it?

No.

"Nothing," she said. "It's crazy, Davis. I have to go home now and stay there. Watch television, try not to think about what's happening to her. That's what I have to do."

"I would think home is a place you may not see again for a while. We just snatched an entire cadre of moneymakers from a guy who's so nasty his own lieutenant is afraid of him."

Davis was exactly right. Until they caught the slavers, she had to lay low. And so did Davis.

His eyes narrowed. "You think there's some information somewhere. And you're going after it."

She should say he was wrong, whale away at him until he finally gave up. But she quailed at the thought of doing this alone.

"What is it?" he asked.

"Ice's house," she said. "I know Ice. He's an ass-coverer. As lackadaisical as he was with the bodies, he's meticulous about his own records. That was part of what pissed Dad off. Ice acted like our system was soooo much trouble; then he'd bring in his spreadsheets with every conceivable piece of information on them. If there are records, he's got 'em. I'm betting they're at his house, in his computer."

"You want to go get them."

She nodded. "Am I crazy?"

Davis seemed to consider. "Maybe. If he's there…"

She shrugged. "You have a gun. I have a gun. That's two to his one."

"Why not let your uncle or your aunt do this?"

"Because they don't know him. I'll find his secret stash because I know how he thinks. They'll find what he left to throw them off. Once they take over here, you and I are prisoners as much as those women. They won't let us move an inch, will pop us in a box of cotton and hide us away until it's safe again. If it ever is. Trust me. I know *them*, too. If we don't move now, we never will." She put her hands on either side of his face. "I have no right to ask you to do this. It's dangerous as hell and stupid, but if we don't and Zan dies, I'll never forgive myself."

He put his hands on her wrists. "I'm in," he said. "We have to go now before it's too late. We have no vehicle."

"Don't be silly. We have two hearses parked in the garage. The keys are hanging on the hook beside them."

* * * *

Ice lived in a white-frame, three-bedroom bungalow in White House, about twenty miles and as many minutes straight up I-65 to the north. She'd been there many times as a child, not so much as an adult, but her memories of it had been pleasant until today. Now, it felt like visiting the home of a long-dead relative. The Ice she'd known and loved *was* dead.

Davis used a long gold key to open the back door. "Where do we start?" he asked as they closed the door behind them.

"His computer," Neva said. "If it's still here."

They found it in his bedroom, which was as clean and as neat as Ice himself. The computer sat on a mahogany desk with ornate carvings and a finish so well polished, burnished embers seemed to glow within the wood.

The laptop was plugged in and running, but when they lifted the screen, they saw the request for a password.

"What would he use?" Davis asked.

Neva leaned over the desk and typed "Paddy." The computer rejected it. She then tried "Paddy's," "Ice Man," "Ice Wagon," all with the same response.

Davis bumped against her. She moved over so he could get to the keys. His fingers lopped off the sides of the keys and made her wonder how he ever hit just one. As he hit each key, the letter showed in the box for just a second before it changed to an asterisk. He typed: N E V A. Instantly, the machine opened to a neat tree of files.

"One thing about Ice," she said as she bumped Davis out of the way in her turn, "he's methodical. These should be in some recognizable order." She ran her finger down the list, ignored the "budget folder" and the "investments." Next came a series that were named with only one letter, beginning with A and ending in Z.

She opened the first one, found a list of names that meant nothing to her.

"They're all women's names," Davis said from her shoulder.

"But what women? Where? This is useless." She scrolled down until the folders ended, then slowly paged through them again. "I need to open every one, read everything."

"We don't have time," Davis said. "When they notice we're gone, all hell is gonna break loose. I'd like to be back at the funeral home before that happens. You work on the computer. I'll see what else I can find. In fifteen minutes, we'll compare notes." He had her check her watch against his. Then Neva was alone with the maddening files.

She wanted a file that said where the women were located and when. On a hunch she chose the "H" folder. Six documents. The first one was named "Phoenix House." It included the location of the house and a list of dates from the past three years. Neva grabbed a pen and jotted the information down on a pad, then moved to the next document, which was labeled, "Springfield." Took her a while to decide it was Missouri, not Tennessee, but when she was sure, she jotted that one down, too.

She'd worked her way through to the last document when a voice wafted out of the kitchen.

"I can't," he said, his voice thin, the stress evident in every word. "You can't make me."

Neva lifted her hands from the keys, turned toward the kitchen, listening to hear more of what could not be possible. Despite Ice's ins and outs at the funeral home, he and Gray had never met because Gray didn't like to be around death. Said it was creepy.

Yet that was Gray speaking in the kitchen.

"Like hell you can't, boy," Ice said.

Neva stumbled, caught herself on the wall, went down the hallway toward the kitchen.

"Your mother," Ice's voice said, "has a past, son. I took you to that ratty motel tonight so you could see what she really is: a whore. I got pictures you wouldn't believe. You do what I tell you, nobody'll ever see them. You don't, they'll be all over the Internet. I would imagine her fine friends at the church and the guy she's working for wouldn't appreciate them, but it's up to you."

Neva stepped through the kitchen door. Davis sat on one of the red chairs with a video camera in his hands. He glanced up and said, "Do you want to see this?"

She managed to nod and fell into the adjacent red chair. Davis turned the camera so she could see its screen.

Gray sat in one of the same red chairs, his face ashen, his eyes red-rimmed and swollen. Neva's head felt like somebody had blown a balloon up inside it.

"It's not so bad," Ice said. From the sound of his voice, he'd held the camera in his hands while he and Gray talked. "I started when I was a lot younger than you are. Hurts at first. You get tired of standing with your pants down around your ankles, but you get used to that, too."

Gray dropped his head into his hands and sobbed. "I can't do it. I can't."

"You worried about Neva?" Ice's disembodied voice asked. "She's outta the picture, boy. You don't want her to find out what you're doing. Nice girl like her, she's not gonna want you after. Sorry about that, but there are plenty of women who *will* want you, who don't get all snooty about what a man does to make a living."

Gray dropped his hands and stared at the camera.

"Hadn't thought about the little red puff, had you? You've had it, right? Good stuff?"

Gray's face twisted. "I'm *not* going to talk to you about Neva."

"Okay, okay," Ice said with a chuckle that sounded about as warm as Neva felt. "We'll let you have a night to think it over. I'll take you home tomorrow. Meanwhile, hold out your hands."

Gray held them out. Ice slipped a pair of handcuffs around Gray's wrists, then put a hand on his shoulder. "Try to get some sleep, son. Things'll seem better tomorrow."

The screen went dark.

Neva's stomach twisted into a tight knot, her head pounded. Ice had—

"Gray couldn't do it," she whispered. "He couldn't do what Ice wanted him to and if he didn't—"

"Ice would have destroyed his mother. He would have lost you," Davis said, his hazel eyes soft, and yet there was a righteous anger in them.

After ten long years, Neva knew why Gray killed himself, understood once and completely that it had nothing to do with her. She should feel relieved.

But she imagined his last long, sleepless night on earth, the anguish of searching for a solution that didn't destroy his mother. Was it around dawn when he realized there wasn't one, that he would have to choose between his mother and his life?

Had he thought of Neva?

Of course he had. That made it so much worse. To think of the promise of their lives together, of the pain he would put both her and his mother through must have torn him apart.

He'd had no choice.

His mother's apology with his blood-covered body in her arms made perfect sense now.

The ember of hatred that ignited when she learned who Ice really was flamed into fire. Her hands curled as if they were around his neck. She'd been disgusted by his treatment of the women. But what he'd done to Gray deserved death.

Davis said, "There were several tapes back there." He opened the camera, slid the tape out, showed her the label. "Gray Ledbetter," it said. "But this one drew my interest. Why would he make it, keep it?"

"I told you he was an ass-coverer. He'd probably already told Drennon about Gray, promised to deliver him. Maybe he kept the tape in case Gray ran away, so he could prove he'd done his best." It wasn't something she could prove, but it fit Ice. "Or he may have planned to use it to make Gray's mother come back into the business." She shrugged. "Once I thought I knew Ice, knew what he did and why, but that's no longer true. I'm glad you found it," she said. "Take it with you. We'll give it to Uncle Rex, let it testify for Gray at Ice's trial."

"Okay," Davis said. "Look, I can only imagine how this must have affected you, but it isn't going to help Zanna," he said softly. "You sit here a while. I'm going to the bedroom. See what I can find."

She dragged herself out of the chair. He was right. She had the answer she'd sought, but that wasn't going to get Zan home. "You take his bedroom. I'll take the spare," she said.

They'd been gone from Oakley's for nearly forty-five minutes, more than long enough to be missed. She regretted the panic her family was suffering, understood how awful it was of her to put them through it. But she wouldn't stop as long as there was any chance of finding something to lead them to Zan.

She grabbed the closet door, jerked it open. She'd seen the four-drawer filing cabinet he kept in there many times when he'd thought she was in the bathroom or finishing her peanut butter sandwich. He'd seemed so furtive as he worked in those drawers. This was what she'd meant when she told Davis she knew Ice's secrets.

The first drawer was full of manila folders, which were, in turn, full of photographs. She tossed them on the bed, let them fan out.

Women in various positions, doing things Neva didn't know humans could do. The second bunch was about as bad, but in the middle of the third, she saw three photos that looked like a schematic. She carried them to the middle of the room so they were directly under the light. Schematic of what?

The longer she gazed at them, the more familiar they seemed until finally she called to Davis. "Aren't those yours?" she asked when he entered the room.

Davis didn't have to look long. "Hell, yes. Pics of my blueprints, the ones in my study. How the hell—"

"He came to your house," Neva said, remembering the disarray she'd found in Davis's study. Ice must have come for the blueprints without knowing another of Drennon's henchman, the unlucky Juan, had been dispatched to kidnap her. Ice had tossed things around, taken pictures of the blueprints and left. If she was right, his rescue of her that night had been pure serendipity.

"So Ice got in my desk," Davis said. "I thought you'd done it."

Neva barely heard him. Her mind was centered on Ice's interest in the old tunnels, how he'd stopped in the middle of a delivery, spent several minutes talking to Davis about them, asking questions, wondering if they were still used for anything. "What's in those tunnels, Davis?"

"Nothing, really. I think the Elks probably used them for deliveries and such, but they've been abandoned for years."

"So what use would Ice have of them?"

"Unless he wanted to set up parties down there… Wait a minute." He turned to her with a gleam in his eyes she hadn't seen since he laid his brother in the casket. "You remember his asking about the Elk's Lodge, if they still rented the place out?"

"Yes," she said, excited now that she saw where he was heading.

"That would be the perfect place to set up. Downtown, so no neighbors to notice what's going on. Big, empty. The people who rent it out don't give a crap what happens as long as it's left in good order. I've talked to them."

Neva could barely stand still. That's where Zan was. "Let's go," she said to Davis, already halfway out of the bedroom door.

CHAPTER FORTY-SEVEN

Rex hurtled Robert's hearse down Main Street toward downtown Nashville. He'd been afraid to take Sims's car now that things were breaking.

That damned Neva.

Running off when she knew her dad had been through hell worrying about her. He couldn't say she knew the FBI was coming because he and Claudia kept that to themselves to keep from spooking the women.

He'd made sure Neva knew he was pissed, even though his conversation had been with Davis, who had the good breeding to insist they contact Rex before they went off on yet another wild-ass chase.

Which part of "you just broke up a sex ring" had she missed?

Rex believed Ice and Drennon were gone, headed for lands unknown, but he didn't *know* a damned thing. If they got a single shot at Neva, her chances were pretty damned slim.

A fact that he would make brilliantly clear to the young lady once they finished checking out the tunnels.

Not much hope they'd find anything. But he'd been a cop far too long to walk away from any possibility, particularly when it involved someone like Rozanna Clark. Neva and Davis were coming from White House, which meant their trip would take much longer than his, but he'd been delayed by the arrival of the FBI. Those guys—well, guys probably wasn't the right term since most of them were women, including Claudia's old college chum. But male or female, they came in the door in a sweat to get the women loaded up and outta there. Doubtless worried about a large-scale shootout when they couldn't trust local law enforcement.

Their panic spread through the women like a case of flu on a cruise ship and made everybody's job harder. Claudia sent Rex after Neva to help calm the women. That's when he discovered both she and Davis were missing.

Rex left Claudia to help with the operation, but he'd hate to be Neva when she finally made it back to her aunt.

He parked the hearse in the Second Avenue garage in a space he hoped was long enough to keep its ass end from getting hit. Davis had given him directions to the mouth of the tunnels, said they would meet him there. Rex had agreed because the boy had a set of blueprints and was bringing them, and because he didn't relish the idea of going in there alone.

There was nobody waiting outside the tunnel, but inside Rex found both Neva and Davis.

"You are in so much trouble, little girl," he said to Neva.

"I know," she said.

Davis had a flashlight in one hand, a group of large photographs in the other. "See here?" Davis put his finger on a spot about halfway down a side tunnel.

"Yes."

"That's one of the rooms. There're three of them scattered through the tunnels. I figure if she's here, they've stuffed her in one of those."

Their eagerness to get going was catching, but Rex took a moment to say, "I don't want you guys to get your hopes up. It would be most unusual for them to stash one woman away from the others to begin with. If they did, they would have snatched her on their way out of town, used her to get rolling again."

Neva's eyes darkened even in the harsh glare of the flashlights. She shook her head. "She's here. I know she is. I can feel it."

"Okay," Rex said, "I hear you, but you need to be prepared for what we find. Or don't find."

Davis stuck the plans in his back pocket.

The tunnel was half lighted. Its roof rose as they walked along its narrow floor. Someone had recently swept the floor. Rocks, dirt and bits of wood lined its sides. It was the first hopeful sign that the tunnels had been used fairly recently. By whom was another matter.

Rex prayed there would be more good signs.

"The first room is just down this corridor," Davis said as they turned to the left into a narrower, lower-roofed tunnel.

The nearness of the walls made Rex breathless. "Man could get claustrophobic in here," he said.

"Right here," Davis said.

"That's the damnedest thing I ever saw," Rex said as he lifted his foot high to step into the room. "What kind of door is that?"

"Very unusual one." Davis put his flashlight on the round wheel against the wall. Rex reached for it and then drew back.

"Like to get into this sometime when we have time," Rex said. "Right now, we don't."

Davis nodded.

Based on the pocks and dips in the stone, the room looked to have been hand-hewn. It was tiny enough so Rex backed out almost immediately. There was nowhere to hide in that cubby.

They stopped at a second, larger room, but here, too, there was no one.

"There's one more," Davis said. "On down the hall."

Rex followed the two young people, but that room, too, was empty. "She's not here," Rex began. "I am so sorry—"

"We're not leaving," Neva said. "There are lots of tunnels. She doesn't have to be in one of the rooms. She could be tied up somewhere. She could be upstairs."

Over her head, Rex shared a long and pregnant stare with Davis. It was not likely the girl was here to begin with. Even less likely if she was stashed in one of the tunnels that she was alive.

"We don't have a lot of time—" Rex began, but Davis cut him off.

"Let's begin at the beginning," he said. He put his flashlight on the picture and stabbed his finger at the main tunnel. "The tunnel ends right here. Let's begin there. I'll mark them as we go through so we won't do one more than once and can't get lost." He turned to Neva, whose eyes were wide. "If she's here, we will find her."

Rex hoped like hell they didn't find a body so badly beaten nobody could recognize it. He steeled himself for what might come.

They rounded the end of the narrow, low tunnel into the big one. Lotsa space between the walls. Rex's chest loosened. He really didn't like tight places.

Davis led the way past the tall stairs and was halfway down the back end of the main tunnel when he slid to a stop.

Took a minute for Rex to see it. "Did you know this one was here?"

Davis's frown was deep, his gaze on the picture. "It wasn't here. See these Xs on the tunnels? I marked every single door. This wasn't here."

"That's where she was, then!" Neva cried. "She escaped! All we have to do is find her."

Rex managed a smile, even though he knew the chances were excellent she hadn't escaped. They'd taken her.

Neva stepped into the room, which was large enough to make three of the others. Rex followed. Davis came behind. The tunnel's light bled far enough so they could see it was empty. Neva sent her flashlight beam around until it landed on a platform with ropes attached to all four corners.

Rex lifted the ropes. They'd been cut. He flashed his light upward, saw the mechanism that would have raised the seat, moved down the wall and saw the rest of the ropes with their counterweights curled on the dirty floor. He put his light directly on the ropes attached to the seat. While the main rope was filthy, the cuts were clean. They'd been made recently.

"Look!" Neva said, excitement making her voice loud enough to reverberate off the stone walls.

Her flashlight was on a plastic water bottle that had at least an inch of dirt on it, but the dirt was rubbed away in a hand-size print. Inside that print, the plastic was clean. Like the rope, that bottle had been handled recently.

"No way to open that door from the outside, you said?" he asked Davis.

"That's right."

"But it could be closed from within."

"That's the only way," Davis said.

A slight hint of hope lighted Rex's mind. Whoever cut that rope had been in here very recently. If it was Zan, if she'd come down the waiter, then destroyed it. If the door was closed when she got here, nobody could get to her.

While Rex was thinking this over, Davis sent his flashlight beam around the room.

"Think you'd better see this, detective," he said.

Rex recognized them immediately. Human bones. He squatted beside them, gazed at the empty water bottles, then rose, sent his light around the edges of the wall. Two more sets of bones met the light, each surrounded by empty water bottles. "Think we'd better back out, folks. We might have a crime scene here."

Davis went first, then Neva, her face drawn.

They were nearly back to the main tunnel when Davis stopped so quickly, Rex nearly ran into him.

The dim lights hanging along the tunnel's roof cast strange shadows that made it hard to distinguish details, but Rex had no trouble recognizing the man who stood shuffling his feet about halfway down the tunnel.

"You lookin' for a redheaded woman?" the giant asked.

"Yes," Neva said before Rex could speak.

"I got her."

"They call you Large George, right?" Rex asked.

"Yessuh."

"You have this woman?"

"She hurt her head," George said. "I been carin' for her, but she ain't wakin' up."

"How'd you know we were looking for her?" Rex asked.

"Them bad men gone," George said with a shrug. "She was the onliest one left. I been knowin' you was a police for a long time. She needs your help."

"Where is she?" Neva's voice was balanced exactly between terror and excitement. Rex offered a quick prayer that the redheaded woman was Zan, that she was alive.

They followed George out of the tunnel.

Going in, the land was easy to traverse, but as Rex exited, he saw how it sloped quickly to the riverbank with soil that was nowhere near stable.

George stepped aside, held his hand out. One by one, they allowed him to help them to higher ground. "That woman, she fall there," he said, gesturing with his hand at the river's edge.

Rex moved upriver and peered over the side. The river was as low as he'd ever seen it, its water a dirty brown, its movement sluggish and strange. As it receded, it had exposed huge rocks, their tops a good two feet above the water.

If Zan had fallen onto those, they'd be very lucky to find her undamaged.

"You ride up front with Davis so you can show him the way," Rex said to Large George. "Neva and I will ride back where the caskets usually go."

Rex stepped out of the hearse near the refinery with a sense of déjà vu and sadness. Sims had made his choices, paid the price. That's how life worked. But it was still sad.

George made them wait at the bottom of the hill.

"You think she's okay?" Neva asked.

Rex put his arm around her, pulled her close. "Zan's alive, pumpkin. That's always a good thing." His anger at Neva had evaporated, which didn't mean she wasn't in for a tongue-lashing later.

Neva huddled against him, her body shaking, until George, who had disappeared near the top of the hill, suddenly reappeared. Zan's bright head was against his shoulder. Her eyes were closed, her limbs loose, her face ashen.

Rex's throat grew tight.

When George reached the bottom of the hill, Rex stepped forward to take Zan, but Davis got there first and took her into his arms with a nod at Neva. They turned for the car, but Rex called them back, handed over Sims's cell phone. "Call 911. They'll be here in a heartbeat, can treat her on the way in."

"I needs to say stuff to you," George said as Rex turned to leave.

Rex nodded at Davis that he and Neva should go on. The ambulance couldn't get any closer to Homeless Town than the refinery.

George said, "You was here before."

"Yes, when those two men were found."

"Naw. You was here last night."

"You were here?"

"Yessuh. I was watchin'."

"You saw the other man," Rex said, suddenly seeing where George was headed.

"He come here all the time. Ain't nobody gonna cry over that one."

"Did the police get his body?"

"Naw."

"You know where it is?"

"That ain't what I gotta tell you." Large George went on to describe the man he'd seen carrying a half-dead woman toward a downtown dumpster, a description that perfectly fit Mike Floyd out of uniform. "She weren't dead," George went on. "I hit him, took her away." George took a half step backward and stopped. "She weren't dead."

"You did right, George. In fact, you deserve a medal."

At first George looked confused; then his face split into a wide smile.

"You want to help me make sure that bad man doesn't hurt any more women?" Rex asked.

"Yessuh."

"You'll have to sign a statement, come to East Precinct, but not now," Rex hurried to add. "I'll tell you when."

"I do it here."

"Okay. We'll do it that way." He stared at George for another long moment before he stuck out his hand and said, "I've been wrong about you, George. You ever need a cop, you let me know."

Another huge smile crossed George's face as he enfolded Rex's hand into his. "You a good man, officah."

CHAPTER FORTY-EIGHT

Robert pulled into his driveway that night exhausted but exhilarated. His baby was safe, although considering what she'd managed to pull off, he probably couldn't think of her as a baby.

His chest expanded.

Quite a woman, his daughter.

Zan was at Vanderbilt Hospital recovering from a concussion, still unconscious, but there didn't appear to be any blood clots. They thought she'd be home soon. Neva and Don wouldn't leave Zan's hospital room until the girl could leave with them. When Zan was well enough to travel, Don intended to take his child home with him, where he could make sure she was safe.

An armed guard was posted outside the hospital room. He would travel with father and daughter.

Robert had asked Rex to recommend someone to provide the same services for Neva and Moya. He would suggest that Davis do so as well.

Until Ice and Houston Drennon were caught, none of them would really be safe.

Robert wasn't privy to the workings of the FBI, but from the snippets he'd overheard, he expected there would be news from both East Precinct and Drennon's funeral home before the month was over. Whether they caught Drennon or not, he was done in Nashville, which meant Robert could begin to pull his business out of the hole. He still had enough money from the second mortgage to pay his bills while he got his business going again.

He listened to the coolant spit against the hot car exhaust.

He'd been harsh with Sylvia this morning—was it just this morning? He couldn't remember ever before speaking to her like that. They'd had fights like every other couple, said things they didn't mean and tried to take back, but he'd never jumped her shit.

At Neva's insistence, he'd done some research on caretaking. Thankless job, physically and emotionally draining. That plus Drennon's relentless pressure had combined to make Robert irritable, but how to explain that to Sylvia. In her mind, she'd asked for a simple drink of water and got a face full of his resentment.

He'd apologize.

The next time she was awake.

With a sigh, he headed for the house, the day's euphoria evaporating with every step. An empty, dark house, something for dinner that Sylvia would refuse to eat, television or a book if he could manage to concentrate. Two fingers of whiskey and fall asleep in the chair.

Just like always.

As he passed through the garage, he noticed how cluttered it was. How long had it been since he cleaned it out? A year? Two? He promised himself he'd get to work on it this Saturday.

Unless he had too much business at the funeral home.

As he opened the door, the mouth-watering smell of fried chicken hit his nose, floating just above the distinct smell of green beans cooking with a fine ham hock.

He shook his head. Olfactory illusions?

She was in the kitchen. Her back was to him. He saw, in the same new way he'd just seen the garage, how thin she was. Her back was bent. Her hair made of straw. She'd aged horribly in the past few months.

She turned. A radiant smile he remembered from long ago first filled her eyes, then spread across her face. She was once again his beautiful bride, the mother of his child, the woman of his dreams.

"You're home," she said, as if she'd thought he might not come.

"Yes." He was afraid to say anything, lest he send her back upstairs to hide under the covers. She wore a pair of jeans and a soft knitted top in deep blue that drove color into her eyes. The jeans hung on her, the top was too large, but except for their trip to the doctor's office, it was the first time in weeks he'd seen her dressed. "You look wonderful," he said. He caught his breath again as tears filled her eyes.

Had he already burst this incredible illusion?

"I am so sorry," she said. "I've been mean to you." She twisted a couple of knobs on the stove, threw herself into a chair, gesturing that he should do the same. "I wouldn't exercise, took anything the doctor handed me without question, blamed you for everything. I went to the doctor today. A new doctor."

Thunderstruck, Robert listened. Beneath his fear, a riotous joy jostled for room. Too soon to trust this. He'd been fooled many times before. But a new doctor and the proof of Robert's eyes were hard to dismiss.

"I didn't take any of my meds this morning, took the bottles with me. He threw them all in the trash, promised that if I would try, he would be right there with me. I'm going to do better than try, Bobby—I'm going to make it work. There'll be bad days. He said there would and I knew it already. Today, I climbed the stairs four times. It was hard, but I feel better than I have in years. He gave me a new drug, something he says should help through the transition. Once all my old drugs are out of my system, we'll design a regimen together, something that will help, but in the end, it's up to me."

He struggled for only a second against the flood of tears and then let them go, allowed their cleansing flow to wash out some of the pain and frustration of the last twenty years. When he could stop, he drew his bride into his arms, careful not to crush her thin frame, and said, "I cannot begin to tell you how happy I am. I was afraid I'd been short—"

She pulled back. "Oh, you were. You were short, to the point. But that was just the splash of icy water I needed to see the truth. All those times you've sacrificed for me were wonderful, Robert. I can't thank you enough. But the best thing you ever did for me was to tell me to get my lazy ass out of bed and get my own water."

CHAPTER FORTY-NINE

Three weeks later, Neva pulled the life-size bust of Gray Ledbetter out of the corner and blessed the peace and quiet of her basement sanctuary.

Zan was with her father.

She, like Neva and, to a lesser extent, Moya, had learned how fragile their lives were, how easily they could be taken. They understood now, all of them, that safety required vigilance.

The world was full of good people, but bad people existed.

Neva's gun lay on the shelf. Firing ranges were a weekly part of her life. The weapon she'd long blamed for Gray's death was once again just a hunk of metal with operating parts.

So far, there'd been no sign of Ice or Drennon. Uncle Rex said the FBI tracked Ice to the Mexican border, but there the trail died. Aunt Claudia believed he'd gone to Russia. The FBI had begun conversations through the State Department to see if they could get any international cooperation. Drennon had poofed like a ghost, leaving no trail, no records, nothing the FBI could use to find him.

They'd captured two of Drennon's men, both of whom were only too eager to make a deal. With the information they'd provided, two more groups of women were rescued.

Her dad hired a new guy to replace Ice. Jim was a quiet fellow who delivered his bodies on time and picked them up with equal regularity. He was a Vanderbilt law student so the hours worked well for him.

Next to Zan's rescue, the best news was that Neva had her mother back. Her dad practically skipped into work every day, often patting his stomach and raving about the wonderful breakfast he'd eaten. It was an uphill battle for both mother and daughter to find common ground for conversation. So far, they'd centered on her dad, his good points and his endearing quirks, topics about which they agreed totally.

She hadn't seen Davis in three weeks. She'd stayed at the hospital until Zan could leave. Davis had promised they'd take a long weekend, but this week he was back in Europe to check out another new drilling technique firsthand. He was scheduled to be home later today.

Their conversations were friendly and warm, but Neva detected spaces between his words, wondered if he still carried Stephen's death in his mind.

Her cell phone broke into "Evil Woman."

"Will you be home tonight?" Moya asked before Neva could say hello.

"Yes. Is it possible I might be blessed with your august presence? Do you still know the way?"

"Don't be a smart-ass. I am furious!" Moya's voice rose on the last word and made Neva wince.

"Sorry. I didn't mean to make you mad."

"Not you, stupid. I'm furious with Ken."

"Why?"

"He broke his other little finger!"

"His other..." Neva gritted her teeth to capture the laughter bubbling up her throat. "How?"

"You remember when he broke the first one?"

"Yes."

"I told him I would be there when he tried to work on that project again."

"And were you?"

"Yes. Standing right by his side, telling him he needed to secure that board before he cut it. But did he listen? Oh, nooooo. Damn thing fell. He tried to catch it and broke his right little finger in the middle of the second joint. I'm sorry, but anybody *that* stupid doesn't deserve to spend the evening with me!"

"I'll be home around dinner time," Neva said. "See you then. We'll have milkshakes."

"Rocky road."

"Stupid nuts get stuck in the straw."

Neva hung up. Poor Ken. Man would be lucky to be allowed to use power tools ever again.

With a wide grin still on her face, Neva spent a minute or two walking around Gray's bust, trying to remember his scent, the feel of his hand in hers, but the connection wouldn't come.

The bust represented her most frequent frustration. She'd started it as soon after Gray's death as she could focus, desperate to capture him as he'd been before the image of him faded from her memory. The head came easily. She put the cowlick at his crown that in life had defied all attempts at training. His pecs got the tiny cleft put there when he chipped his breastbone in a bicycle accident.

She'd worked a week on his cheekbones, another week on his mouth, ripping features away, then recreating them, as if her hands were stuck in some bizarre Groundhog Day repetition.

Over the years, she'd gone back to it, but no matter what she did, no matter how rested or relaxed or sure she was that she'd finally moved past the trauma of his death, she created the same face.

In the first year after Gray's death, the shrinks said she couldn't finish the bust because she didn't know why Gray killed himself, that since Gray took that knowledge to his grave, she would never know. So, they said, she was in a loop. When she finally accepted that fact, she would give up on the bust.

Now she knew why he'd committed suicide. Now she was free at last to finish what she'd started. She'd seen Gray's face in this clay a thousand times. Now she could coax it out.

She collected a new bag of clay from the refrigerator, selected what she needed, inhaled the scent of dirt mixed with mineral oil. As her hands shaped the clay into ropes, her body warmth moved into it, made it pliable. She moved her conscious mind out of the way, began the high cheekbones, patting and tweaking the mound of new clay, shoving it up from beneath so the lift would be in alignment, spreading it back toward the ears.

The cheekbones arched up under where the eyes would be, then smoothed toward the nose.

She closed her eyes, allowed her hands to feed the image back to her. It was perfect. She experienced a tiny flare of hope as she began on the nose, feeling for it as she had earlier, making her mind see what her hands felt.

She'd never sculpted this way before, but it felt right.

Her hands slightly—oh so slightly—lifted the end of his nose until it was open enough to inhale all the air God would give him, to stoke the incredible energy that sent him running when walking would be better. Her hands told her it was good, too. Silent tears sneaked from beneath her lashes.

She wasn't just sculpting now, she realized. She was stroking the clay as if it were his flesh, feeling its warmth, connecting to the feelings she once had for him.

She lost sense of time and of herself. Instead of the oily clay scent, her nose filled with the smell of Aramis, the cologne he wore because she loved it. Aramis mixed with the clean, fresh smell of the wind. These remembered scents swept her back to the time before her heart broke and her life spun out of control.

Gray's eyes had been wide and the blue that happens in exotic tropical lands where the sun dominates the sky and the water looks like air. They'd mirrored a perfect soul, the innermost part of a man-child who wanted only the best for everyone.

She released what was left of her consciousness, let the energies take her, piling clay on clay, smoothing it into the right shape for eyebrows. As she reached for the eye sockets, doubt tried to drag her back, but she shifted, re-centered, let it go. Soon she was in the zone again—blind, deaf, a kindred creature with the clay, both of them bent on getting it right.

At last, her hands dropped to her lap, finished. She sat sightless for a moment, fearing to look until curiosity finally drove her eyes open. "Oh, Gray," she said as she stared into the face she remembered, wide-eyed with wonder and poised for joy.

She held her hands beside his cheeks so they almost touched him. "I loved you so. A part of me will always love you. I blamed you for my pain. You knew that, right? But I was wrong. It wasn't your fault, Gray. None of it." She dropped her hands because as glorious as the likeness was, it offered her no connection. She needed to talk with her hand on his stone as she had so many times before. It was time to lay the past to rest.

* * * *

The pull against Neva's leg muscles felt good as she climbed the hillside with her new bodyguard's tall frame beside her, but the wind was stiff, and high November clouds blocked any warmth from the weakened sun.

She dropped down toward the grave and then said, "Josh, this is going to be a personal visit. See those bushes there?"

Josh nodded his blond head.

"I'd like you to stay just outside. Are you okay with that?"

"Let me check it out first, Miss Oakley, and then I'll make sure nobody bothers you until you're through."

She smiled, grateful the service had sent her a guard with enough sensitivity to understand that life must go on and people cannot always be slaves to complete safety.

Josh lifted the lowest branches of the bushes until he seemed satisfied nobody was lurking there ready to jump her the minute he left. "I'll be outside," he said softly. "Let me know if you need me."

She nodded, already judging the best piece of ground for her to use for this most important moment. Finally, she chose a spot near the right side of Gray's flat stone, picked up a large rock that lay beside it and settled down.

With little grass and no rain for so long, the land was as hard as concrete.

What a waste his death had been. A fine mind, a good heart lost. As naïve as any other pair of teenagers, they'd been sure *their* children would be high achievers, go to Ivy League schools, perhaps save the world.

She laid her hand on his stone, waited until she felt the familiar connection. When it came, she poured out her love for him, her agony over what had driven him here. When she ran out of words, her chest was as raw as if she'd torn something from it, but for the first time, it felt less like a festering sore than a cleansed wound.

Through a haze of tears, she gazed at the trees that swayed in the light breeze, thought of the good moments between them, the laughter and promise. The wind picked up. She shivered.

"Uhnnnn."

It came from behind the bushes.

Something heavy hit the ground with a thud.

Neva leapt to her feet, the rock still in her hand.

Ice stood at the edge of the bushes, his pale blue eyes red-rimmed, as if he'd not slept in a while. He'd lost weight. "Yeah," he said, "I look bad. Being on the run can do that to a guy. Did you know my picture is in every post office, on the Internet and in every police station in the country?" He wiped blood off the blade of his knife onto his pants as he stared at her.

"What did you do to Josh?"

"Josh? Oh, the cowboy outside? He won't be bothering us."

A frigid block grew in Neva's belly. "Is he—"

"Quit worrying about the cowboy. He knew the job when he took it. You ruined my life."

"You ruined your life. I didn't let you ruin mine."

"I tried to help you, goddamn it. Look what you did to me."

Random thoughts blasted through Neva's mind like shooting stars. He had a knife.

She had nothing.

He was taller than she, stronger than she.

Her arms and legs suddenly felt weak, but she wasn't weak. She had a rock. Aunt Claudia had told her a thousand times to fight until she could not fight another second.

She would fight for her life, for the life lost just outside those bushes, for the lonely, frightened children Josh left behind, for his grieving widow, for Bianca and Luisa and the lives Ice had taken for his own pleasure and use.

But most of all, she would fight for Gray, who'd never had a chance against this monster, whose life had been lost due to greed and avarice and perhaps resentment that Gray's mother had somehow escaped the business, put her broken life back together, found a good man, married him and developed a family.

Things Ice had never done.

A sense of peace swirled up from her feet. This moment was ordained the day Ice walked Gray into a filthy motel room and made him watch his mother's degradation. It was written again in blood when Gray took his life.

She was not alone.

She tightened her hand on the rock. Ice would not leave here with her. He would have to kill her first.

Ice watched her. "You wanna make this hard or easy?"

"I think we'll try it the hard way." She forced her stiff lips into a smile. "If you're sure that's what you want to do."

"I like you, Neva, but you should learn when to quit."

"I'll work on that, Ice. After we're done." She watched him while she talked. Thinner, tired, if the red-rimmed eyes were any indication. He might not be as strong as she'd first thought.

"Better come with me," he said.

"Right, Ice, because you only have my best interest at heart."

Even though clouds still covered the anemic sun, the world seemed to grow bright. She gazed at the knife. She'd have to handle that first.

She stood her ground, her gaze boring into his ice-blue one, cold now where it had always before been full of warmth for her. She shook off her feelings about Josh, shoved Gray's last moments out of her mind and waited.

The space between them developed a strange ripple, a line of colorless writhing air that began at his chest and disappeared at hers. It sparked, twitched as if a type of energy was being fed into it.

Ice frowned as if he felt it, too. He kept his hand behind him, walked slowly toward her. "We gotta be going," he said as he neared. "Got a long way to go."

Neva turned sideways to give her the best angle to crack his skull.

"Don't make me cut you," he said.

She waited for him to get near enough.

One more step. The rock filled her hand, solid and effective. If she could hit that broken finger, he'd drop the knife.

He came closer; she slashed out with the rock. It slammed into his hand. He dropped the knife, whirled back for it. She got there first, kicked it high. It arced, flew into the bushes. Swept by a sudden glacial fury, Neva swung again and hit him on the side of his head, a blow that trapped her fingers between the rock and his hard skull. She lost her grip and rock followed the knife into the thick brush.

Iced struggled up. "That'll cost you," he said. Blood trickled down his cheek.

"Sorry. Next time you want to carve my face, I'll try to be more obliging." She moved downhill.

Ice glanced at the bushes as if he wanted to find the knife, but it was a boxwood, evergreen, woven tight. With a slight shake of his head, he turned back to her. "I'm stronger than you are," he said.

"I'm smarter than you are," she countered, watching his eyes, looking for something to tell her he'd made up his mind. "That's why I can recreate people and all you can do is destroy them."

A dark flush began at his neck.

Working off the fact that she'd hit a nerve, she said, "It's true. You're a destroyer."

With a low growl, he charged her.

She stayed still, her knees bent, ready to dodge him, watched where he placed his feet until he was nearly on her. Then, as she'd done behind the house across from Paddy's, she stepped aside. His momentum carried him down the hill.

When he turned, his face was dark red.

She'd outmaneuvered him, but now *she* was uphill. If he charged her again, his run would labor against the rise. "You won't get out of here with me, Ice. Dad's working down there. He knows what time I left. Thanks to you, he's a little protective these days."

Ice shot her a pitying look. "He's nowhere near this place. I've been watching you since you pulled in this morning."

She struggled to regain the upper hand. "Your boss ask you what army took you down?"

"Shut the fuck up!"

With a strange skip, he charged her again, hit her a glancing blow that sent pain shooting through her left shoulder. She fell hard enough to rattle her ribs.

Instantly he was on her.

He grabbed at her hands, squeezed her ribs with his knees so hard she could barely breathe.

His face bounced around above hers, scant inches from her nose.

She grabbed his left hand with her right, trapped it just long enough to slam her long, thin thumb into his right eye, shoved, twisted.

He screamed, threw himself onto the ground, writhing his hands over his face.

She leapt up, searched for a weapon.

The fall winds had scoured the ground.

There was nothing.

She measured the distance to the driveway.

Too far.

Even with his eye streaming, Ice would outrun her.

She moved downhill, reached again for the peace that had sustained her so far, and waited.

He struggled up with his right eye closed, climbed to his feet, obviously in pain and just as obviously furious.

He rushed her.

Neva moved back and angled herself as Claudia had taught her, stood steady until the right second and launched herself at his legs.

His long limbs flew over her.

Furious, she shoved her hand high and clawed at his heel with her fingernails, dug them deep.

The pressure changed his arc.

He reached toward her, his head turned sideways, hovered against all logic above Gray's grave. She stared into his eyes. Waited.

Gravity re-exerted itself. He slammed to the ground like a felled tree with his foot still in her hand.

It twitched once, then was still.

She leapt up, prepared to ward off another attack, but it was obvious there was no life in his body. She kicked him in the ribs, both to be sure he was dead and because it felt good. His body lifted, then settled. Neva's chest expanded. She barely managed not to throw her head back and crow. And yet, she had to admit a tiny sliver of regret that the hero of her early life was such a shit.

She crawled to his head, saw Ice's blood flowing around the letters "better," and sucked in a quick gasp of air. He'd fallen flat like somebody doing a belly-buster into a pool of water, only he didn't land on water. His body landed on hard-packed earth; his head crashed onto Gray's gravestone.

She put her fingers on the edge of the stone, careful to avoid Ice's blood, waited for the connection. "He's dead, Gray. You can rest now."

A sudden wind tossed the trees. She looked up. Was it nerves or a trick of the light that made her imagine she saw a tall, lithe figure move down the hillside, stop at the river's edge, turn back with a wave before he disappeared entirely?

CHAPTER FIFTY

Rex was tired. He'd spent most of last night helping Claudia and Field Agent Gregory work through how to handle Ice's death. They were still sorting through things at East Precinct, trying to decide who was involved and who was not. Mike Floyd was cooperating.

Since Mike was still in the hospital, reporters couldn't get to him, but that wouldn't last much longer.

If they could keep Ice's death under wraps until they had everything tied up in a neat package, they could release it all at once. The mayor would appreciate that. One bad week.

Information they'd so far gathered was pretty tight.

Drennon was the boss they all talked about. He had ten different operations around the States, a couple more overseas. His funeral homes were covers. They'd still not found him, but they would. They had the names and locations of all his safe houses. They'd broken his organization, arrested or scattered his employees, frozen his bank accounts; they had eyes on his wife 24-7.

* * * *

Pratt Architectural was a three-story glass building built before the word *terrorist* made it across the Atlantic. Didn't build them like this anymore. Too dangerous.

Rex hoped the glass was bulletproof. He parked his car behind the building. He'd never met Davis's dad.

This was one was hell of a reason to make his acquaintance.

Inside the enormous lobby, the receptionist sat behind a desk large enough to hold the control panel for a jet plane. She had a Bluetooth receiver in her ear and was staring fixedly into a computer monitor larger than Rex's modest television screen.

He waited for her to see him. After three or four minutes, he figured out that wasn't going to happen. "I'm sorry," he said finally. "I'm Detective Rex Mason. I need to speak with both Mr. Pratt and his son Davis."

She disengaged her gaze from the monitor, turned to him with a quick smile. "I'm sorry. I get lost in these figures sometimes. Have you been waiting long?"

"Not too long."

"You want to see both of the Messrs. Pratt?"

"That's right."

"May I ask what this is about?"

"I'm afraid I can't give you that information. Mr. Davis Pratt knows me." Rex flashed his badge.

Five minutes later, Davis came in wearing what Rex decided was an Italian suit with a snowy white shirt and a tie that couldn't decide whether it was black, gray or white. It was the first time Rex had seen him in business attire. "You clean up well," he said as they shook hands.

"Marie said you wanted to see me and Dad. Is something wrong?"

"I'd like to tell you and your dad at the same time."

Davis led the way back through the tall door into a conference room with tables that looked like they might have come from a *Jetsons* set. "Sit down," he said, waving a hand at the first chair on the right of the table. "I'll get Dad."

John Pratt was as tall as his son. He was probably once as buff, but years of working with his head instead of his hands had softened him. He was also one of those lucky people on whom gray hair is perfect.

"Detective Mason," John said as he took the chair at the head of the table. He waved Davis into the one to his left. "Davis tells me you were helpful during his recent bad time."

"Your son is a hell of guy, sir. His knowledge helped us when nothing else could have."

John nodded. "I just wish my other son had not... Well, you understand, detective. The boy would have been equally good, I'm sure, but when he was taken, circumstances intervened."

"In fact, that's why I'm here," Rex said.

"To talk about Stephen?" John's eyes widened.

Rex laid the folder he'd brought with him on the table. "Your son Stephen *is* dead, sir, but it was not Davis's bullet that killed him. In the tunnels Davis showed us, we found bones of several young boys. It's taken a while to get the DNA back, but there is no doubt at this point that Stephen died within days of his abduction. The man Davis shot was someone who *looked* like your son."

Rex lifted his gaze to Davis just in time to see the man's face drain. "What are you saying?" Davis asked, half rising. "All this time, Stephen was dead? The man I shot—"

"—has no DNA on record in this country, Davis. We don't know who he was, but he absolutely was not your brother."

Tears leapt to Davis's eyes. He stumbled from the room.

Rex kept his gaze on the tabletop until John Pratt said with tears in his voice, "God bless you, detective. God bless you. He was never going to forgive himself, no matter what his mother and I said. We didn't blame Davis." John lifted his hands. "How could we blame him when he saved Neva's life? He's not slept well since it happened. I don't think he's seen Neva, either. I hate to think of what this could have done to him."

"I'm just the guy who gets to bring the good news," Rex said and then stopped himself. "I didn't mean— I know your son is dead. That's not good news."

"My son was already dead, detective. He was lost to me. What you did today was give me back the other one. I cannot thank you enough."

"Dad?"

Davis stood in the doorway. His eyes were still glassy from his tears, but the set of his jaw was granite.

"Davis! I'm so glad you came back—" John began, but Davis stopped him with an upraised hand.

"You know who gave me those plans?"

"Frank Gorman."

"Forgotten tunnels, Dad. Forgotten by everybody except Frank."

Now it was John's turn to pale. "You think he might have…" He shook his head. "If it were Frank, son, he would never have given you those blueprints."

"Not necessarily, Mr. Pratt," Rex said. "Criminals sometimes almost ask us to find them. Guilt, especially guilt over murder, can eat a man from the inside out. Gorman may have given Davis those blueprints for the express purpose of helping him find your younger son's body." Rex gazed from one face to the other, so alike, yet so different.

"He was always fond of you boys," John Pratt said with another shake of his head. "Taught you both how to climb. Took you on camping trips, particularly Stephen. He really liked Steph—" John stopped, stared across the table for a moment, seemingly seeing nothing. Finally, he turned to Rex. "That's how they operate, isn't it? The pedophiles?"

"There are no hard and fast rules, sir. Mr. Gorman may be a fine man, but if he knew about the tunnels, we should probably talk to him." Rex thought fast. If he didn't move quickly and Gorman was the killer, he'd lose him. On the other hand, with East Precinct in a mess, he didn't quite know how to go about this. Finally, he said, "Do you think he'd mind answering a few questions?"

CHAPTER FIFTY-ONE

The air in Neva's mother's kitchen smelled like heaven. Perfectly browned pork chops sat on the table beside fluffy biscuits and Miss Sylvia's signature mashed potatoes.

"Mom, if you don't stop feeding me so often, I'm gonna be fat as a pig."

"You'll never be fat, Neva. You have my mother's metabolism. You will always be thin."

"Did your mother eat pork chops with gravy, hot biscuits and mashed potatoes for dinner?"

"Often," Sylvia said with a smile. "Never gained an ounce."

"Good to hear," Neva said. She set the tall glasses of iced tea, an Oakley family staple in all seasons, on the table. "I'll call Dad."

She made it to the living room before the doorbell rang.

"Now who can that be right here at dinner time?" her dad grumbled. He set aside his newspaper, went to the door. Light from the porch spilled through, showing the shadow of a man. One of her dad's business pals, probably. He'd invite the man for dinner. Neva turned toward the kitchen. Have to set an extra place.

"Davis!" her father said from behind her. "Good to see you, son."

Neva whirled back, unsure what to do: go to the kitchen and wait to see if he wanted her or follow her heart into the living room.

She turned back for the living room just as Davis stepped inside. He raised his hazel gaze to hers. She searched it, expecting to find the same muddle of conflicting emotions she'd seen the last time they were together, but to her surprise, his eyes were the hazel glories of old, clear and sparkling, obviously glad to see her. An enormous smile spread across his face.

"Can you stay for dinner?" her father asked.

"Actually, sir, I hate to delay it, but I'd like to talk to you for a moment if you don't mind."

Her dad shot a quick glance over his shoulder at her, then nodded. "Of course. Have a seat."

"I'll help Mom get dinner on the table," Neva said unnecessarily. She felt funny, like butterflies were testing their wings in her belly. What could Davis need with her father?

She carried the lima beans to the table, set them down, telling herself sternly that she would not eavesdrop, but somehow as she walked toward the table, her body angled itself so she passed right by the door. All she heard from the living room was a low murmur.

"What are they doing in there?" Sylvia asked. "Dinner's ready."

"Something they don't want us to hear."

Sylvia got an extra plate, fork, knife, spoon and napkin. "Get Davis a glass of tea, honey. Your dad's not going to let him leave without dinner." When it was all set, Sylvia dropped into her chair. "I guess we'll wait 'til they deign to come in."

Neva sat down beside her. "I really appreciate all you're doing, Mom."

Tears filled Miss Sylvia's eyes as they did so often these days. "I am so sorry about all the time I wasted, baby. You should have had much better."

Neva put her hand on her mother's arm. "I did fine. You were here, after all. Just not feeling well sometimes."

"You don't have to whitewash it, honey. I know exactly how often I was not here. Your dad took great care of you. I owe Rosita Vargas about a million dollars for her help. If God gives me enough time, I hope to make it up to you by being the best mother in the world."

Neva kissed her mother's cheek. "You already are."

"Of course you'll stay for dinner," Neva's dad said. "I'll hear nothing more about it. Sylvia, do we have an extra plate for this young man?"

Sylvia merely gestured at the extra plate. "Good to see you, Davis."

They ate and chatted about mundane things: politics, shared tidbits about people they knew. When dinner ended, Neva shooed both her parents out of the kitchen. "I'll take care of this," she said. "Least I can do for such a great meal." Davis insisted on helping, so it was quite late when he said, "Wanna go for a ride?"

"Sure."

"Where are you two off to?" her dad asked as they came through the living room.

Neva kissed his forehead. "For a ride. Or if you'd prefer, we could stay here and chaperone you two. You know how you are."

Neva's mother blushed a deep crimson, which made her dad laugh as he said, "Get out of here. No telling what we old folks might get into."

The night was crisp but the sky was filled with clouds. Once a cloud-filled sky would have heralded rain, but lately they were just clouds that gathered, then faded away.

Davis's truck was parked right outside the garage. He took her arm but said nothing as they walked toward it. He slid her into her seat and closed the door.

When he got in, she said, "Are you going to tell me what this is about?"

"I have a jillion things to tell you," he said, his eyes shining in the dash lights. "This is the first one." He told her about Stephen, about how he really died.

"They've arrested Frank Gorman," he said. "He kidnapped them over time, kept them in that room doing— I don't want to think about that part. He climbed in and out on the dumbwaiter. He was an expert climber. Even I remember that." Davis was silent for a minute. "I guess you never really know somebody."

She said the right things, but inside, her sorrow at his loss competed with a wild joy. She now understood his clear-eyed welcome to her earlier. They might still not have a future together, but at least it hadn't been destroyed by Stephen's death.

"Okay," he said. "That's the first thing. I have many more. But I want to say them in the right place."

"Where's that?"

"You'll see."

They rode in silence until he turned off on the road beside Oakley's.

"We're going to talk in the funeral home?"

He smiled at her, passed the home, drove into the cemetery.

"Where are we going?"

"Just wait."

He parked the truck in the cemetery, grabbed a flashlight and opened her door. "This place," he said, sweeping his hand at it. "This is where it began. I was digging graves. You came to see if I was doing it right. I'll never forget it. The sun blasted pure gold among the auburn in your hair. Your eyes were the prettiest I'd ever seen. I think I fell in love with you before you got up the hill." He walked as he talked, leading her.

"You looked pretty good yourself," she said. "Those muscles all bunched up where you'd been working with the shovel. Nice tan. Gorgeous eyes. Those damned dimples. Where are we going?"

"There's something we have to do," he said.

He led her across the hill.

When he moved downward, she realized where he was going.

He'd decided to tell her she would have to choose between him and Gray. She would choose Davis, but it pained her to think of completely shutting out the part of her that would forever love Gray Ledbetter, the boy who'd first stolen her heart, then destroyed it. She wanted Davis to be so secure in her love he could leave a tiny part of her for Gray.

Probably too much to ask.

Davis led her around the bushes, stopped at Gray's grave. "I know how much he meant to you," he said. "He died young. Your memories must be of a perfect boy. No warts or faults to blemish it. I may be that way now, too, but it won't last. I'll say something thoughtless or you'll discover I squeeze the toothpaste from the top or a million things that will make you want to kick my butt."

"The same will be true of me."

"Yes, but you are my first love. I am not yours."

"Davis, I—"

"Wait. Let me finish. I need you to know. I understand he will always be a part of you. I hope in time to root him almost all the way out of your heart, but I'll take whatever you can give. I love you, Neva." He dropped to one knee, pulled a velvet box from his pocket, held it out.

"You have got to be kidding me," she said. She plucked the box from his hand. "You're proposing in a cemetery?"

"I am proposing," he said, "in front of Gray, telling him as I just told your father that I will always treat you well, always cherish you, always keep you safe."

Tears filled her eyes. He rose, pulled a flashlight from his pocket, trained it on the box as she opened it.

She had no idea about diamonds, couldn't have told if the center stone was a half-carat or a carat and a half, didn't know if the side stones were chips, didn't care. It was perfect, as if he'd reached inside her head and found the ring she'd seen in her dreams.

He slipped it on her finger, where it glowed like a star. "It is customary," he said, "for you to say something at this point."

She put her hands on either side of his face. "I think Gray left me when Ice died. His story was over then. Justice was done. I moved on, as well. You're right. I will always love him in the part of my heart that will forever remain a teenager. But that love is minuscule compared to what I feel for you. Yes, Davis, I will marry you. Yes, yes, yes, yes—"

She might have gone on forever had he not found her mouth. She clung to him, saw her life reel out. Children, grandchildren, maybe even great-grandchildren. She'd meet them all with her hand in his.

Lightning flashed overhead. Thunder rumbled.

Raindrops hit Neva's head.

Then she and Davis were rushing for his truck, laughing like crazy people while rain slashed at their shoulders and poured over their heads.

THE END

ABOUT THE AUTHOR

Nancy Sartor, a Nashville-born writer, is a charter member and current president of Word Spinners Ink as well as a member of Romance Writers of America, Mystery Writers of America and Sisters in Crime. She is an enthusiastic graduate of Donald Maass's Breakout Novel Intensive Workshop, Don Maass's workshop on micro tension and the Writer's Police Academy. She is a member of the prestigious Quill and Dagger writing group in Nashville, Tennessee.

Because her favorite books always do, Nancy believes a novel should enlarge understanding, raise awareness, plead for the less fortunate, define a better way of life, provide a personal story so poignant it brings tears to every eye or in some way contributes something of substance to the reader. She lives in Nashville with her husband, the classical composer David P. Sartor, and two Maine coon cats, Ginger (yes, *that* Ginger) and Autumn Fire.

Did you enjoy this book? Drop us a line and say so! We love to hear from readers, and so do our authors. To connect, visit www.boroughspublishinggroup.com online, send comments directly to info@boroughspublishinggroup.com, or friend us on Facebook and Twitter. And be sure to check back regularly for contests and new releases in your favorite subgenres of romance!

Are you an aspiring writer? Check out www.boroughspublishinggroup.com/submit and see if we can help you make your dreams come true.